BOUND BY Lies

REBECCA SHEA

BOUND BY Lies

REBECCA SHEA

COPYRIGHT

ISBN-13: 978-0-9864288-4-5
Edited by: Beth Lynne, Hercules Editing and Megan Hand

dedication

To my family for always believing in me and encouraging
me on this journey, and for allowing the voices in my head
to make their way into our lives. I know it's not easy sharing me
with fictional characters. Thank you for allowing me to live my
dreams. I love you more than you'll ever know.

Emilia

PROLOGUE

Death.

My eyes snap open, and I struggle to sit up and catch my breath. I'm suffocating in my reality. I tremble and a loud gasp finally comes from me; the sound of me breathing—or rather, trying to breathe. I finally feel my lungs expand, bringing in the cool air of the dark bedroom. My chest is tight as I exhale, and I try to breathe again, but it's the pressure of my heart constricting along with my lungs that causes me such immense pain.

The memory is on a constant loop like a train wreck. There is no way to bury the images. The gun pressed to his head. The yelling. The slow pull of the trigger. The blood.

"Alex!" I scream his name over and over, willing him to live. "Keep your eyes open!" I yell, reaching for his outstretched hand. The cool tile beneath me is slippery with his blood. I slip and slide in the warm liquid as I try to reach him. "Alex," I mumble, my voice hoarse from yelling. I struggle, trying to make my way to him. The sounds of more yelling and gunfire play in the background like a television show. Except this isn't TV...this is really happening.

Danger. Death. All of it hangs in the air around me, except I'm not afraid of dying. I'm afraid to live without Alex. Tight arms pull at my waist, tugging me further away from Alex's outstretched hand. All I see are Alex's amber eyes begging me not to leave him, pleading with me as his eyelids begin to slowly close. My name falls from his lips, barely a whisper as he reaches for me one last time. And then, nothing. I see nothing but black.

I gasp again, my breaths coming heavy and fast as I hear the final gunshot, but I see nothing. I feel pain in my head, but I'm covered in safety.

Sam.

I struggle to push him off of me so that I can get to Alex, but his grasp is too tight. When I'm finally free, I see him—Antonio. He pulls the trigger, and I watch the final bullet pummel into Alex's chest before Antonio turns to me.

Fear.

Pure evil dances in his dark brown eyes, and hate flashes across the light brown skin of his face as he looks down on me, his gun pointed at my head. As I stare at the barrel of the gun, images of the things I used to fear flash through my mind, but nothing compares to the moment you know you're going to die...and then hearing the gunshot before everything goes black again.

Pain.

That's all I'm capable of feeling in this moment. My lungs burn. My heart aches. My head screams.

Physical.

Mental.

Emotional.

Pain.

That's all I feel.

ONE

Emilia

I sit with my back pressed against the headboard of Sam's bed, my knees pulled tightly to my chest. "Why" is the question that haunts me—has been haunting me all night.

Why Alex? Why me? *Why?*

My arms are wrapped tightly around my legs in hopes that this uncontrollable shaking that has racked my body for the last twelve hours will stop. Twelve hours since I've seen him. Twelve hours since he left me. He promised he'd never leave me.

Promises. I don't believe in promises. Every promise ever made to me has been broken.

I roll my neck as my muscles ache and scream at me. It seems when you can't shut off your mind, your body pays the price. Except this is nothing. Alex paid the price—with his life.

All I can see is blood. Blood is everywhere. On his chest. On the floor. On me. Did you know that blood smells? In large amounts, blood has a metallic smell to it. I'll never forget that smell. Twice in the last six months, I've knelt in the blood of people I love, begging them not to leave me. Twice that metallic smell has hung heavy in the air around me. And the images, scents, and sounds never leave you once you've experienced them. The smell, mostly, is something I'll never forget—ever.

I've barely even noticed that I'm half-naked. Only in a bra and pair of panties as my shorts and tank top lay in a pile on the floor, covered in Alex's blood. My skin is caked with it, dark crimson and brown. It's disgusting and I must look terrifying, but right now, I'm not ready to wash it off.

It's all I have left of him.

My mind continues to play like a broken record, repeating everything that happened in slow motion. Andres walking through the front door of Alex's condo, heads turning, guns pointing, and then, without warning, gunfire.

I plug my ears to block out the sound of the gunshots and the screaming in my head. It amazes me how the memory not only remembers just sights, but sounds and smells also. I can still hear the gunshots ring out. I can still smell the gunpowder.

My fingers flit around the base of my throat, searching for the gold compass necklace that Alex gave me, the only thing that'll comfort me right now. But it's gone. Tears sting my eyes as my hand rests in the hollow where the necklace should be. I toss my head back and hit the edge of the headboard while choking back the impending tears. My head is pounding with a terrible headache that throbs from my temples down to the base of my skull. It's most likely a concussion from hitting my head on the tile floor when Sam threw himself on top of me as the gunfire rang out.

"Em," Sam's voice calls to me quietly from the doorway. He's standing with both arms raised above his head and he holds on to the doorframe. He's changed out of his grey suit pants and white dress shirt that were also covered in blood, and now he's wearing a pair of sweatpants and a t-shirt.

I glance at him out of the corner of my eye but keep my head dropped back against the headboard. I'm numb, unable to feel anything at the moment.

"Em, come on. We need to get you cleaned up." He offers me a sympathetic smile because that's Sam. Safe, caring, concerned. I always told myself he was safe where Alex was dangerous, but I shake those thoughts aside as Sam moves toward me, his feet shuffling softly against the wood floor as he sits down on the edge of the bed. Concern clouds his dark eyes. "I should've taken you to the hospital," he says quietly, resting his hand on my forearm. "We need to have your head looked at." He brushes his fingertips across my temple, pushing back a strand of hair that was stuck to my face. Safe. His touch is safe.

"I don't have insurance, and I can't afford it. I'll be fine," I mutter through dry lips. My mouth is also dry, and I try to swallow but can't.

He sighs. "You're still shaking. I think you're in shock. Come on. Let's get you cleaned up, and I'm taking you to the ER." He tugs at my arm, my muscles are stiff as Sam begins lifting me from the bed. Listlessly, I rest my head against his shoulder and wrap my arms around his neck as he carries me to the en suite bathroom.

Safe. I should feel safe in his arms, but the only arms I want around me are Alex's.

"Hold on to the counter," he says gently as he sets me down and my toes touch the cold tile floor. "Bath or shower?" He pulls an oversized towel down from the towel rack and rests it on the edge of the tub.

"Bath," I answer him, emotionless.

Sam turns on the faucet in the large bathtub and plugs the drain. Reaching under the bathroom sink, he pulls a box of Epsom salt and sprinkles it in. "For your muscles," he says as he closes the box and puts it away. Then he pulls out another bottle and squirts some purple liquid in the running water, bubbles beginning to fill the tub. "Lavender mint." He runs the bottle under his nose before closing it. "Ex-girlfriend," he mumbles and puts the bottle back under the sink. Tossing a sponge into the sudsy water, he stands back with his hands on his hips. "You going to be okay to get yourself undressed and all?"

"Yeah." I nod and rub the back of my head. I look at Alex's blood on my hands and then back to Sam.

"Okay, if you need anything, just holler. I'll be in the living room returning a few phone calls."

He closes the door behind him, and I catch a glimpse of myself in the full-length mirror attached to the back of the door. With all the dried blood on me, I look like I was murdered, which isn't far from the truth. A piece of me died right alongside Alex. Black mascara caked under my eyes, my pale skin, and wild hair only add to the horrifying picture.

Lifting my hands, I turn them over and inspect them. Alex's blood. Without warning, tears spill from my eyes and I fall to my knees as I think of Alex bleeding on the floor of his condo. Loud, bellowing cries escape me as I crawl to the toilet, lifting the lid to throw up. My stomach clenches again and again, and I gasp for breath once the contents of my stomach are gone.

"Jesus Christ!" The bathroom door flies open, and Sam runs over to me. On his knees next to me, he grabs me by the shoulders and tilts my head so he can look me over. His fingers wipe tears that have pooled under my eyes. I should hate his touch, but I don't. "What happened, Em?"

I reach out and press down on the toilet handle, flushing it, and close the lid. Leaning back against the cool bathroom wall, I look Sam in the eyes. His fingers brush my long hair behind my ears. Safe. Sam is safe, I keep telling myself.

I close my eyes and take a deep breath. Then I open them and look down at myself. I should feel vulnerable, almost naked and covered in blood, but I don't. I hold my hands out to Sam and he looks at them, sympathy falling across his face.

"Em, come on. We need to get you cleaned up. I'm really worried about you. I know you have a concussion and now, with the vomiting, I think it's serious." He pulls me up by my elbows, and I squeeze his hands tighter. He's so strong and confident, but I can see the fear and the sadness in his eyes. He's buried it, because that's what he does. He's all business. Meanwhile, you can read me like a book. I'm a hot mess. Everything I've ever felt or seen can be easily seen on the outside.

Carefully, he guides me by the shoulders and unclasps my bra, sliding the straps down my arms, where it falls to the floor. Normally, I'd be embarrassed that Sam is seeing me naked, but right now, I don't even care. His hands fall from my shoulders, down my back, and to the waistband of my panties. Tugging them, he pulls them down and taps my ankle for me to lift my foot. He does the same with my other leg.

With his hands back on my shoulders, he guides me to the bathtub. "Step in carefully; it's slippery," he says, not releasing my shoulders until I'm safely in the tub. I sink into the warm water and rest my head back on the edge. The hot water pricks at my skin almost painfully. Sam pulls a small hand towel off the towel rack and rolls it up. "Lift your head." When I lean forward, he slips the rolled towel behind my neck. "I'll be back in just a minute. Just relax," he says, slipping through the door again. This time, he leaves it open.

I close my eyes and let the warm water try to soothe me. I stretch my legs and feel the muscles begin to slowly relax. I inhale deeply, trying to get my mind to mimic my legs. *Relax*, I tell myself.

"Here." Sam's voice pulls me from the sounds of my deep breathing, and I open my eyes. He's holding out a glass of ice water. "You can brush your teeth when you're done, but I thought you might want some water."

I take the glass from him and sip the cool, refreshing liquid. Only the slight bones of my shoulders peek out of the bubbly water and the ends of my long hair hang heavily around my shoulders.

Sam pulls out the floating sponge and squeezes it. Taking the bottle of body wash, he squirts some onto the sponge, then sits on the edge of the tub and squeezes the sponge until it bubbles. "Give me your arm." He taps my left shoulder. Lifting my arm from the water, he begins running the soft sponge over my skin in small circles, starting at my shoulder, down my arm, and lifting to do the underside and my armpit. He takes his time with my hand and cleans my fingers methodically, scrubbing the cuticles to remove all traces of Alex's blood. Tears pool in my eyes as I watch all that I have left of Alex disappear in the sponge. He repeats this same process on my right arm, then he scrubs my neck and back.

"Sam, my necklace is gone." My voice breaks with emotion.

"What necklace?" His face twists in confusion.

"The one Alex gave me. It was a compass. I think it fell off at the condo."

"It's probably in evidence. I'll see if the crime scene technicians found it."

"I need that necklace, Sam." Tears spill from my eyes. "It's all I have left."

He swallows hard. With a curt nod, he pulls the removable showerhead off the wall and turns on the water, wetting my hair and letting the water run down my face. He's gentle and caring and quiet. Squirting a small amount of shampoo into the palm of his hand, he lathers it and begins rubbing it into my scalp. As he washes the blood of his brother away, I wonder what he's thinking and what he's feeling, except I'm too afraid to ask. My head falls back as his fingers begin to slowly massage me, releasing some of the tension and easing my headache. Turning on the handheld showerhead again, he rinses the shampoo from my hair and hands it to me before reaching down between my feet and pulling the drain plug.

"I loved him," I say, my voice quivering with emotion. I'm not sure why I feel the need to tell Sam. Maybe because it's his brother. Maybe because I feel vulnerable with him taking care of me right now. But I need Sam to know how I feel for Alex; I mean, "felt." My stomach sinks when I speak of him in the past.

He nods and sits on the edge of the tub. Finally, he stands. "Rinse off. I'll be just outside the door if you need me."

I close my eyes when I glance down at the water. It's no longer clear. It's turned pink from the blood on my hands…on my body. Alex's blood. I use the showerhead to rinse the remaining suds off my body. Turning the handle, I shut off the water and wrap myself in the large towel that Sam left on the edge of the tub, pulling down another towel to hand dry my hair.

"You okay in there?"

"Yeah, I'm good," I lie. *I'll never be the same*, I think to myself. Everyone close to me dies.

When the doorbell rings, I hear Sam leave and close the bedroom door behind him, then I move quickly into the room and slip into a clean bra and panties, and pull a gray tank top over my head. My cut-off jean shorts are on the top of my pile of clean clothes, and I step into those.

There's a knock on the door and it opens slowly. Sam looks at me and hesitates before finally speaking. "Em, you have to give a statement. I've put them off for almost twelve hours, but they're here and really need to get this done. I've told them to make it fast, then I'm taking you to the hospital."

I nod and take a deep breath. A statement. For a fleeting moment, I contemplate bolting. Sliding out the window and running away, away from the police, away from the bloodshed, away from my reality. I almost chuckle as I realize that was what I did in Illinois and it led me here. But this is my opportunity to get justice for Alex, for my mom. I take a deep breath and nod.

"It won't take long; just tell them everything you know and remember. Just be honest."

"Okay," I say weakly.

Swallowing hard, I pad down the hallway to the living room and take a seat on the leather couch. There are two men in chairs across the sofa table from me, both wearing suits and holding leather portfolios with notepads in them.

"Emilia Adams?" the old bald one asks as I pull a pillow into my lap for a measure of comfort, although nothing can really offer me comfort right now.

"Yes, I'm Emilia Adams," I exhale a long breath.

"I'm Special Agent Jonathon DeMartini with the ATF, and this is Special Agent Jorge SanFilipe with the DEA. We're going to need to get your statement about what happened last night at the residence of Alejandro Estrada."

I hesitate and fake a stiff smile for the detectives. For the next hour, I'm pummeled with questions, many of which I can't answer. When they begin to ask similar questions over and over, Sam steps in and politely ends the interview. Everyone stares at me as I twist my fingers nervously in my lap. A few hushed words are spoken, and then the men step into the kitchen. I hear Sam walking them out a moment later.

"You did great," he says, locking the door. "Your statement matches mine, so they shouldn't have any additional questions. They typically come back for another round when there are inconsistences."

I follow Sam with my eyes as he walks over to the couch and sits down next to me.

"How's your head?"

"Throbbing." I run my hand over the back of my neck.

"Let's get you to the hospital. I should've taken you last night." He reaches for my hand and pulls me up from the couch carefully. In the garage, he opens the passenger door of his car, and I slide numbly into the warm leather seats.

The drive to the hospital takes no more than five minutes, but I can't seem to get out of the car once we've parked. I stare at the automatic doors opening and closing as people enter and exit.

"Em, we need get you inside and registered."

"I've never been in a hospital before," I say absently.

"Well, they're not all that exciting, but I promise we'll both feel better after you've seen a doctor. Come on." Sam shuts his door and jogs around to open mine. He offers me his hand, but I ignore him and push myself out, steadying myself on the car door. Inside, I'm greeted by a woman at a large gray desk.

Sam glances at me before stepping forward and speaking discreetly with her. There are rows of chairs lined up, all facing a television that hangs from the ceiling in the corner, airing the local news. I take in the faces of the people waiting. Young and old, light and dark. Nothing similar about any of them.

My head throbs in tune to my heartbeat. I can feel the pulsing in my inner ear, and my vision begins to blur under the bright lights. The antiseptic smell of alcohol hangs in the air, and I shuffle across the floor, choosing a seat away from everyone else. I couldn't take it if someone wanted to talk to me. What would I say? That the man I loved died only a few short hours ago, and less than two hours ago, I was still covered in his blood?

Sam sits down next to me, his knee bobbing as he fills out paperwork. The scratching of his pen agitates me, but I close my eyes and rest my head back against the wall.

"Birthdate?" he asks quietly, nudging my arm to get my attention. "What's your birthdate, Em?"

"October second, nineteen ninety-three."

His pen begins to scrawl across the paper again before he flips it over and writes on the back. "You're going to have to help me with the medical history, okay?"

I nod just as a nurse steps out of the double doors and calls my name. Sam stands first, and I follow him as we cross the waiting room. The nurse, a young blonde, escorts us to an exam room, then asks Sam to wait outside for just a few minutes.

"Go ahead and take a seat in the chair," she says to me, offering a kind smile. "I'm Marcie, and I just need to ask you a few questions, then he can join us again. Why don't you go ahead and tell me what happened?"

It takes a moment to process everything she's said before the words come out in a monotone voice. "I hit my head pretty hard on a tile floor last night, and since then, I've had a severe headache, some nausea, a little bit of blurred vision."

She clicks away at the small laptop on the desk, casting careful glances at me in between her typing. "How did you hit your head?"

"My friend Sam," I point with my thumb to the door, "tackled me to keep me from getting in the crosshairs of some gunfire—" I stop abruptly when I realize how crazy this sounds.

Marcie's eyes widen. "Around what time did this happen last night?"

"Last night around seven, I think." Everything just spills from me. The honesty…the truth of my brutal reality spills from my lips. I should be embarrassed, but I'm not.

"You should've come to the emergency room immediately," she says, tapping on the keyboard again. "Before we let your friend back in, state law requires me to ask you if you are the victim of domestic violence or feel threatened in any way at home."

I almost snort. *At home.* I don't have a home. I shake my head gently, but it hurts, so I stop. "No," I whisper.

"Okay. Let me send your friend in, and I'll be back to take your blood pressure and get some additional medical information." She opens the door and steps out just as Sam enters.

He takes a seat in the chair next to me and sets the clipboard in his lap. "You okay?"

"Yeah." I nod, then instantly wince at the pain.

Marcie joins us back in the room, pushing a small cart with a blood pressure monitor on it. "Let me get some vitals from you, and I'll go through a quick medical history before the doctor comes to see you." She wraps the cuff around my arm and presses a button on the machine. Pulling a thermometer off the same machine, she sticks it under my tongue and holds it in place until the machine beeps. "Temperature and blood pressure are normal," she says as she peels the Velcro cuff from my arm. Sitting down again, she clicks away at her keyboard.

"Paperwork?" She reaches for the papers in Sam's hand and

glances at them before entering a few more things on the computer. "Okay, so let's get some additional medical information from you."

I take a deep breath and hope that I can answer some of her questions.

"Any known drug allergies?"

"No."

"Date of last menstrual cycle?"

I pause, trying to remember the last time I had a period. Sam turns to look at me, and I shrug. "I'm not sure. A couple of months ago, I guess. I've never really been regular."

She types a few things into the computer. "Smoker?"

"No."

"Do you use any illegal drugs?"

I catch Sam glancing at me out of the corner of his eye. It's a valid concern; I was living with the leader of a drug cartel.

"No, never," I answer quietly, and Sam visibly relaxes.

There is a quick but loud knock on the door just as it swings open. A doctor enters the room and holds out his hand to me. "I'm Doctor Jacobson. Nice to meet you."

"Emilia Adams," I say, shaking his hand in return.

"Sam Cortez," Sam says, shaking his hand after me.

Dr. Jacobson spends the next ten minutes examining me, asking me more questions, and finally deciding he'd like me to have a CT scan. Marcie takes me down the hall to weigh me, and then she hands me a sterile cup for a urine sample.

"Write your name on the cup and leave it on the small table in the room. When you're finished, I'll meet you back in the exam room before transport comes to take you to radiology."

"What's this for?" I point to the small cup she holds in her hand.

"Routine." She smiles at me. "We always screen urine for a multitude of reasons. You have nothing to worry about."

I do everything I'm told and wash my hands. Glancing at myself in the mirror, I see that my hair hangs in long, messy waves. My face is still pale and dark circles are finally setting in under my eyes. I feel numb as I splash some water on my face and use a paper towel to pat it dry. With a deep breath, I toss the paper towel in the trash and find my way down the hallway to my exam room. Sam is noticeably absent, so I take a seat and wait for Marcie or the doctor to return.

Minutes tick by and exhaustion is taking over. My eyelids are heavy and I finally close my eyes and listen to the hustle and bustle of the emergency room fluttering with activity on the other side of the door. Voices echo in the hallway, but I'm too tired to listen. My mind, along with my body, is finally shutting down.

There's a quick knock as Dr. Jacobson opens the door and enters the exam room. "Change of plans." He rests his hip against the edge of the counter and folds his hands together. "Your urine tests came back as positive for a pregnancy. Since we're not sure how far along…"

He's still talking, but all I hear is "positive for a pregnancy," and I lose it. Pregnant? How? I mean, I know how, but *why?* Why now? No. I can't have Alex's baby.

No, no, no! My mind screams at me!

Burying my face in my hands, I just shake my head and cry. The throbbing in the back of my head seems to get worse, and I feel my chest tightening as I try to breathe. "No!" I yell at Dr. Jacobson, to myself, to anyone that can hear me.

His voice trails off and the room is now silent, with the exception of my gasping cries.

"Ms. Adams," he says quietly after a moment. "Since you took a pretty hard fall, and we're not sure how far along you are, I'd like one of our obstetricians to take a look at you as well. I can see you're surprised by the news, but I do need you to listen to me in regards to your head injury."

Tears fall as I nod. Where is Sam? *Where the hell is Sam?* My heart beats so rapidly in my chest, it feels like it's bouncing off my ribs. I try to compose myself and look through my blurry eyes at

Dr. Jacobson, who's begun slowly giving me instructions for my head, and I only half hear him because of the loud swooshing sound in my ears.

"I believe it's a concussion. For the next few days, I'd like you to rest. No strenuous activity. Limit the amount of time you're using a computer, watching TV, or reading. Mostly just rest. Give your brain time to heal. I want you to see your primary doctor in two days. If anything worsens before then, you need to get back to the emergency room immediately."

He pauses and begins pulling open the cabinet over the sink, pulling down medical supplies and setting them on a tray before quietly leaving the room.

I can't believe this is happening to me. Leaning forward, I rest my elbows on my thighs and bury my face in my hands again. I gasp for air between deep sobs. "Why is this happening to me? Why?" I cry to myself. I'm not sure how much more I can take before I break. I was never whole to begin with and every loss, every setback, chips away at me more.

"Emilia, what the hell is wrong?" Sam's voice says as he closes the door.

I just shake my head in my hands and inhale sharply. My throat is tight, and I don't have the strength to explain everything to Sam right now.

He squats in front of me and grips my forearms, pulling my hands away from my face.

"Em, tell me what's going on."

There's a knock on the door, and a doctor and a nurse step in. The nurse is pushing a large machine with a small screen on it. My heart races as the doctor begins powering up the machine. I bounce between denial and shock and I feel nauseous.

"I'm Dr. Anderson and this is Shelly." She gestures to the nurse. "Dr. Jacobson tells me we have a fairly new pregnancy, and we need to check things out after a fall. Is that correct?"

Sam is now standing next to me, and he inhales sharply. His

face is pale and I see his throat tighten as he swallows. He looks as scared as I do. His hand rests on my shoulder in a supportive gesture.

I nod and swallow hard as she pushes the large machine closer to the exam table and the nurse begins carrying over the medical supplies that Dr. Jacobson had left on the counter.

"Why don't you hop up here on the bed? We're going to do an abdominal ultrasound."

Sam rests his hand on my shoulder before giving it a comforting squeeze.

I slide onto the table and lie down as Dr. Anderson powers up the ultrasound machine and types a few things into the computer attached to the cart.

"Just confirm for me your full name and date of birth, please," she says, typing away.

"Emilia Adams, October second, nineteen ninety-three." My voice is timid…weak.

"Okay, Emilia. Go ahead and unbutton your shorts for me," she says in a comforting voice. I unbutton the shorts, and she tucks some paper into the front of my jean shorts and folds it over the waistband. "This is supposed to be warm, but it's never warm enough. My apologies if it's cold." She shakes a bottle and squirts a large amount of gel on my lower stomach. With a small wand, she presses against my stomach with one hand and presses buttons on the machine with her other hand. She presses and pushes, at times causing me to catch my breath.

"Everything looks really good, Emilia." She smiles at me. "You're very early. From just my measurements, I'd say five weeks or so. Everything seems to be progressing just fine, but I'd schedule an appointment with your OB/GYN immediately." She presses a few more buttons on the machine, and a long picture strip prints out. She looks at it and smiles as my stomach turns and my reality sets in. She smiles at me sympathetically and takes a calming breath. "Dr. Jacobson said this wasn't a planned pregnancy."

I nod at her and fight back tears.

"You have options, Emilia. There's a lot of support available to you while you determine what's best for you," Dr. Anderson says quietly, gathering her items.

"Okay," I'm barely able to get out.

Sam leans against the wall, his hands tucked behind him. He's staring straight ahead at the door, a look of shock on his face. Sam hasn't said a word; his support has been silent. A squeeze on my shoulder during the exam has been all that he's been able to do. I know he's in shock as well.

"I'm going to send in one of our social workers to speak with you. She'll have more information for you," Dr. Anderson says as she slips out the door, her long, blonde hair bouncing around her shoulders as she leaves.

The next thirty minutes are a blur as a social worker hands me a stack of pamphlets and gives me information and phone numbers for clinics, organizations, and doctors. Sam disappeared somewhere during that time, and I find him out in the waiting area. He looks as exhausted as I feel.

Without a word, we leave and drive to his home in silence.

TWO

Sam

For the last two hours, I've paced the floor between my living room and kitchen in a complete state of shock. Em being pregnant was not part of the plan. *Fuck.* I pinch the bridge of my nose as I feel the pounding in my head begin. With a deep breath, I follow the hall to where Em lies in my bed. My bedroom door is cracked open, but I knock quietly anyway. "Em, are you all right?"

She's lying in the fetal position in the center of the bed and shifts slightly at the sound of my voice but keeps her back to me.

"Are you hungry?" I ask, but she remains silent. "Come on, Emilia. Talk to me."

She didn't say a word to me on the way home, and she retreated to the bedroom the moment we walked in the door.

"No," she finally manages, her voice raspy.

"No what? You won't talk to me or you're not hungry?" I want her to talk to me...open up to me.

"Hungry," she mumbles.

"Emilia, you have to eat something. Even something small." I push the door open further and step into my room. I feel helpless and all I want to do is help her.

"My stomach is still bothering me. Maybe later." She pulls a pillow up tightly to her stomach, tucking it between her chin and her knees.

"Alex told me you won't eat when you get upset." She stills, and I flinch when I realize I said Alex's name so casually and how it affects Emilia. "I'm so sorry, Em."

"When did he tell you that?" Her shoulders begin to bob gently, and I can tell she's crying again.

I swallow hard. "When he called to tell me you left. He followed you to the church, and he was worried about you, so he called me to come and get you."

She nods, her face buried in her hands.

"Em." I reach out and skim my hand along her forearm, but she pulls it away and buries her face in her hands.

"What am I going to do?" she sobs.

I move toward her and sit on the edge of the bed. Emilia watches me tentatively as I sit down.

"I need Alex. I can't do this without him." Alex. She'll always love Alex. I swallow down my bitterness.

You can, Em. You have me now. But I bite my tongue and rub her back. Conflict settles in me as I realize I'm in love with a woman carrying my brother's baby. Since I can't tell her that I'm in love with her, I settle for, "Em, everything is going to be fine. But you need to rest and you definitely need to eat. Everything else will be fine. I promise." I try to comfort her, but she shakes her head back and forth against the pillow.

"I can't do this," she stutters between breaths. "I'm not strong enough to do this alone." She uses the back of her hand to wipe her nose.

"You *can* do this, and you *are* strong enough," I encourage her.

She takes a deep, cleansing breath as she tries to compose herself and pushes up to a sitting position, crisscrossing her legs. Her breaths are staggered and deep, and she takes a moment before exhaling loudly. She looks so small and helpless, and just…sad. "I have so many questions," she says quietly. "I don't even know where to start."

"Just ask me." Not that I'm a fount of baby information. I clear my throat and amend, "I may not be able to answer all of them, but I'll tell you what I can."

"The truth?" she asks. I hate that she even doubts me, but she should. Alex and I both lied to her.

"Yes, the truth."

"Do you know where your dad is? He got away, didn't he?" Her fingers twist around each other as she looks directly at me and stutters through the question. She watches me as if she'll be able to read whether or not I'm lying to her.

"Antonio," I say, disregarding him as my father, "got away. However, we have a pretty good idea where he is, and we have every agency and police force in the state working on locating him."

"Where do you think he is?"

"Mexico."

"Does he want me dead?" She swallows hard, and I do too.

"I don't have confirmation of that, but considering how much you know about his business now, my guess would be yes."

She exhales slowly, and her eyes drop from mine.

"But, Emilia, as long you're here with me, nothing is going to happen to you. I won't let anything happen to you." Over my dead fucking body would I let anything happen to her.

"I can't stay here forever," she whispers, leaning back against the wooden headboard.

"You're going to stay here for as long as you want, and I promise I won't let anything happen to you." I will not let her walk away from me. I *want* her as much as she *needs* me.

"Sam." Her voice breaks. "Will there be a service or funeral?" Her eyes are trained on the ceiling, but I can see tears glistening in the corners.

I pause, wondering what to tell her. Regardless, it's all lies. "If we do something, it'll be small, private. You won't be able to go, Em. If Antonio is looking for you, he'll expect you to be there. My guess is he'll have his guys watching."

"I need to be there," she says, her voice somber. "I need to say goodbye." Tears fall freely from the corners of her eyes and roll down her cheeks to her neck. I feel her pain, and I want nothing more than to pull her into my arms and take it away. "There's so much I need to say, Sam. So much I need to tell him."

"I know, Em." I sit quietly and watch her try to keep it together. Her chest constricts and her body trembles as she tries to control her emotions. God, I hate seeing her like this. I want to pull her into my arms and wrap myself around her. Comfort her; tell her I'll always take care of her—and her baby.

Her sniffles are the only sound filling the space between us. In the bathroom, I snag the box of tissues from the counter and set it on the bed next to her.

She takes two. "Thanks." Then we sit silently again for a long time, no words spoken as she wrestles with her thoughts and emotions. She wavers between shock and sadness, but it's the fear I see in her eyes that saddens me the most. Is it her reality that she fears? Is it me? Finally, she takes a deep breath and clears her throat. "Will I be able to go back to work soon? I need to keep my job…I need the money."

My heart sinks. She's worried about money? Of all the things, this is something she should not be worried about.

"You probably won't be able to work anytime soon. But you don't need to worry about money, Emilia."

"I won't take your money, and I can't let Jax and Megan down. I need this job," she pleads with me. She's stubborn. This was what made me fall in love with her. "You can't do everything for me. I need to learn to live on my own, Sam."

I sigh loudly. "Let me see what I can do. It'll be at least a few weeks. You need to heal, physically and emotionally, and not jump back into things." I can do everything for her, and I will if she'll let me. Plus, there is no way I'll risk letting her out of my sight until Antonio and his associates are behind bars.

"I'll go crazy if I don't get back into a routine—"

"You'll hurt yourself," I argue with her, "or worse, your baby if you don't take care of yourself."

She rubs her eyes with her palms and exhales loudly in frustration.

I take a moment to calm down. The last thing she needs right now is a lecture. I want to show my concern for her, but not drive her away with crazy expectations. "Listen, I don't want to tell you what to do, Emilia. But you're not thinking clearly right now. Give it a few days. A lot has happened in the last twenty-four hours. Take some time to absorb everything. Financially, you'll be fine. Mentally, I'm worried about you."

She nods and lies back down, resting her head on my pillow, her long hair spilling onto the pillow next to it. Everything about her is beautiful. Even when she's sad and broken and defeated, her natural beauty is all I can see. I brush my knuckles across her soft cheek and take a deep breath as I take in her beauty.

"I need to run to the office to get some files. I'm going to work from home for the next few days. I'll grab some food on my way back. You *need* to eat." I hesitate. "I won't leave you, though, if you're not comfortable being here alone."

"Go. I'll be fine. I'm going to try to take a nap anyway. I can't shake this headache." I run my fingers through her hair and she watches me as she closes her eyes. Her head falls to the side as my fingers flit through her silky hair. She turns to me when I stop and looks at me. She opens her mouth to say something but stops, pressing her lips together. I brush my fingertips across her bottom lip and up her cheek, finally stopping near her ear.

"There is a phone on the nightstand. If you need anything, you call me." I don't want to leave her, but I have to get to the office to get my files so I can work from home.

"I will," she whispers and closes her eyes.

I lean down and press a quick kiss to her forehead. I want so badly to taste her lips, but I know now isn't the time—I just hope she'll eventually learn to love me.

The antiseptic smell of the hospital stings my nose as I enter the sliding doors. A rush of cool air greets me, and I scan the main reception area. Just behind the main desk is a set of elevators that I take to the third floor. Anxiety bubbles to the surface as I'm deposited at the end of a long, sterile-looking hallway. I scan the area for a reception desk on the floor, finding one on the opposite end of the hallway from me. As I near, I pull my wallet from my back pocket and show the receptionist my badge and identification. My hand shakes and I'm not sure if it's because I'm nervous or exhausted.

"Alejandro Estrada," I announce quietly, glancing over my shoulder to see if anyone else is around.

She looks at her computer screen, tapping away at the keyboard before she smiles at me and points. "Room two-seventeen, just down the hall. Keep your badge and ID available. You'll need them to get into the room."

I take note of all the empty rooms as I walk down the long, sterile hall. The long hall leads me to a police officer standing outside Alex's room. I approach the uniformed officer, who stands a few inches taller than me and looks like a professional wrestler. I hand him my badge and ID. He checks it closely and nods before opening the door. After stepping inside, the door latches behind me. The sound of a television plays quietly behind a pulled curtain, and I step forward. When I peek around the curtain, a pair of eyes meets mine, followed by an exaggerated sigh.

"You here to finish the job?" He cringes through gritted teeth.

I actually let out a little laugh. "You are one lucky motherfucker."

Alex gives me a pained smile as he tries to reach across himself for a remote on a bedside table. His arm is wrapped in thick gauze and rests in a fabric sling, which is propped up with pillows. Annoyance roils through me as I see him smirk, and I think of Emilia at home on the brink of a breakdown.

Shoving aside my annoyance, I step over to the side of the bed, pick up the remote, and hand it him. I realize it's the first nice thing I've done for my brother in twenty-some-odd years. Not that I've had many chances. "Here you go."

His dark brown hair is messy and both eyes are lined with dark circles, similar to Emilia's gaunt look. His skin is ashen grey, and he looks as if he's just skirted death—because he has.

"Thanks," he says, pressing a button on the remote, which raises the back of his bed. He cringes as the bed adjusts him to an upright position. "So what brings you to see me, *Agent* Cortez?" A smirk tugs at the corner of his mouth and he says the word "agent" sarcastically.

I take a seat in a chair next to him. "First, how are you feeling?" I expect him to say "like shit" because he looks like hell and word is that he's damn lucky to be alive.

Alex exhales loudly and rubs his shoulder. "They said the bullet missed anything major. I broke my collar bone and, aside from tissue damage, that's it."

"Like I said, you're one lucky motherfucker. You took three bullets to your shoulder and upper arm and you only have minor damage. Most people die from one bullet," I snap at him. "You were bleeding pretty good; I thought you might bleed out before we could get medical attention on site."

"Do you really care or are these pleasantries part of the job?" Alex snaps at me bitterly.

I clench my jaw and decide it's best not to respond. I offered an olive branch and he declined. Point taken, moving on. "So, I think we have a deal."

"You *think* we do, or we do?" He narrows his eyes at me, skeptical.

"We have a deal if you're willing to accept it." *Take the fucking deal and leave. Leave Emilia, leave town, and just get the fuck away from here.*

"Talk."

I open my leather portfolio and pull out a typed agreement with the terms of the deal in which he will provide everything on the Estrada cartel in return for witness security protection and his liquid assets that have not been seized.

"It's cut and dry. Should be an easy decision," I try to persuade him, then slide the paper onto the bedside tray. "It's a fair deal, Alex. Take it," I urge.

His eyes scan the bulleted items outlining the terms and he sets it back on the table. "So that's it?"

I give a curt nod. "We have the files from your house. All you have to do is sign. Of course, for the next four to six months, you'll be at our disposal, providing us anything and everything we need to build our case against Antonio. You'll remain in a safe house while we build our case, and once we have sufficient information, the witness security agreement will be enforced."

"What about Emilia?" His eyes search mine, looking for answers.

I pause. This is where it gets complicated. I rub the stubble along my chin and sigh, figuring out how to best explain this. "The agency wouldn't..."

"Deal's off," he interrupts me, tossing the paper back at me. It flutters to the ground next to my feet.

"Alex, listen to me. This is it. This is your one chance to get out. This is what you wanted," I reason with him. "This is your opportunity for a better life. You can redeem yourself—"

"I was doing this to protect Emilia," he cuts me off with a growl. "If she's not a part of the deal, I'm not doing it. I need her safe—and without witness security, she won't be." The blood pressure cuff attached to his arm begins to inflate and the machine starts beeping. He tosses his head back onto his pillow and takes a couple of deep breaths.

"You're making a huge mistake. Don't turn this deal down, Alex. This is your chance to live without looking over your shoulder. This is what you wanted," I yell at him.

"I won't do it if we can't protect Emilia." He changes the subject. His eyes lock on mine, and I hold his stare. I know I'll never get a deal for her, but I choose not to tell him this right now.

The door to Alex's hospital room opens, and the officer stationed out front clears his throat. "Everything okay in here?"

"Yes, sir," Alex says. "I'll let you know if I need anything." The police officer closes the door and Alex looks back at me. "So I'm in custody, I take it. That's why he's here?" he asks bitterly. Alex is always questioning my motives.

"No, he's here because I asked for you to have protection." *Good deed number two*, I think to myself. Not that I'm counting.

"How is she?" he asks me, looking away from me. His voice cracks and he clears his throat to choke back his emotion.

"She's a mess." *She thinks you're dead. She's pregnant. She doesn't have any family.* I shake my head, thinking about what she's going through right now. "You knew she wasn't going to handle this well." I exhale deeply and lean forward in my chair, resting my elbows on my knees.

"I need to see her." It's a demand.

"I can't do that. We need to keep her thinking you're dead. If she slips up and Antonio finds out you're alive, you're as good as dead—and so is Emilia. I've got my hands full protecting her. I can't protect both of you," I snap at him.

"I don't need you to protect me," he snarls at me and narrows his tired eyes.

I sigh loudly. "Look, if the organization thinks you're dead, you're no longer a threat to them. You know this."

"What about Emilia? They think she's still a threat because

they believe she has information on them, right?" I can see the fear in his eyes when he speaks of Emilia and his concern for her.

"Right. Which is why I need to focus my energy on protecting her, not both of you." I clench my jaw.

"Fuck!" He slams his only free hand on the bedside table. "I need to see her. I need to protect her!" he yells at me. Only he's tired and hurting and his yelling is nothing more than a raised voice.

I get it, though. Of course he wants to protect her. We both do. "Alex, I'm working on it. Emilia is safe right now, but I need you to take the deal to protect yourself. I'll try my best to see what I can do for her."

"She's a part of the deal or there is no deal, Sam. Do you understand?" he yells at me angrily.

I reluctantly nod and bite my tongue. Without Alex's signature on that agreement, this case is screwed—and the only thing I want is my father in prison.

"Where is she?"

"Staying with me." I look away from him for a brief moment before turning back.

He closes his eyes, and I can see the veins in his neck throbbing. He's angry. "So help me God, if anything happens to her on your watch, I'll take you to Mexico and fucking cut you into pieces with a goddamn chainsaw, then feed you to the fish. Do you understand me?"

And he would. I'm sure of it.

"I care about Emilia just as much as you do, Alex," I sneer at him. "I'm not going to let anything happen to her."

"And if you fucking touch her, so much as look at her, or act in any way other than that of a professional federal agent, I'll fucking kill you with my bare hands. Mark my words. Dead. Gone. I'll make you disappear," he says through clenched teeth.

"Careful, Alejandro. Threatening a federal agent isn't going to help you." Just then, the curtain opens and an older male doctor with white hair pulls a stethoscope from his neck.

"I can't have you two arguing in here," he says, giving me a dirty look. *Me.* I didn't even hear the door open. "Mr. Estrada needs his rest. He's in ICU for a reason. He's not supposed to have any visitors, even the 'law' kind."

He looks over his wire-rimmed glasses at me, then presses the stethoscope to Alex's chest. I sit back in my chair and rub the bridge of my nose. Reasoning with him seems pointless. Alex always had the temper—clearly, he still does.

"Your blood pressure is elevated and your heart rate is accelerated. Either you calm down and rest or you'll be on strict hospital orders, Mr. Estrada," the doctor scolds Alex.

"He's my brother," he mumbles under his breath, as if it pains him to admit to that fact. "It was just family business."

"I don't care who he is or what you're arguing about. Keep it down and *rest*." He wraps the stethoscope around his neck and looks pointedly at me. "Five more minutes and you need to leave."

"Yes, sir." Believe me, I don't want to be here any longer than I have to. I'm already starting to crack under all this.

"We're almost done, Doc." Alex winces as he lowers the back of his bed just a bit. I stand and help Alex readjust the pillow under his arm—good deed number three. When the doctor leaves, the room is quiet except for the background noise from the television.

"I'll come back tomorrow. But Alex, you need to seriously consider this deal. Please." I sound like I'm fucking begging him. I am begging him, and I hate that I have to beg him. I hate asking my brother for anything.

"I'll think about it," he replies, his jaw hard. "Make it right with Emilia and I'll do it."

"I'll see what I can do. Get some rest."

Juggling my laptop case, keys, and bags of Chinese food, I scramble to shut off the alarm before it goes off and scares Emilia. The house is dark with just the moonlight illuminating the family room through the large windows and the glass French doors. After turning on lights in the kitchen, I pull out the white takeout cartons and set them in the middle of the round kitchen table, opening each box carefully.

"What time is it?" a raspy voice asks from behind me, startling me. Emilia rubs her eyes as she steps into the kitchen. Her hair is messy and falling out of the ponytail she had it pulled up in earlier. Even with her loose tendrils, she looks stunning.

"Hey." I glance over my shoulder at the clock on the kitchen wall. "It's almost seven. Did you get some rest?"

She nods sleepily. "What's all that?"

"Dinner. Chinese food. I didn't know what you like, so I got a little of everything."

She scrunches her nose and rubs her stomach as she turns around and walks into the family room, sitting down on the couch. Tucking her legs up under her, she pulls a blanket off the back of the couch, draping it over her.

"Are you cold?" I frown at her. "It's a hundred and ten outside."

"But it's freezing in here." She rubs her arms and shrugs. The air isn't even set low, but it's because she's so thin and exhausted.

"Sure you're feeling okay?"

"Yeah." She nods quickly, surely to ward off my suspicion.

From the cupboard, I pull down two large dinner plates and begin heaping a little of everything onto each plate. Lo mein, fried rice, broccoli beef, cashew chicken, and egg rolls all on display for Emilia to choose from. I walk the plate of food and a fork over to her, and she tilts her head, rolling her eyes in feigned annoyance at me.

"Eat. There has to be something on this plate you'll like."

She scrunches her nose again, but takes the plate and balances it on her lap. I take two bottles of cold water from the fridge and grab my plate as I head back into the living room. I take a seat on the floor in front of Emilia and place the water bottles on the coffee table. She twirls her fork in the lo mein noodles, bringing it to her mouth taking a small bite. *Good.*

"Did you sleep the entire time I was gone?" I ask between bites of food.

"I did. I finally feel rested," she says, and I know she's lying. She still looks exhausted. Stabbing a piece of cashew chicken, she pulls it from the fork with her teeth. "This is really good. I guess I didn't realize how hungry I was."

I'm just glad she's eating. We sit quietly, picking at our food. The only sounds are the metal forks scraping against the glass plates.

"Did you get what you needed from the office?" she asks, taking another bite of chicken.

I shrug and take a drink of water before responding. "I did."

"You were gone a long time," she says, looking at me skeptically.

"I was. I got pulled into a couple of briefings—"

"Do they have any information?" she asks as she wipes her mouth with a napkin.

I shake my head no and push food around my plate. We sit quietly, the mood heavy around us.

"I know we have a lot to talk about," I say, finally breaking the silence. I twist my body around so I'm looking at her. Her hand stills before setting the fork down on her plate. "I'm sure you have a lot of questions, and when you're ready to talk, Em, I'll tell you everything."

"Promise?" Her face tells me she's wary. "You won't lie or hold back?"

I shake my head once. "I won't."

She feigns a small smile for me. Pushing the blanket off of her, she swings her legs off the couch and carries her plate to the kitchen. I'm happy and surprised when I see her helping herself to a second serving of fried rice and cashew chicken. Her long, skinny legs peek out from under short cut-off jean shorts, and she wobbles a little as she steps over me and back to her spot on the couch. I never realized how skinny she was before, but the bones of her shoulders are obvious as well. No wonder Alex was so concerned about her eating—and now she's eating for two.

I reach for the television remote control and push the power button. "How about some Netflix?"

She looks at me like a deer caught in the headlights. "Net huh?" she asks with a mouth full of fried rice. I almost laugh at the sound she makes.

"Netflix. You can watch movies, television shows, all from the comfort of your couch. It'll be your new best friend, trust me."

She casts me a sideways glance at the words "trust me." Obviously, I don't blame her. I wasn't entirely honest with her about my association with Alex and the Estrada family.

"So what do you recommend?" She twists the cap off of her water bottle.

"What do you like? Scary? Romantic? Comedy?"

"Not scary. I don't like horror or blood." She shivers when she says that. I don't blame her there either. She's been living in a nightmare these last few months. She's seen enough blood to last her a lifetime.

"How about funny? Dodgeball!" I say excitedly. "It's got Ben Stiller and Vince Vaughn. It's hilarious."

She looks at me like I have two heads, and I feel guilty once again. "Sure. I have no clue who they are, but I could use a laugh."

It's then that I see the sadness in her eyes, the worry she carries on her shoulders, weighing her spirit down. I want to take away all of her pain if she'll let me. Settling in, I sit on the opposite end of the couch and she lies on her side, resting her head on the arm of the couch. Her knees are pulled up and tucked in close to her chest. She looks so innocent, so naïve. Only I know better. This girl has seen more in her short life than most will see in a lifetime.

For the next hour and a half, my attention is split between the movie and the beautiful girl on other end of my couch. She makes attempts to laugh at the funny parts, but I can tell her heart isn't into it. By the time the credits roll, her eyes have closed and her lips are slightly parted, her chest rising and falling in a steady pattern. I'm glad she's sleeping again. She needs it.

With a sigh, I shut off the TV and pull the blanket off of her, folding it and placing it back on the sofa. Sliding my arms under her back and her knees, I easily lift her and walk her down the dark hall to my bedroom. She can have the bed again; I'll take the couch. One more glance at her under my comforter and I leave her to rest. And as I lie on my couch, I make plans to buy a bed for the spare bedroom. It's time anyway. It's been empty since I bought this place.

As I stare up at my ceiling, I feel my thoughts and emotions wrestling to break free. Anger, sadness, resentment, hostility, and even guilt settle in. I'm angry with Alex for bringing Emilia into this mess. I'm sad. I lost my brother, and even though we're still enemies, I miss him. And it's all my father's fault. All of it.

My anger for him burns the hottest. Just thinking of him being out there and still free to conduct his "business" has me tensing with fury. He was the one that tore Alex and me apart. He was the one that murdered our mother. And if it's the last thing I do, I will kill him with my bare hands.

Suddenly, a tiny voice in the dark startles me. "Sam." I hear her feet softly shuffle across the floor as she comes into view.

"What's wrong, Em?"

"I can't sleep."

"You've only been in bed for twenty minutes."

She sits down on the end of the couch near my feet, and I push myself up.

"Can I ask you something?" she asks shyly.

I swallow hard. I promised her the truth and that's what she'll get. "Of course."

"What happened to your family?"

I never knew such a tiny question could make me feel so vulnerable. Her voice is so small, so desperate. I want to tell her, but… We sit in the dark facing each other. Maybe it's easier to tell the truth in the dark. You can hide the emotions on your face—no one can see your fear, your hurt, and your despair.

"God, Emilia…" I trail off and wonder how to even explain it. "My mom was the glue. That woman loved Alex and me more than anything. She was the best mom—" My voice breaks, and I clear my throat, shoving down my emotions. "When my dad started his business, I remember them fighting often. She cried a lot and used to talk to my *tia* about how scared she was. She hated the business. She hated guns and drugs. My dad didn't care. It was always about money to him."

Emilia shifts on the end of the couch and pulls her legs up under her. I watch her for a moment to make sure she's okay hearing all of this, then I continue. "Alex was the one that found my mom. I'll never forget that day." I run my hands over my face and press the tears back into my eyes. "He ran home from school when she wasn't outside waiting for us. He knew something was wrong—and so did I, but I was a coward. I was afraid to go home. He ran and didn't stop running until he got there. By the time I finally got home, I could hear Alex screaming inside the house. Screaming and crying, and I watched my dad from the driveway. He was sitting on the front steps, smoking a cigarette… And when he looked at me, I saw nothing but pure evil." I can't believe I even acknowledged Antonio was my father.

"So what happened? How did you end up with your aunt and uncle?"

"They took both Alex and me, and tried to keep things as normal as possible for us. Taking us to school, picking us up, making sure we went to church. Father Mark really stepped in to make sure we were handling everything okay mentally. He'd pull us from class, to talk to us…I guess almost counsel us." I remember this fondly and am so thankful we had him.

"I can't believe you've known Father Mark for that long."

I blow a puff of air from through my lips. "I know. That old man is the one person, the only person I've ever trusted other than my aunt and uncle. Anyway, my aunt and uncle wanted to become Alex and my legal guardians. They knew what my dad was doing and didn't want us in that environment. My aunt begged Antonio to let us stay with her, but he wouldn't leave Alex." I choke back the hate I have for my father.

"Why?" There's a sadness in her voice as she questions me.

"He always loved him more, I guess. If that's what love is. I don't think my father, I mean, Antonio really even knows what love is." My heart drops when I admit this openly to Emilia. Even though I hate my father now, as a child, I wanted nothing more than his love and acceptance.

"I'm sorry," she says quietly.

"Don't be. I was the lucky one. My aunt and uncle did an amazing job raising me. They gave me everything I ever needed and more. The day Antonio took Alex home with him was the last day Alex ever talked to me. He switched schools and life just moved on for us." I remember the hurt I felt at losing my brother. He was the one person I had left, my other half.

"I feel bad for both of you," she whispers.

I swallow hard. "I always felt bad for Alex, but that sympathy vanished when I found out he was following in Antonio's footsteps. I think it was in high school. I overhead my aunt and uncle talking about it late one night. They'd heard from family that Antonio was priming Alex to take over. That was the day I decided I'd do anything in my power to bring that organization down. I went to college and worked my ass off. Graduated and applied as a special agent for the ATF, which brings me to where I am today."

We sit in the dark, silence now filling the space between us.

I've bled all my dark family secrets to Emilia and while it should feel good to get it off my chest, it doesn't. I'm just—sad. Minutes turn to hours, and we remain silent, taken in by the comfort of each other's presence.

As the first hint of the morning sunrise peeks through the glass patio doors, Emilia clears her throat. "Sam?"

"Yeah."

"I'm scared," she says weakly. I want to pull her to me and wrap her in my arms, but I refrain.

"I know you are. But I promise I won't let anything happen to you."

I wonder to myself how many times she's heard that lie, and if I'll ever be able to truly protect her.

THREE

Emilia

I reach my arms above my head and exhale slowly while I stretch. It takes me a few minutes to wake up as the fog in my head begins to clear. The clock on the nightstand reads twelve thirty-four, and I hastily kick the soft sheet off of me. I can't believe I slept past noon.

The house is quiet as I peek around, looking for Sam. Through the glass patio doors, I see him sitting on the back porch. His broad build is shadowed by a large wooden pergola covered in a flowery vine, and he looks distracted as he types away on his laptop at the patio table.

Glancing over his shoulder, he catches me standing there and gestures for me to come outside. I'm greeted with a blast of hot air when I step out, although it's comfortable in the shade.

"Did you sleep okay?" he asks before pulling a glass of orange juice to his lips.

"I did. I can't believe it's already this late." I slink down into a wrought-iron chair padded in a thick cushion. I'm not used to sleeping late. I was either up early for work or to take care of my mom. I've never had the luxury of sleeping the day away.

"What can I make you to eat?" he asks with a smile. I appreciate Sam always looking out for me and being so attentive. Pushing his laptop aside, he rests his forearms on the table.

My stomach grumbles at the thought of food, and suddenly, I'm craving Rosa's Belgian waffles. *Rosa.* My heart stills when I think of her. I have no way of getting in touch with her, not that I would be allowed to.

"Sam, did you know Rosa, Alex's housekeeper?"

"I didn't know her personally, but we know of her. We've investigated everyone that's ever worked for the Estrada family."

"And…" I drawl, wanting him to spill the beans on what he has on Rosa.

"And we found nothing. She seems to be legitimate. Why do you ask?"

I contemplate what I should say, if anything at all. Despite his kindness, I'm still wary of Sam. I know I need to trust him, I'm supposed to, but I'm not sure I can. "She made the best Belgian waffles." I reply simply, leaving it at that.

"You want waffles?" he asks with a hopeful smile.

"It's more than waffles. I miss her. I grew close to her in the short time I was at Alex's. I guess I'm worried about her too. She was kind of a mother figure to Alex, and I wonder how she's handling all of this."

Sam sits back in his chair and inhales sharply. "I see," he says, rubbing his chin. His eyes shift back and forth between me and his glass of orange juice. "I don't know where Rosa is or how she's doing, Em."

"Can you find her?" My voice hitches with hopefulness.

He hesitates. "I don't know if that's a good idea, honestly."

"Why?"

"Em, I'm trying to keep you away from that life. Yeah, she wasn't directly involved, but for all I know, Antonio is watching her too."

"Then we need to warn her."

"Em," he snaps at me. "I've got my hands full right now. Please…"

"Please what?" I challenge him. Surely he wouldn't let someone who means so much to me fall prey to his father. "I didn't ask for you to protect me—"

"No, you didn't, Em, but Alex did."

I freeze when he says this.

He exhales loudly and slowly, tension passing through the air between us. Finally, he blows a puff of air through his lips. "Look, I'm not Rosa." He laughs. "But I can try to make you waffles. I know I have a waffle iron somewhere, and I promise I'll see what I can find out about her."

I try not to get my hopes up too much. "You will?"

"I promise." He rests his hand over his heart.

"Okay." I nod. "But I don't really want waffles. I'm kind of nauseous." All the talk of Rosa has upset my stomach.

"You need to eat something. How about some fruit?" He leans forward and rests his hand on my arm in concern.

Fruit actually sounds good…for a split second, until my mouth begins to water and that familiar feeling of bile begins to rise. Jumping up from the patio chair, I sprint inside the house. I can hear Sam calling my name, but I can't respond. I barely make it to the hallway bathroom before I heave into the toilet.

"Emilia!" Sam finds me over the toilet and kneels next to me, pulling my hair back. "It's okay," he says softly. His other hand rubs small circles on my back as my stomach clenches one last time and I vomit again.

Reaching up, I blindly find the handle and flush the toilet. Tears sting my eyes, and I fall back, leaning against the bathroom wall. Sam sits quietly next to me, both of our legs outstretched next to each other.

I wipe my mouth with my forearm as a sob escapes me. "I can't do this, Sam."

He reaches out and rests his hand on my thigh, giving it a

tender squeeze. "You can, Em. You will." He encourages me, but even he doesn't sound convinced. "Come on." Sam pushes himself up and reaches his hand out to me, pulling me up and steadying me by my shoulders. "Let's wait a little bit to eat, let your stomach settle." I nod in agreement. "There's something I wanted to give you."

"What is it?"

"Let's go." He slides his hand into mine and guides me to the living room. "Sit down." He gestures to the couch and hands me a large, white plastic bag. "Open it."

I slide my fingers through the drawstring opening and pull out a white box with the profile view of a slim laptop. Peeling the plastic wrap off, I lift the lid and gasp at the sleek silver laptop. "Sam! This is too much."

"Do you like it?" he asks as I pull the laptop out of the box and rest it on my lap.

"I love it. I have no clue how to use it, but I love it." I've always wanted my own laptop, but could never afford one. I always used the clunky old computers at the public library.

He chuckles. "I'll get it all set up for you. It's easy to use once you play around with it for a while."

"This is too much, Sam." I hate owing people anything, and right now, there is no way I can afford this laptop.

"This is a gift, Em. All you have to do is accept it. That's it." He smiles sincerely at me.

"Thank you," I say quietly.

Two hours later, Sam has me all set up and ready to browse the Internet. He's shown me a website that all the women in his office rave about: Pinterest. It's a website that has every idea imaginable to save ideas on home décor, cooking, crafts, fashion, and so much more. I'm already hooked. Although he's made me vow not to set up social media in case Antonio is looking for me—and he's also asked me to stay off my email in case that's also being monitored.

Apparently, Pinterest and I are going to become close friends because that's about all I'm allowed to do.

Evening begins to settle in, and Sam is out on the back patio, grilling dinner. I give the laptop a rest and join him, settling into a patio chair while he mans the grill. I fight back tears as my memory still replays everything that happened just a day ago.

Dressed in a pair of athletic shorts and t-shirt, it's easy to admire Sam's impressive build—except all I see when I watch him is Alex. His arms flex and relax as he flips chicken breasts one-handed while gripping a cold bottle of beer in the other hand. He's got an Arizona Diamondbacks baseball hat on backward, which allows me full access to view his chiseled jaw and dark brown eyes. Eyes just like Alex's, just a little darker.

His lips twist into a smile when he catches me watching him. "Like what you see?"

Rolling my eyes, I reply, "You wish." I rub my eyes with the back of my hand so that he doesn't see me crying again.

Which causes him to bust out laughing. "Dinner will be ready in a few."

"Can we eat out here tonight? On the patio?" I ask and smile at the thought.

"Sure. It's a little warm but not terrible. Let me turn on the misters; that'll make it more comfortable."

I jump up go back into the house to gather the place settings from the kitchen table so I can and move them from the kitchen table to the backyard. While I'm in there, I grab the tossed salad and dressings and the pitcher of ice water, bringing them outside and them placing in the center of the large, iron table. Sam sets the platter of grilled chicken and veggies between us as we sit, and whispers a quiet prayer before plating me a healthy serving of chicken, veggies, and salad. The sun is just beginning to set and an orange hue lights up the afternoon sky. It's peaceful, calm here.

"Tomorrow, I have to go into the office for a while. I don't like leaving you here alone, but it's more dangerous if I take you with me."

"I hate that I'm an inconvenience to you," I say, stabbing a piece of chicken breast with my fork. Sam's cooking is delicious, but I seem to only be able to eat a little bit at a time because of my nausea.

"You're not an inconvenience at all, Emilia. I wish we could locate Antonio and his men, then I wouldn't be so concerned about leaving you alone—or taking you with me." He sighs. Reaching behind him, he pulls another beer from the small outdoor refrigerator that's built into the stone grill area. Twisting the cap, he takes a long pull from the glass bottle before setting it on the table.

"Are you close to finding him?" I ask, pushing the tossed salad around my plate. I set my fork down after suddenly losing my appetite. The hair on the back of my neck stands on end every time I speak about Antonio.

"Negative," he responds and takes another sip of beer.

"If he finds me, Sam, he'll kill me, won't he?" Sam just stares at me. His refusal to respond tells me his answer. "He smiled at Alex before he pulled the trigger and shot him. I saw him smile. If he'd kill his own son, I know he'll kill me…" My voice trails off as a new round of tears form in my eyes.

Sam rests his hand on the table and stares at me for a moment. A flash of concern rolls over his face. "I don't know, but we have to assume he will. That's why it's important for you to stay here. Obviously, you'll have to leave for doctor's appointments, but we'll figure that out—"

Is he joking? "So I'm basically a prisoner in your house?"

"You're a guest. Not a prisoner, Em," he says defensively.

Same thing, I think to myself. I take a bite of grilled asparagus and chew slowly. Wiping my mouth with the napkin, I push my plate away from me. "Well, if I can't go out, can you arrange people to see me here?"

"Em, it's best if nobody knows where you are." Sam is tense and grips his fork tightly in his hand.

I sigh loudly, annoyed. I'm tired of arguing. It's amazing to me how alike Sam and Alex are. No wonder they hate each other; there's no negotiating with either of them. It's their way or no way.

"Well, then," I say, indignant. "I at least need to call Jax and Megan. I can't just disappear from my job and not let them know why."

His face is guarded. "What're you going to tell them?"

"The truth."

Sam sighs again. It's our universal language of annoyance with each other. He sighs, I sigh, and then we both sit in silence until one of us finally admits defeat and speaks first. I poke at the grilled vegetables on my plate and Sam sits back in his chair, his fingers locked together behind his head.

"Okay," he says, and I smile. I've won this battle. "You can call Jax and Megan tomorrow, but I'm going to stop by and talk to them as well. And Em, you cannot tell them where you are."

"That's fine." I smirk at him and take a bite of chicken.

"Now eat. I want that plate empty," he orders me as he tips his beer bottle back and finishes it.

"Sam, I have to schedule two doctor's appointments—"

He cuts me off with a nod. "Yeah, I've been meaning to ask you about that. Go ahead and schedule them. Just let me know and I'll take you."

I cringe as I tell him, "I don't have a primary care doctor or insurance." I can't even remember the last time I went to a doctor before I went to the hospital the other day.

"Don't worry about insurance." He waves me off. "I'll leave you the name of my family doctor. You should be able to get in quickly for a follow-up for the concussion. For the other doctor, you're going to have to look through the materials the doctor at the hospital gave you. I don't have a recommendation there," he says as he blushes.

The patio is getting dark, and Sam walks over and flips a switch. Suddenly, hundreds of little white twinkling lights light up the patio area. The lights are woven into the vines covering the pergola. Wow. If I thought it was beautiful in the morning, now it's breathtaking.

"This was the one project I did myself after I bought this house. Everything else I contracted out. I had the house gutted and redone on the inside, but the outside is just as it was twenty years ago; just freshened up the paint and replaced the windows."

"You knew what this house looked like back then?" I sip from my ice water.

He nods and stares fondly at the large tree in the middle of the backyard, lost in thought. "I do. This is the house I was raised in until I was sent to live with my aunt and uncle."

What?

My heart stops. "This is where you and Alex lived?" I ask cautiously.

"It was." His eyes are full of pain—regret.

"So this is where your mom was…" I shudder to say the rest.

He nods his head quickly, his face twisted in anger. "Yes, it was. Ridiculous as it sounds, though, it's the one place I'm the most at peace. I lost everything when that happened. My mother, my brother, my father…and I should hate this place, but I don't. I'll admit, when I first bought it and everything was the same, it was hard. I hired an architect to redesign the inside. To make it mine but also my mother's. She was so proud of this little house." The emotion in Sam's voice is so thick as he talks about this house and his mom, and I want him to keep talking.

"There used to be a little garden out in the back corner of the yard. She'd grow whatever she could keep alive over there." He laughs, clearly lost in a memory. "It can be hard to grow anything here, but she could get some vegetables to grow. She insisted that corner to the right was the only place that would get the morning sun, but was shaded from the harsh afternoon sun. My mom made

Alex and me dig and dig, and she mixed in more soil and fertilizer until she finally had a garden she was happy with. Alex and I just loved getting dirty." He pauses.

"And that tree over there." He points to a medium-sized tree to the left that looks like it's been trimmed into a perfectly round ball. "That's an orange tree. She planted that. She never got to see the oranges, though." I turn back to look at him as he swallows hard. "And that tree right there," he points to the giant tree with large limbs, "there used to be a tire swing that hung from that branch." There is a large, sturdy branch that reaches out to the center of the yard. "My Uncle Tommy hung it for Alex and me."

"Was it still there when you bought the house?" I don't know why I'm compelled to ask, but I am. I wonder what Alex would think of Sam living here and if his memories would be as bittersweet.

"It was. There were a few things that were too painful to keep. I had the landscapers remove it. Besides, the thick rope was frayed and the tire was completely dried out and cracking."

I envision what this backyard must've looked like twenty years ago. Simple yet family friendly.

"When I saw this house was for sale, I needed to buy it—for me. I guess it was closure," he says, his voice cracking.

I let Sam have his moment with his memories. I can imagine how painful they are for him. Finally, I say softly, "I'm glad you bought this place too. Does Alex know you live here?" I ask and catch myself. "I mean, did he know?" Sadness fills my voice.

He shrugs. "Not sure. I'm pretty sure he kept tabs on me, but I'm not sure if he knew where I actually lived."

"I wish he could've seen this place again," I say, almost a whisper.

"Why?" Sam questions me.

"He talked about your mom and you…although he never mentioned you by your name, so I never knew he was talking about you."

Sam puffs through his nose loudly. "What did he say?"

"He loved your mom's baking. He talked about her cookie dough."

A giant smile reaches across Sam's face. "She made the best chocolate chip cookies. Alex would always eat the dough, though, and there was only a little bit left to make cookies."

Sam's story is so similar to Alex's, it's almost as if I'm listening to Alex verbatim. I bite my lip hard as the sadness envelops me. "I wish you two could've made amends," I admit somberly, hoping I don't elicit an angry reaction from Sam.

He holds his gaze on me, looking like he wants to say something but shakes it off, and then I add, "I hate that your father was the wedge that drove you two apart."

Sam's face turns cold. "Antonio ruined a lot of lives, Em. Not just mine and Alex's. I have to find him."

"And I have no doubt you will." I pray that he finds him and gets the closure he needs for himself, and the closure I need for Alex. Hate is an awful emotion and I'm sure I've never felt it before until I think of Antonio and everything he took from me.

As I lay in Sam's bed, I reflect on all that's happened in the past forty-eight hours. I sob quietly into a pillow in hopes of not waking Sam, but it's in the middle of the night when I miss Alex the most and I'm unable to contain my emotions. Not being able to reach over and brush my fingers across his chest, or stretch my leg out and wrap it around his. It was the comfort of his presence that brought me peace—and the fact that I knew he'd do anything to keep me safe. I felt his love even when he couldn't bring himself to say it.

Now I press my eyes closed and push the memory of his touch, his smell, and his voice to the back of my head. I swallow down the lump in my throat and vow to my baby that I'll be strong for him or her. It's tonight that I make a decision that'll ultimately change the course of my life forever—but I make the promise to Alex to take care of his baby, our baby. I promise to be the best mom in the world, despite my fears and my doubts. I promise to give my baby everything Alex ever wanted for himself—a normal life, free of the Estrada cartel.

FOUR

It's before six in the morning when I leave the house. Emilia is sound asleep in my bed, and I scribble a quick note for her and leave it on the kitchen counter. I'm hoping she'll sleep late like she did yesterday and I make it back here before she's up.

Even though it's less than fifteen minutes to my office, I'm not the first one here. Trey is already at his desk with a Styrofoam cup of piping hot black coffee from the break room. I don't know how he stomachs it, though. The coffee here is shit.

"Hey, buddy," he greets me as I toss my laptop bag on my desk.

Pulling out files and docking my computer, I grumble a short greeting back to him.

"How's it going over there?"

Not really ready for conversation until I've had some caffeine, I spin in my office chair and offer to buy him coffee from Café Au Lait. Five minutes later, we're walking through the still empty, early morning streets of downtown Phoenix. I'm briefing him on Alex, explaining that he's turned down the offer until we can work something out for Emilia.

"They won't go for it," Trey hisses at me. "She's not a concern to them."

"I know. But we need them to take an interest in her or we lose Alex. Without his evidence and testimony, we're fucked. Antonio is tight; you know that. The little we have won't stand for much in court. There's no way the prosecution will have a leg to stand on without Alex."

"Shit," he grumbles as he holds open the door to Café Au Lait for me.

Jax is behind the counter, filling the glass case with pastries from a large cardboard box, and I lower my voice to keep our conversation discreet. "We need a deal for Emilia or we lose him. He'll walk. Especially once he finds out Emilia's pregnant."

Jax glances over to us but drops his head and continues stuffing pastries into the case.

"Whoa, whoa, whoa…" Trey's eyes are wide with shock, and I realize I haven't told him about Emilia yet. "She's pregnant? With Estrada's kid?"

I barely refrain from rolling my eyes. "No, with Charlie Brown's, you dumb fuck. Yes. With Alex's."

He chuckles and stuffs his hands in his pockets. "How are you feeling about that?"

I glare at him, shoving my disgust down. "Can we focus on the topic at hand? We need a deal for Emilia."

He sighs. "I'm out of favors, man. Getting one for your brother was my last one, and let's just say *no one* was happy about that deal. The DEA wants to prosecute Estrada's ass—bad. The favors I had to call in will take me years to repay." We lower our voices to just above a whisper as we move toward the counter.

"Morning, gentlemen. You're here early. The usual?" Jax asks. He closes the pastry case and tosses the tongs in a small sink behind him.

"Early meeting today, but we need our java first," Trey says, tossing a ten-dollar bill onto the counter.

I don't stop him, even though it's my turn to pay.

Jax pours our coffees and hands Trey his change, then glances at me. "Hey, Sam, think I could have a word for a minute…in private?" His eyes cut reluctantly between Trey and me.

Trey nods behind him. "I'll grab a table. I have a quick call to make."

Jax leans on the counter, both of his hands pressed to the light-colored stone top. "Hey, have you heard from Emilia? I haven't and I'm worried. Word gets around, and—"

I cut him off, coming close so only he can hear. "She's fine, Jax. I promise. It's complicated and she wants to talk to you and Megan, but right now," I pause, "there's a lot going on. She feels terrible leaving you and Megan hanging, and she's been asking about you both."

Jax nods and twists his lips into a frown, so I add a little more for his peace of mind. "I promise, as soon as it's safe, she'll come by. Do me a favor, though, will ya? If anyone, and I mean anyone, comes by asking for her, let me know. Oh, and don't tell them anything."

"You got it," he says, but I see the hesitation in his eyes. I offer him a small, reassuring smile when Jax leans in and whispers, "Just tell me she's okay? I mean like, really okay. Not what you think I want to hear. I heard it was pretty bad—and bloody." His face twists with disgust.

I give a firm nod, not wanting to divulge more than I have to. "I promise she's okay, Jax." I can visibly see him exhale and relax.

He nods, finally accepting my answer. "Thanks, Sam."

"You got it, buddy. Thanks for the coffee." I raise my cup in lieu of a wave, and Trey follows me out the door with a cellphone pressed to his ear, juggling his own cup of coffee.

We make it back to the office just in time for today's status meeting. The good news is we've stopped all Estrada business operations. We've shut down all of Estrada's known drug routes, confiscated shipments of guns, frozen bank accounts, and secured property and real estate. We've essentially crippled the business. The bad news is Antonio and his men are nowhere to be found. The compound in Mexico has been cleaned out and everyone seems to have vanished, leaving no clue as to where they could be.

I decide to pay another visit to Alex to see if he'll give up any details as to where he thinks everyone is hiding, specifically Antonio.

"Hey, hold up." Trey jogs up to me as I wait for an elevator. "You headed to see Estrada?"

"Affirmative." *Why?* He usually leaves dealing with, or tailing, Alex up to me.

"Mind if I tag along? Maybe with two of us putting the pressure on him, he'll cave and sign the—"

"Not happening," I cut him off. "He won't sign anything until Emilia is protected with a deal."

"And what if we can't do that?" He pushes his suit jacket back, propping his hands on his hips.

"We're fucked," I tell him bluntly. "It's as easy as that, Hoffman. We. Are. Fucked." Unease simmers just under the surface of my skin, and my patience is wearing thin with Alex, with this case, and with finding Antonio. I need Alex to accept this deal in return for his testimony and evidence. It's the only way we'll put Antonio away for life—if we can find the bastard.

At the hospital, Trey and I both present our credentials in silence to the guard still positioned outside Alex's room. With a stiff nod, he lets us in. Alex is sitting up in his bed, staring at the sterile grey wall in front of him. At the sight of us, his head turns slowly, his eyes narrowing on Trey with a look of disgust.

"What's he doing here?" he barks, although his anger is directed at me.

Who cares? I'm not in the mood for his shit today. "Agent

Hoffman and I are out on business, and I wanted to stop by to give you a few updates." I look between Trey and Alex, both of them glaring at each other. I roll my neck, trying to relieve the tension I feel take over me every time I'm in Alex's presence.

Alex's face is now covered in short, dark stubble and his hair is messy. He looks more like an Afghani terrorist than the sleek mastermind of a criminal organization. His one good fist is balled at his side in a weak show of testosterone.

"How are you feeling?" I ask, trying to show some concern for his condition and not jump right into business.

"How does it look like I'm feeling?" His tone is sharp, bitter.

"You'd look better in the fucking morgue," Trey spits out with a cocky smirk. "Quit playing games, Estrada. Are you going to sign the deal or not?"

Alex seethes, his breaths coming short and fast. The vein in his neck is throbbing as his balled up fist tightens to the point that his knuckles are white, and my own anger simmers just beneath my skin. We're all on the edge of losing it, but I need to remain calm.

"We've been chasing your ass for four years, and quite frankly, I'm getting bored." Trey props his hands on his hips again, intentionally exposing his gun holstered on his hip.

Alex rolls his eyes. "Get rid of this fucker before I do."

I let out a long breath, again trying to defuse the situation, and shoot Trey a stern look that tells him to simmer the fuck down.

I position myself between Trey and Alex in an attempt to end this pissing contest. "We lost Antonio. He's cleaned out the compound in Mexico. We've frozen all the bank accounts and seized all his property. So where the fuck is he, Alex?"

Alex lets out a condescending laugh. "He has millions stashed here and there and God knows where. Your guess is as good as mine."

"Don't fuck with us, Estrada," Trey warns, stepping out from behind me.

"I have no idea where he is, that's the truth. And if you two assholes are here, who's with Emilia?" Alex looks like he's on the verge of losing it.

I ignore his question. "Alex, you're in danger and so is Emilia until we can find him. If we can get him, Emilia won't need a deal or protection. She'll be safe and can leave all of this behind her. Isn't that what you wanted? To give her a life? For her to be safe and happy?"

A flash of regret crosses his face. It's brief, but I catch it, and it makes me wonder. Maybe Emilia is the best route. I should've played this card a long time ago.

After a moment, Alex turns his head and stares out the window, his one good hand now balling the white sheet like it's his lifeline.

I take a calmer approach. "We've got the account set up for her with the money you told me about. That'll last her a lifetime. She'll be able to go back to school, buy a house, and never worry. You're giving her a life, Alex, but we need Antonio."

A muscle jumps in his jaw, and I know I have him now. There is no doubt she's my golden ticket.

Tension hangs thick in the room. For several long seconds, the only sounds are the light beeps from the machines Alex is still tethered to. The quiet and the sterile smell of this room are enough to make anyone go mad, including me. I'm ready to finish this conversation and leave. Trey is quiet, his eyes bouncing between Alex and me.

Clearing his throat, Alex finally speaks. "I want her with me. I don't want to let her go."

I almost scoff. Of course he doesn't want to let her go, although his admission may be the first honest thing that's rolled from his tongue in years.

"Do you think of anyone other than yourself, you selfish prick?" Trey fires off in a tirade next to me. "Let her go. Give her and that baby a fucking chance. Don't drag them down with you, you piece of shit." Fuck! He did not just say that.

Alex's head snaps to Trey, his eyes full of rage. "What did you say?"

"Everyone calm down," I say, but their voices carry over mine.

"You're a fucking death sentence, Estrada. Give them a chance. Emilia got tangled in your web by chance. Now be a man and let. her. go."

Alex is turning red with seething rage. I don't think I've ever seen him like this. "Agent Hoffman, get the fuck out of my room. I need a few minutes to talk to Agent Cortez…*alone*."

Fuck, fuck!

I want to strangle Trey. My hands are clenched into tight fists at my side and my shoulders rise and fall quickly as I breathe. This is not how I wanted Alex to find out about the baby—in fact, selfishly, I didn't want him to find out at all. *Fuck!*

Trey remains rooted in place, and I want to punch the fucking smirk off of his face.

"Now!" Alex growls and, in one swift motion, throws the pitcher of ice water on his hospital table directly at Trey. The plastic pitcher bounces off Trey's chest and falls to the floor, water now dripping off Trey's suit. "You fucking—"

Before he can finish, the hospital door flings open and the guard steps in. I take matters into my own hands before this gets ugly, and grab Trey by the shoulders, pushing him back. "Not now, Hoffman," I bark at him.

He tries to shake me off of him, pointing a finger directly at Alex. "You will pay for that, Estrada!" he hollers over my shoulder. Shrugging me off of him, he stalks toward the door. The guard holds it open and Trey steps out into the hall with the guard right behind him.

I inhale sharply and turn around. "Let me explain," I say, raking my hands over my face in frustration.

Alex's eyes are full of rage. "When were you going to tell me?"

I shuffle nervously from foot to foot and finally just tell him. "I brought her to the emergency room the other night to have her head looked at. She hit it pretty good when everything went down. I guess it's routine that they check for any signs of pregnancy before a CT scan, and that's when we found out."

"We? Like you were there?" He flexes his hand, open and closed, open and closed, like if he weren't chained to the hospital bed, he'd lunge at me and strangle me with that one hand. I'd like to see him fucking try.

"I just told you, I brought her to the hospital," I bark in frustration.

One of the machines he's attached to begins to beep loudly, and Alex takes a deep breath. The beeps begin to slow and finally stop all together. "How is she?" he asks.

I run a hand over my face, pinching the bridge of my nose and then my chin. "She's scared. She's fucking scared to death. She believes she has no one. She's worried about money, and she can't go to work. She doesn't know what she's going to do about the baby. She's holding it together, but barely."

"She's considering not keeping it?" His voice breaks, and he tries to conceal it by clearing his throat.

"She's not sure," I say honestly. "The hospital gave her paperwork with all of her options."

Alex lays his head back against his pillow and shifts in his bed, wincing as he adjusts his bandaged arm. His head rolls to side, and he stares at the grey wall in front of him.

"She's doing the best she can," I tell him quietly. "I've told her money wasn't an issue, and I promise I'll do everything I can to keep her safe."

Alex doesn't respond, but I see the muscles in his neck move and shift as he swallows.

"I'll keep them safe, Alex." It's a promise to the brother I've hated for years, and it's a promise I worry every minute that I won't be able to keep. "I need to find Antonio to make that happen, though. As long as he's free, none of us are safe."

He nods his head slowly and turns back to me. "I don't know where he is. I really don't," he says honestly, his eyes glistening.

Shit, I believe him. I wish I didn't.

I rake my hands over my face and look at Alex who, for the first time ever, looks defeated. "I have to plan your funeral. I've already told Emilia she couldn't go. I told her it would be small, formal, and quick. She's obviously upset, but understands that for her safety, she needs to stay away. I'm hoping this might draw Antonio out."

"It won't," he grinds out, sounding more hopeless than angry now.

I can't let myself believe that. "Don't be so sure of yourself. If he thinks Emilia will be at your service, he may show up—and if he doesn't, he'll send someone on his behalf. Someone we can pick up and will hopefully lead us directly to him."

"Sam?" Alex says my name somberly. "You're not going to find him. I guarantee you he's gone. His connections in South America are extensive. There are names in the files, but there are people he's connected to that even I don't know. My bet is he's setting up shop in Southern Mexico or Columbia."

I nod and take that in. It's not something I haven't considered. "We've got every agency on the case. We'll find him if it's the last thing I ever do." I shift uncomfortably as the heavy silence weighs on us.

Alex's eyes are glossy and red, and I can see he's lost in thought. "If I take the deal, what does it mean?" His eyes are fixed on the window again. He won't look at me.

"The details were outlined in the document I gave you. Once you've accepted the agreement, you'll be briefed by the U.S. Marshall Service and be taken to secure housing. You will remain there as long as we need to meet with you while we build the case, and maybe even once we go to trial. Could be a few weeks, could be months. Once we've established our case, you'll be given your new identity, a housing subsistence, and medical care. If you need job training, we can arrange for that too. You'll meet with the prosecutor and can request that in the final details. The most important thing you must follow is you cannot, and I mean cannot, have any contact with unprotected family or business associates. That means Emilia. You cannot find her if you accept this agreement."

He swallows hard and his jaw ticks. I feel for him, I do. But he needs to know the severity of the situation.

"You need to let her go," I say quietly.

He clears his throat and moves to speak, then closes his lips and just looks at me. I give him a moment to collect his thoughts and respond, but he shakes his head slowly and remains quiet.

"Another part of the agreement is that you cannot return to Phoenix. You'll be set up in a new city, a new state, and once you've acclimated to your new city and your safety is ensured, you'll only need to check in with the government once a year, or if you move. You won't have twenty-four-hour protection like you will while you're in secure housing. It's a top-notch program, Alex. And the U.S. Attorney's office doesn't agree to this often."

"I know," he mumbles almost incoherently. "If I agree to take the deal, to walk away from this, I need to see Emilia first. There's a lot I have to explain to her and things I need to tell her. Things I didn't get a chance to say before."

I shake my head. "Alex, we can't do that, you know that. You've given her what she needs for a fresh start. The baby and her will be fine. I'm going to recommend she change her last name, and I'm sure we can get the court records sealed for her protection—"

"I *need* to see her!" he bellows.

I take a calming breath, hoping that Alex will also take note and get his rage in check. "Stop. Think about her for once. Think about your baby. Let her grieve you and move on. If she knows you're alive, she'll never move forward. Alex, if you love her, give her this. Give *them* this gift."

I can't imagine how he feels right now—the information received today and how he's processing the decisions he needs to make, but I can't let him risk her. Or the baby.

"I'll sign the agreement," he replies, his voice reluctant and almost heartbroken, twisting with pain. "Bring it to me in the morning and I'll sign it."

I look at him for a moment, genuinely surprised, even though this is exactly what I wanted, what we needed. The one person I swore didn't have a heart or a care for anyone other than himself just made the most selfless decision of his life.

I nod once at his anguished face, keeping my own emotions in check, then I slip out of the room. The walk back to my car is long, and my heart feels heavy. For the first time since taking this case, I want to quit.

FIVE

Alex

Tears pool in my eyes, and I fight the urge to blink. It's such a foreign feeling; the sting, the burn. I can't remember the last time I cried.

Actually, I can—at my mother's funeral.

The lump in my throat is so big, it's hard to swallow, and I finally stop fighting it when Sam steps out, the click of the latch telling me he's gone.

I rest my head back against my pillow and inhale a shaky breath. Traitorous tears slide down my cheeks, and I brush them away aggressively with the back of my hand. The taste of salt in the back of my throat chokes me, and I finally swallow. I wonder how many times Emilia has cried. Sam said she was scared, and I fucking hate myself for the pain I've caused her.

I should've left her alone that first day. I never should've stopped my car. She'd be safe right now.

But I wouldn't trade the time we had together for anything. My chest clenches when I think of how much I love her…and a baby I'll never know—*my* baby. Lying here in this goddamn hospital bed, I wrestle with the choices I've made in my life. Some good, most shitty. Not that I had a huge say in my career choices. Still, nothing scares me more than the decision to leave Emilia and our baby behind and never look back.

My hospital room door clicks again, and I quickly brush away any evidence of my emotion. I was trained to always have a poker face. Never show my emotions. I'd mastered it until Emilia came along.

An older doctor with grey hair sticks his head in the door. "Mr. Estrada?" I nod. "I'm Dr. Rusten." He steps inside room. "Is now a good time?" he asks hesitantly, possibly sensing my emotional breakdown.

"Yeah, now is fine." I take a deep breath.

He sets his laptop on the side table. Sliding the sling off my shoulder, he gently guides my arm out. "I was reviewing the notes in your chart," he says as he begins unwrapping the gauze from my arm and shoulder. "You're healing quite nicely. Everyone is in disbelief that you've rejected all your pain meds, and depending on how your wound looks, you may be out of here sooner than we expected."

"How soon?" I cannot wait to get out of this damn bed.

"The next day or two?" He raises his eyebrows when he says it. "You're young and healthy, and with the right physical therapy, you'll be as good as new. You'll have a few scars here along your shoulder, but with proper care, even those will fade." He points to the incision along the front of my shoulder where they opened me up to pull the bullet out. "Are you able to lift your arm at all?" he asks as he props my elbow in his fingers.

"A little," I wince in pain as I try to lift my arm.

"I expected it to hurt," he smirks at me. "You're doing great. Another week or two of rest and we'll get you into physical therapy. I'm going to recommend a release date of tomorrow as long as you feel up to it. Does that work for you?"

I nod as he begins rewrapping my arm and shoulder in fresh gauze, and my mind wanders to everything coming for me. Sam said I'd be put into protective housing until they're done with me, which is when the witness protection and my new alias would take effect.

"You'll be as good as new in no time." Dr. Rusten slides the sling back onto my arm and over my shoulder. He reaches for his laptop, pulling it under his arm, then leaves me to wonder what my new life will look like once I'm free of protective custody and the Estrada cartel. I should be ecstatic that freedom is just around the corner, only it feels like a noose around my neck because I won't be with Emilia.

I shift uncomfortably in the hard bed and reach for the call button, then wait for a nurse to appear. A minute later, the door opens and an older, heavyset woman enters.

"Everything okay?" she asks as she visually inspects me.

"Yes. I'd like to try and shower." I press the button on the side of my bed, raising the back.

She gives me a regretful smile. "No showers yet. I can bring a small bowl of water, and we can give you a sponge bath, but you can't get your bandages wet."

I sigh loudly in annoyance. I know it's not her I should be annoyed with, but I am.

"I can bring you a razor and shaving cream if you'd like," she says kindly.

"That would be great. And if it's okay, I'd like to remove this blood pressure cuff and try to walk for a bit."

Another regretful smile. "You can't leave the room, but you're free to move around here." She waves her hand through the air of my small hospital room as if it's some grand space. Sure, sounds like a fucking party. "Just push the cart with your IV bag with you. We're not ready to detach that yet. I'll be right back with some water for a sponge bath. You can shave in the restroom."

She flips on the light of the attached bathroom on her way out, and I slowly dangle my legs off the side of the bed. I struggle to sit up straight, the weight of my bandaged arm and shoulder causing me to lean forward. But for the first time in days, I'm able to inhale deeply, my lungs stinging at the sudden intake of air. I slide forward until my toes touch the cool tile floor, and I finally balance myself as I stand. Damn, that feels good.

I take two steps forward and lean my forehead against the window. The setting is beautiful. The late afternoon sunset is lighting up the Phoenix sky, a fiery bright orange, and the outline of palm trees line the horizon.

"Whoa," a voice says from behind me, and I turn slowly to see the nurse juggling a bowl of water and an armful of towels. "You should not have gotten up without help," she scolds me.

"I'm fine."

She frowns at me in disapproval. "Yeah, I know, tough guy. I read your report. You've refused all pain meds, which is crazy. You need to rest to be able to heal. The meds will help you sleep." She sets the bowl of water on the side table. "Sit down on the edge of the bed."

I stifle a growl as I obey her order, sitting down and wincing when my arm shifts in the sling.

"See." She raises her eyebrows indignantly at me. I shake my head as she scolds me.

Reaching behind me, she unties the hospital gown and pulls it carefully down over my shoulders, resting it around my waist. Squirting something into the water, she swirls a sponge around and goes to work, gently wiping my free arm, my neck, and my chest. I close my eyes and let her help me. She works quickly and quietly, paying special attention to my injured shoulder.

"You want to clean yourself?" She gestures to my waist and below.

I smirk and shake my head again. She's funny and doesn't take any shit.

"It's nothing I haven't seen a million times, tough guy. Won't embarrass me in the least,"

she says gruffly.

I like her. I like her no-nonsense attitude. "I got it," I say, taking the sponge from her.

She shrugs and shakes her hands dry. "I'll go run a sink of water and get all set up in the restroom to shave you."

"Just leave it on the sink. I'll do it," I say as I lean forward and wipe my legs.

"No can do. Not allowed to leave the razor."

"Seriously?" I quirk an eyebrow at her.

"Seriously," she says over her shoulder and she lays out a towel on the edge of the sink. Discreetly, I wipe myself down, tossing the sponge into the bowl when I'm done. Surprisingly, I feel a little better. I hold on to the hospital gown so it doesn't fall down.

"What's your name?" I ask her as she walks back over to me. She sees me struggling and pulls the gown back up, securing the ties behind my neck.

"Shelly. Sorry, I should've introduced myself." She smiles and reaches for my arm. She's short and round, with a head full of curly brown hair. Latching on to my free arm, she guides me to the bathroom slowly, almost too slowly, and positions me in front of the sink. I stand a good foot taller than her, and she reaches up to apply the shaving cream. Standing on her tiptoes, she gently rubs it around my cheeks, chin, and above my upper lip.

Shelly's hand shakes as she reaches up and runs the razor down my cheek, and I hold my breath. A shaky hand and a razor to the neck are not my idea of a good time.

"Shelly. If you don't mind, I'd really like to try and shave myself."

She hesitates, her blue eyes shifting between mine before she smiles tightly and hands me the razor.

"I won't tell if you don't," I say jokingly, praying she'll agree. "And I have no plans to do anything with this razor other than shave."

She visibly relaxes and takes a step back, watching as I methodically run the razor down my cheeks, my chin, and down my neck. I take my time, savoring the feel of the smooth metal gliding over my skin.

When I hand the razor back to Shelly, she hands me a wet washcloth, and I wipe the remaining shaving cream off my face. I brush my teeth as best I can with my left hand, and Shelly collects the washcloth and towels before guiding me back to the bed.

"Feel better?" she asks as I settle in and she adjusts the pillow under my arm.

"I do. Thank you for your help."

"Well, you just push that call button if you need anything else." She dims the lights as she quietly leaves, and I lie back on the bed, anxiety now coursing through me.

All I can think about is Emilia.

I wake up to a light rap on my hospital door before I hear it open. Agent Hoffman enters the room, along with Dr. Rusten.

"Mr. Estrada," Dr. Rusten says as I rub my eyes and yawn. "Today is your lucky day. You're being discharged into the custody of the U.S. Marshals service."

"I haven't signed anything yet," I say, narrowing my eyes at Agent Hoffman. "That would make me a free man."

"Negative," Hoffman barks at me. "We have enough evidence to hold you on multiple felony charges. So, I can take you with me, and we can get you booked into jail, or you can sign the agreement you told your brother you were going to sign, and I can turn you over to the U.S. Marshals. Your choice." He smirks at me, his demeanor arrogant.

My heart rate picks up, but I force back my anger and nod politely. "I just need the agreement, and I'll sign it."

"Emilia Adams isn't part of the agreement. You understand that, right?"

"I do," I say quietly, my heart sinking. It's what's best, I tell myself. It's best for her and our baby. She'll be free of me and the train wreck of my life that I brought her into, and our child will never know the madness that I lived. I'm conflicted as I sit here. One part of me feels peace, the other sadness of never knowing what our lives could be like together.

"Cortez is busy this morning, but I'll take you with me to the office, and I'll have a copy of the agreement for you to sign. We'll arrange for the U.S. Marshals to take custody of you there. The location is secure," he says.

As if I'm worried about my own life at this point. I don't give a fuck if I live or die. I'm worried about Emilia. This is all for Emilia.

I swallow hard and simply nod as he speaks. I'm not even sure what he's saying as my heart pounds and blood swishes through my ears. My final moments as Alejandro Estrada are here—now. I'll be someone new by morning.

A backpack lands at the end of the bed, and Hoffman gestures to it. "Some clothes from your place. I'll be waiting outside."

He turns quickly and disappears into the hallway, leaving me with Dr. Rusten. The doctor quietly goes about his business, clicking away at his laptop before he stills and looks at me. "I've printed discharge orders. They'll be waiting at the desk. Please pick them up on your way out. You'll need to follow up with a physician and get your physical therapy arranged." His voice is quiet, somber, like he can feel the heaviness of my decision weighing on me. "I'll send in a nurse to help you get dressed. And..." He pauses, giving me a small hopeful smile. "I wish you the best, Mr. Estrada."

"Thank you," I barely manage on a whisper. I hope for the best too.

When Dr. Rusten leaves, I sit at the edge of the bed for a few moments. Staring at the backpack. This is all I have left of my life —clothes. I shake my head at the thought when I remember Emilia. Beautiful Emilia who walked into my life with nothing more than what I have sitting right here—a backpack of clothes, and that was all she needed. She was happy with what she had—even when she had nothing at all. I can learn from her. I have learned from her.

I unzip the backpack and pull out a pair of boxer briefs, jeans, t-shirt, socks, and tennis shoes. I lay them on the bed next to me when the door behind me opens.

"Let me help you with that, my man." A young man in scrubs saunters over and reaches for my clothes.

"First time I've had a male nurse," I mutter as I check his badge that reads "Michael Clark, RN."

He chuckles under his breath at my ignorance. "Just be glad it wasn't me to give you a sponge bath." He laughs as I step into my boxers and he pulls them up. He unties my gown and releases the sling from my shoulder, then helps me into my jeans and socks, but there's no way that t-shirt is going over my shoulder.

He pulls the backpack off the bed and rummages through a few more items. "A button-down. Perfect." He pulls a plaid button-down from the bag. "This'll fit over your bandages," he says, sliding the arm carefully over my shoulder.

I slide my feet into my Nikes, and he ties them for me. I shove my t-shirt back into my backpack and zip it up.

"Thanks for the help," I mumble and pull the backpack over my good shoulder. He follows me to the door, and I pull it open with my left hand. Hoffman is talking to the guard outside my door and turns his head when he sees me.

"Wait here. We have transport coming," the nurse says as he steps around me and heads to the reception desk down the hall. He comes back with a stack of papers just as a man with a wheelchair shows up.

"Alejandro Estrada?" the older gentleman asks.

"Yes."

"Take a seat. Your chariot awaits." He grins at me.

Agent Hoffman rolls his eyes but directs the man where to take me. "We've got a car out back. We'll need to leave through the shipping and receiving dock."

"Yes, sir," the man says eagerly as I settle into the wheelchair.

"Put these on." Hoffman hands me a pair of sunglasses. I look at him, and his eyes widen in annoyance. "Just in case."

I slide the pair of aviators on my face, and we take off down the quiet hallway. When we reach the loading dock, Agent Hoffman pushes a large metal door open and sunshine temporarily blinds me, even with my sunglasses on. Two unmarked cars are waiting for us, just down a flight of stairs.

"Here we are," the man from transport says as he flips the brake on. "It's been a pleasure." He gives a little bow. I smile at his enthusiasm.

"Ready, Estrada?" Agent Hoffman barks. I'm getting sick of his voice already.

Holding in my retort, I stand up and pull the backpack over my shoulder. "As I'll ever be," I respond hesitantly.

I balance myself on the railing and take the concrete steps slowly, still a little unsteady on my feet. Another agent jumps out of the front seat and opens the back door as I approach. Sliding in, I sink into the warm leather seat as the agent leans in and helps me secure my seatbelt.

The ride through the congested downtown streets of Phoenix is silent. My stomach drops as we drive down Central Avenue, right past my condo. Then I inhale sharply as Café Au Lait comes into view, and I imagine Emilia behind the counter. For the remainder of the ride, I just close my eyes and bury memories, both good and bad, and resign myself to the fate I chose. It should feel good. It should feel like goddamn freedom being out here, not in jail, but it feels like a fucking life sentence in solitary confinement knowing I'll never again get to see Emilia or meet our baby. My heart sinks at this realization.

With my elbows rested on the conference room table and my head buried in my hands, I listen to the two U.S. Marshals explain the details of my witness protection agreement. Agent Hoffman is next to me, bouncing his knees in anticipation. I want to punch him in the fucking throat.

Yeah, you're getting your damn agreement. Calm the fuck down.

I feel my lungs constrict when the written and final agreement is presented to me. Hoffman pulls a black pen from the pocket of his dress shirt and slides it across the table to me, and I barely refrain from breaking it in two.

I know I should have an attorney look at this, but the price is too high that an attorney would snitch me out to my father or other associates. Time stands still as I review each sentence carefully, stalling. What for, I don't know. I've already agreed. I don't have any other options.

"What happens if I don't sign today?" I ask, looking at the marshal seated across the table from me. His eyes cut to Hoffman, who is growing more agitated by the second. At least I get to see him squirm.

"Nothing," Hoffman says. "We'll still ask you to cooperate in the investigation. We'll still take witness statements. You'll have full access to protection during the trial, and then you can sign the agreement. We'll enforce the agreement once we have secured the proper credentials for you. New identity, housing, etc."

"I'd like to wait then." I push the paper back toward Hoffman. His hand visibly shakes in anger, and he snatches the paper off the table. "I've given you everything you need. I'll sign anything you need proving I gave you those files. I'll cooperate, but I just want to wait to sign this. Not yet." Something inside me stirs. My gut is telling me to wait to sign.

Clearly angry, Hoffman's jaw ticks and his nostrils flare, but he remains quiet, his eyes fixed on me.

"Mr. Estrada, the sooner you sign, the sooner we can get to

work securing everything you'll need. You can wait, but we're asking that you don't wait too long," one of the marshals says, but I'm not sure which one. I'm holding Hoffman's angry stare.

"I understand. Thank you," I say, dismissing them. For now, this is what I want.

The U.S. Marshals excuse themselves, and Agent Hoffman sits back in his chair, fixing his eyes on the ceiling. "I don't know what fucking game you're playing, Estrada, but I'm done with you. I'm ready to set your ass loose and let your father have his way with you. Nothing would make me happier than finding your body parts scattered across Phoenix in garbage bags like the trash you are."

Don't hold back.

I flex my hand and will myself not to lunge at him. Picturing him bloody will have to do for now. I turn my head and stare out the skinny window next to the conference room door. People come and go down the long hallway, going about their lives, their daily routines. Nothing is routine about my life anymore. I'd give anything to walk out of this room and down the street for a coffee. To just blend in with everyone else, to walk the streets knowing I'm not being hunted.

Minutes pass and we sit in silence until Hoffman finally jumps up from his chair. "Let's go," he barks, yanking his file folder off the table. He ambles toward the door and I follow him.

But then he stops suddenly near the door, causing me to run into him.

"Jesus Christ," I mumble as I take a step backward.

Then…*Holy shit.*

Over his shoulder, I see what's caused him to stop dead.

Emilia.

She's with Sam, coming down the hallway. Her long hair is pulled back into a ponytail, and she's wearing a sundress, Sam's hand pressed to the small of her back.

Fucking-mother-fucker.

My blood is instantly boiling. I warned him. I fucking warned him, and he doesn't listen. Of course he wouldn't.

I reach angrily for the door to call to her when Agent Hoffman almost slams it shuts on my fingers. He turns around and blocks me from leaving, shoving his back to the door.

"Sit down, Estrada," he grinds out.

I have to take several deep breaths as I step back and assess the situation. I'm taller than he is. I could take him in a heartbeat. But I'm too distracted to really care about him at the moment.

Through the window, I watch Sam open an office door and hold it open for Emilia. She ducks in and Sam follows, closing the door behind them. She's so close. My heart is racing, and my palms are damp with sweat.

"I said sit down, Estrada!"

I take a bold step forward into his personal space. "Open. The goddamn door." My voice is deadly.

"What makes you think she even wants to see you?" he says through gritted teeth. "Haven't you hurt her enough already?" His question angers me, but it's the truth. I've taken everything good about her and destroyed it. She was innocent and pure, and I was selfish and greedy. I pulled her into my world without giving her a choice.

Still...*She's right fucking there.*

"I need to see her." My voice breaks as I stare at the closed door down at the end of the hall.

"Need and want are two very different things," Agent Hoffman says. "What you want could screw everything up for you—for us," he hisses. "I'm not going to let that happen." He pulls a set of handcuffs from behind his suit jacket and orders me to turn around.

I reluctantly comply. More so because I'm afraid I might beat him to death if he doesn't stop snapping at me. My fuse is short as it is.

Snapping the cuffs over both wrists, he leans into me from

behind. "Watch yourself, Estrada. I will make your life a living hell."

Like it isn't already? I know hell. I was living in hell when Emilia became my bright spot, my hope. But I have to let her go now, I tell myself. It's the promise I made to myself in the hospital. I'm letting her go, our baby go. It's for the best, for both of them.

Feeling drained, I let Hoffman pull me out of the conference room and lead me in the opposite direction of Emilia.

SIX

Emilia

I rub my arms furiously, willing the goose bumps to go away.

"Are you cold?" Sam asks, shrugging out of his suit jacket and handing it to me.

"I'm not cold. Your office just kind of freaks me out." I look around cautiously because I feel like someone is watching me.

Sam looks at me like I've lost my mind. "How so?"

"I don't know. I just get a weird feeling here." I shiver as I say that. Unease settles in me. There are cameras everywhere, federal agents—guns. I feel out of sorts here, like I'm being watched or recorded.

"I just have to grab a couple of things, then we'll be out of here. What time is your appointment again?"

"Noon, but since I'm a new patient, I have to be a little early to fill out paperwork. The appointment shouldn't take long, though. My head feels better, and I don't have any of the symptoms the paperwork mentions. It should be a routine follow-up."

He shakes his head slightly. "No, you still have nausea."

I sigh. "You know that's not related to my head bump. I had nausea before the injury." I pick at my fingernail nervously to avoid eye contact.

"Em," he says quietly as he gathers file folders from his desk. "I'm worried about you."

I sigh. "Don't be." He shouldn't be worried—I'm not his mess to clean up. I've already inconvenienced him enough. "I'm sorry." I don't know why I say it. I mean, I know why I said it, but it's an apology for so many things.

"For what?"

"For everything. For being such an inconvenience to you. For complicating your life." I rest my hand on my stomach. "I promise as soon as you find Antonio, I'm leaving."

"No," he blurts out. "I don't ever want you to feel like you're an inconvenience." He rounds his desk quickly and stands in front of me. His voice is panicked. "I want you to stay." He reaches out and grips my upper arms, forcing me to look at him. "I *want* you to stay, Em."

"Why?" I ask him, confused. I'm pregnant with his brother's baby. I have nothing to offer him. I'll just be a burden. "I'm a burden."

"You're not. You'd never be a burden." His thumbs rub soft circles into the sensitive skin of my arms. "Come here." He pulls me to him, wrapping his arms around me in a comforting embrace. "I want you to stay," he whispers into my hair as he holds me. "I need you to stay." My mind struggles with *why* Sam would need me to stay, but it feels good to know he wants me here with him.

Two hours later, we're leaving the doctor's office. "Well, that was good news," Sam says, opening the car door for me.

"I told you I was feeling good, no weird symptoms." I smile at him as he slides into the driver's seat.

"The doctor said you're still not out of the clear. I'll be watching you." He smirks at me.

I have no doubt he'll be watching me. He hasn't stopped

watching me. It's comforting and unsettling at the same time. I'm so used to being by myself. Even with Alex, I had a little more breathing room.

We merge into traffic, and I sit quietly, taking in the streets of Phoenix. "Is this still Phoenix?" I ask as he turns onto a palm tree-lined street, wondering where we're going.

"It is. Phoenix is huge. This is East Phoenix. Just a mile that way," he points, "is Scottsdale."

The radio is on low, and Sam takes a work call as I press my forehead against the warm glass window and admire the beautiful houses and the quaint shops that line the road. When I first came here, imagining myself in one of these houses was impossible. But now I lose myself momentarily in daydreams of living in one of these houses, with Alex, raising our baby. The lush green yards, kids biking in the streets. It's the American dream. And maybe I would've never really had that with Alex, but I can't help but picture it.

The car rolls to a stop at a red light as Sam ends his call.

Before I can stop myself, I blurt out, "I'd like to see where Alex will be buried."

Sam's fingers tighten around the steering wheel. "I don't know if that's such a good idea."

My voice is soft but strong. "I need to do this. You won't let me go to the service, but I need to know where he's going to be. I need this closure." Tears suddenly flood my eyes, and my lips begin quivering so badly I can no longer speak.

Sam watches me swat tears away and offers a tight smile. "Okay," he says as we accelerate.

We make a U-turn and, within a few minutes, we're pulling into the cemetery. The place is tucked away behind a sprawling neighborhood and hidden behind large trees. We pull in slowly, Sam carefully navigating the winding path. It's an exquisite place —beautiful and peaceful. The grounds are immaculate and perfectly cared for. Large trees line the perimeter and are sprinkled throughout to provide a lush and shaded resting place. If I'd had a say in where Alex was laid to rest, I would've picked this place too.

Sam pulls off the paved path and kills the engine.

"Point me in the direction," I tell him, and he nods and purses his lips.

"See that large oak tree? Just to the right, you'll see the headstone for Emma Estrada. Alex will be laid to rest with her." Sam's voice is tight, and he turns his head to look away from his mother's headstone.

I feel myself beginning to unravel; Alex's final resting place is just out of my sight. I need to see it. I need to know where he'll be. "I'll be just a few minutes," I say weakly as my shaky hand pulls on the door release.

The late afternoon sun is hot, but a light breeze whips my hair around my shoulders as I tread carefully across the plots, studying each headstone I pass. My heart races in my chest the closer I get to the old oak tree. Then, in front of me is "Emma Estrada" engraved in a large granite stone, with her date of birth and date of death. "Loving wife, mother, and friend" is scrawled beneath it. My mouth suddenly dries, and I can't seem to swallow down the giant lump in my throat.

The opposite side of the stone is blank, and my stomach flips when I envision what will be written there. Under my feet lies the spot Alex will be laid to rest. I struggle to breathe as I look at the trimmed grass beneath my feet.

Without warning, I'm engulfed in a wave of heavy grief, and I fall to my knees, tugging at the soft grass as tears flood my eyes again. "No," I cry to myself, to Alex, to anyone that can hear me. "You promised you wouldn't leave me," I stutter through ragged breaths. "You promised!" I feel anger mixing with my sadness like a poison, and I pound the ground with my fists. *How dare he! He promised!*

My cries are loud, and my vision is blurred when firm hands

suddenly pull me up. "Em," Sam says sympathetically. "I didn't think this was a good idea. Not yet, anyway. It's too soon." He holds up my limp body when all I want to do is fall to the soft grass below and cry for everything I've lost and everything I'm missing.

"Let me go." I struggle to free myself. It takes a moment, but he stumbles when I break free of him. Then I kneel at the headstone and begin praying through my tears. I pray for Alex, I pray for me, I pray for Sam, but mostly, I pray for my baby. I whisper prayers as quickly as they come to me. Sam stands behind me as I sob, pray, yell, and pray some more. I press my hands to the headstone, where Alex's name will go, and warmth radiates from the marbled stone. Warm, just like his touch.

"Em," Sam says gently as he kneels next to me.

"Why, Sam? Why did he have to die? Why Alex?"

His eyes are downcast. "I don't know." He rubs his forehead and looks at me. "But I think we should go." He stands up quickly and holds out his hand for me.

Reluctantly, I reach out and he helps me up, wrapping his arm around my shoulders. We walk to the car, the warm breeze blowing on my face, drying my tear-stained cheeks.

Sam opens the car door for me, but before I can sit down, he pulls me into an embrace. His firm arms wrap around me; I'm enveloped in him. He's not Alex, but I need his comfort right now. Breathing in the scent of him, I instantly begin to calm down. So much like Alex, yet so different.

Alex was my love—dark and dangerous.

But Sam is now my rock—my safe place.

And I need him. Probably more than I want to admit. "Thank you," I say on a ragged breath as I pull away, and I can't help but notice something in his eyes as he glances at the headstone one last time.

I wake up to the smell of something cooking. I passed out on the couch when we got home. I'm so tired lately. Although I'm not sure grief and pregnancy were ever meant to be experienced together.

Stretching, I kick the blanket off of me and stumble into the kitchen to find Sam on his phone and stirring a pot of pasta. At the sight of me, a huge smile spreads across his face. He sets the spoon on the counter and pulls me to him, his arm snug around my waist. I struggle with Sam's affection. On one hand, I love it, finding comfort in his closeness. On the other, it makes me uncomfortable, yet I'm a glutton for physical closeness and can't turn him away. Shifting the phone to his other ear, he rests his chin on the top of my head.

Surprisingly, the food smells amazing. I had no idea Sam could cook. My stomach growls when I spot the garlic bread in the oven and the pasta sauce bubbling in a pan on the stove.

"I have no updates today," he says into the phone.

Feeling funny that he's still holding me, I wriggle out of his grasp and pick up the spoon, stirring the spaghetti noodles for him. He presses a gentle kiss to the top of my head before he steps away and finishes his call.

"Good timing," he says as he sets his Blackberry on the counter. "I didn't want to wake you up, but it's getting late and we need to eat." He leans against the granite counter, the sleeves of his dress shirt rolled up. He ditched his tie in the car earlier and the top two buttons of his shirt are now open. It's interesting how his complexion is a bit fairer than Alex's, but he's perfectly handsome in his own way. How he's not taken yet surprises me.

"It smells really good." I offer him a smile.

"Well, I hope you're hungry, because there's enough to feed an army." He chuckles and reaches into the fridge for a beer, popping the cap off and pressing the bottle to his lips for a long pull. My stomach growls again, causing me to blush.

Sam sets his beer on the counter. "I'll take that as a good sign."

He smirks and opens the oven, setting the garlic bread on the counter. Just then, the doorbell rings, and he looks at me quickly before sauntering over to the front door. I recognize the voice instantly when Sam opens the door, and I momentarily freeze before turning to look at him.

"Jax," I say and run over to him, leaping into his arms.

"How you doin', sunshine?" He picks me up off of my feet and twirls me around.

"Wait, how did you know Sam lived here?" I look between Jax and Sam. Sam just smiles and picks up his beer.

"Had a visitor at the coffee shop." He winks at me. "He thought maybe you could use some company."

"Your visitor is very smart," I joke in return.

"You're right on time, Jax. Let me drain the pasta and we'll eat. Have a seat." Sam gestures to the kitchen table that I hadn't noticed was set with three place settings. I need to learn to be more observant, I tell myself, then sit down between Jax and Sam.

Sam sets a large ceramic bowl of spaghetti in the center of the table and the pot of sauce next to it. In another bowl, he sets the garlic bread, and there was already a tossed salad on the table. Everything looks and smells amazing.

"So, sunshine," Jax says as he plates some pasta. "We have a lot to catch up on." He smiles at me. "Let's do that after dinner, but I wanted to tell you how much I miss you. Megs, too. She's going crazy without you."

And oh how I've missed them too, but it makes my heart swell to hear I'm missed. I'd grown to love Megan and Jax in the short time I'd worked at Café Au Lait. "I miss you both too. I'm going crazy here," I tell him honestly, shooting Sam a look out the corner of my eye. "I'm used to always working, so spending the days sitting here—is hard," I admit.

"I'm sure it's for the best," Jax says quietly as he serves himself a bowl of tossed salad.

"It is," Sam interrupts, offering me a stern look.

We spend the next hour eating dinner, laughing, and catching up. Jax's band landed a gig at a bar in Tempe near the University, and he's over-the-moon excited. I smile as I listen to him talk about the plans he has with his band. I even tease him about his ponytail and the beard he's grown. Even under all that hair, though, I can see his perfect square jaw. His smile is contagious, and my heart calms a bit in his presence. This is the most "normal" I've felt in days.

"Why don't you two go out to the patio and catch up while I clean up in here," Sam says, standing up.

"Sounds great." Jax grabs his glass of red wine and heads for the French patio doors.

I shoot Sam a thankful look and grab my glass of ice water as I head out behind Jax. I flip on the little twinkle lights before taking a seat on the plush patio chair.

"So what's going on, sunshine?" Jax asks, relaxing his arm along the back of the outdoor couch.

"I don't even know where to start," I say with a sigh. "So much to tell you." I take a sip of my water and sift through what I'm allowed to tell him, what I can tell him while also still keeping him safe.

"Then start from the beginning. I've got all night." His smile is comforting, and I know I can trust him.

"So…there are some things I'm going to tell you that you can't share with anyone, okay?" I glance over my shoulder and through the glass French doors where Sam is still cleaning up.

"I'd never tell a soul," Jax promises, then takes a sip of wine and sets the glass on the wood side table.

"So remember my roommate, Alex?" I ask hesitantly. It's still hard to even mention Alex's name and internalize that he's gone forever.

"Roommate?" he says, raising his eyebrows at me. "You mean 'boyfriend'?"

I roll my eyes at him and smile. "Fine. Boyfriend."

"Mr. Tall, Dark, and, Dangerous?" He chuckles.

"What do you know?" I ask, feeling guarded.

"Only what I've heard on the news. Alejandro Estrada, notorious son of Antonio Estrada, the Estrada drug cartel's leader, was shot and killed in a shootout in his upscale, Central Phoenix condominium complex." He sounds like he's the news reporter.

I shiver when he says Alex's name and "killed."

His eyes turn sad. "I'm sorry, Em. I didn't mean to sound insensitive. I was just repeating what I had heard…and that's it. They've been quiet ever since. No news reports, newspaper articles, nothing."

"It's because Antonio Estrada got away. They're looking for him." I speak quietly, as if someone other than Jax could potentially hear me.

"Shit," Jax hisses. "So you knew all about the business? If you were dating him, why the hell were you working at Meg's coffee shop? I'm sure he could afford to take care of his girlfriend."

"It wasn't like that. I didn't want his money and I didn't know until a couple of weeks before everything happened about his business. Alex finally confided in me. I didn't know what to think. I tried to convince him to just leave, that we could go somewhere, anywhere…and start a new life. But he said you couldn't walk away from a business like that."

"You can't," Jax says abruptly.

"Everything happened so fast, Jax. He told me about the business, then he disappeared to Mexico for a week, and then he came back." I glance over my shoulder, into the house again, to see Sam pacing the living room and talking on the phone. "He lied to me."

"About?"

"A lot. He and Sam are brothers."

"Holy shit," Jax drawls.

"Yeah," I whisper, still remembering how I felt when I found out. "I found out the day of the shooting."

"How did you find out?"

"I found a picture on Sam's dresser. Alex had the identical picture in his condo."

"Hold up a minute. How did you find a picture on Sam's dresser?" Jax leans forward, curious.

I sigh deeply. "I found some pictures on Alex's computer. Pictures of me, my mother, my father...."

"What?" he asks, confused.

"I know." My hands fidget in my lap. It's unnerving telling him all of this, but it feels freeing at the same time. "I confronted Alex, and he claims they came from his father's computer in Mexico. I didn't believe him. I panicked and ran. Alex panicked about me being safe, so he called Sam to find me. I stayed at Sam's house that night."

"Jesus Christ, sunshine. Please tell me nothing—"

"No!" I say loudly. "And I know. It's not like that though, Jax. I've always felt safe with Sam. He's the law. I loved Alex, but he was the dangerous one. I fled to what was safe. They are polar opposites, but both made me feel—"

He nods in understanding. "Continue."

"Anyway, Sam left the next morning for a meeting, which I later found out was with Alex. Alex was in the process of making a deal to turn in everything on the business over to the ATF, DEA, and FBI for immunity."

"This is like a goddamn movie." He shakes his head and picks up his glass of wine. "Keep going."

"After Sam left, I saw the picture. I freaked out, Jax. I lost my shit. They'd both been lying to me. I took the picture and went to Alex's to confront him." I take a deep breath and a sip of water. "Anyway, when I got there, Sam was there. They told me everything. There's so much more, Jax...Things about my dad, my mom...I just..." I pause, needing a moment. It's still a lot to process, let alone talk about.

"You need something stronger than that water, sunshine. Here."

He holds his glass of wine out to me. "This is the craziest shit I've ever heard."

I shake my head and decline the drink. "I can't."

Jax's eyes widen suddenly. It takes a moment, and then realization sets in. "No."

I nod, feeling the weight of my reality bearing down on me again. "Yes."

"Unbelievable," he whispers, shocked.

"I know." I give a humorless laugh. "How much more fucked up can my life get?" My bottom lip begins to quiver.

He stands up quickly and sets his wine glass down. "Stand up."

I set my glass of water on the table and stand facing him.

"Come here." He pulls me into an enormous hug, and I find tremendous comfort in the embrace of my friend. "If you need anything, you know who to call, right?"

"I don't have a phone anymore," I sadly admit, "and I'm under strict instructions that I can't leave here, or even go back to work until Antonio is found. Apparently, because Alex told me about the business, I'm at risk now."

"I don't doubt it." He sighs. "You'll always have a job at Café Au Lait. Don't worry about that. You do what Sam asks you to do."

I nod against Jax's chest. "I'm scared," I whisper, and he rubs his hands along my back.

"I know you are."

"Did you two get a chance to catch up?" Sam's voice is loud, almost angry.

"We did," I say, pulling away from Jax.

"Good." He looks pointedly at Jax. "Remember what I told you. No one knows Emilia is here. You never visited me at my house. You have no recollection of tonight."

"Understood." Jax looks at me cautiously. "Sam, I really appreciate you letting me come by."

"Emilia needed a friend," he says, his tone softening. "I imagine it's not easy being confined to the house—"

"Or losing the person she loves," Jax interrupts him. His tone is condescending and he's putting Sam in his place—reminding him it's Alex that I love.

Sam's mouth snaps shut, and he looks away. The tension in the air is palpable and I shift nervously from one foot to the next. "Or that," he finally says, bringing his attention back to us.

"I'm going to get going. Thank you for the wonderful dinner and inviting me into your home," Jax addresses Sam. He reaches out to shake his hand, but Sam won't take it. He stands with his hands on his hips and blows a heavy breath of air through his nose.

Jax leans in and hugs me again, whispering in my ear. "Call me at the Café Au Lait if you need anything. Anything."

I nod and squeeze him back, then Sam walks him to the front door, while I stay on the patio, sitting back down in the chair and enjoying the mild summer evening. The evenings in Phoenix are finally becoming more bearable as late summer turns to fall.

"Did you have a nice visit?" Sam asks, appearing with a bottle of water.

"I did until you made it uncomfortable," I say, refusing to look at him as I focus on the stars in the dark sky.

"I don't like him touching you like that."

I snap my head to look at him, incredulous. "Like what? Hugging me? Because I hug my friends, Sam. I've hugged you, haven't I?"

Sam's jaw ticks in response. He doesn't respond but takes a seat across from me. "Sorry," he says on a deep exhale.

"Please don't try to run off Jax. I only have two people now. Two. You and Jax." My voice cracks. I hate that it takes so little for me to become emotional these days. I'll have to learn to control that eventually. "Do you have any idea how lonely that is? Add in the fact that I'm confined to your house, I'm ready to lose it."

"I know, Em. I know," he sighs

"I need a little space. I need to be able to go for a walk, go to the grocery store, something."

"It's not safe," he argues.

"It'll never be!" I yell at him. I'm agitated and upset, and I can't take it anymore. "You'll never find Antonio. I have to be the one to decide if I'm going to live in fear of the Estradas, or take a chance and live my life."

"It's not just about you anymore, Emilia. Don't you understand that?" He yells back at me.

I go silent for a moment, gritting my teeth. He's right, and I hate it. "I do understand. But I will always live in fear of the Estrada cartel. With or without Antonio, there will always be someone from the business to fear. I can't just stop living."

Sam closes his eyes and rubs his temples aggressively. Sighing, he sits back in his chair, propping his foot over his opposite knee. Sam's gestures, his posture, even his behavioral characteristics are so much like Alex's, it's eerie.

"You remind me so much of him," I tell him softly.

He pauses as he runs his hand over his face, his fingers resting on his chin.

"He used to get so frustrated with me for the very same things and rub his temples." I crack a small smile, remembering. Because that's all I have now—the memories.

"Obviously, we both care about you…very much," he says, folding his hands in his lap. "And obviously, we'll both do whatever it takes to protect you."

We'll both do whatever it takes to protect you.

What does he mean by that?

It bothers me that he speaks of Alex like he's still alive. Like he's here. And it frustrates me that he shows no emotion toward the brother he just lost. Even though their relationship was strained, they were still brothers.

"Do you wish you'd had the opportunity to reconcile with him?" I ask, knowing I may not like the answer.

He shifts uncomfortably in his seat, and his eyes drop to his hands. "I have no regrets for the choices I've had to make in regards to my family," he says quietly. "He's my brother by blood —but I don't believe there would've been reconciliation between us." Abruptly, his eyes become dark, lost in thought. I feel his pain, and my heart hurts at his admission.

The backyard is dark, the only light filtering through the glass doors from inside the house and the small twinkling lights from the pergola, but I can clearly see the regret in Sam's eyes, even though he believes his denial. We sit for minutes not saying anything, just absorbing our reality—a life without Alex, a life without a brother he never got to make amends with.

"Let's go inside," I say somberly.

Sam lifts his head and looks at me. I stand up and reach out my hand to him. He hesitates for a moment, then takes it, my hand, my peace offering. But instead of standing up, he pulls me into his lap. I want to leap out, but I don't. I like it too much, his arms around me; safe, warm. My legs dangle over the side of the chair. His head rests on my shoulder, and I can smell the faintest hints of beer from his breath mixed with the light scents of his cologne—all masculine and sensual.

Sam's fingers trail softly down my arms, igniting goose bumps across my skin. His touch is tender, yet firm, and I'm at war with myself. Part of me wants to pull away from his touch; another part of me wants to fall into it. He'll never be Alex. Ever. But right now, he is a safe place for my heart to land. His touch causes me to visibly shiver.

"You okay?" he asks, his fingers pausing on my forearm.

"Yeah," I respond.

"You shivered."

I nod.

"Do you want me to stop?" he asks, swallowing hard. My eyes fall from his soft brown eyes to his pink lips as his tongue sneaks out to wet them. *He's not Alex,* I remind myself.

"I should go inside," I admit, gently pulling my arm from his grasp.

"You didn't answer my question, Em."

I pause, conflict coursing through me. There's no denying I feel things with Sam, maybe for him too. And I feel guilty for allowing that. I'm mourning Alex, the man I love, the man I'm certain I can't live without. The man who I'm dead without. Yet here I sit, in conflict as his brother makes me feel alive.

I shake my head slightly and decide to answer honestly. "Do I want you to stop? No. Do I need you to stop? Yes." I slide off Sam's lap, my bare toes hitting the concrete pavers, his arms falling from around my waist. I take off to the safety of the house, where I can momentarily escape my conflict.

"Emilia," Sam calls after me, but I can't turn back. It's too much. Too soon.

My fingers struggle with the door handle just as his tan fingers cover mine. He turns the handle and my heart races inside my chest. He pushes the door open, and I step inside, greeted by a rush of cool air. Sam steps in behind me, locking the door. We stand inside the dim living room, staring at each other, our faces wrapped in emotional conflict.

Taking a step forward, Sam trails his fingers along my jawbone, from my ear down to my chin. Then he lifts my chin with his thumb and forefinger and, without hesitation, leans in.

The moment our lips connect, I lose myself in him. His soft lips devour me gently. He kisses and nips at my lips as my head falls backward, allowing him greater access. He walks me backward slowly as he continues to kiss me, my back finally meeting a wall. His firm chest presses against mine, and his hips hold me in place. Where Alex was aggressive, Sam is sweet. He takes his time exploring my lips.

I gasp for air when his lips suck gently on the tender skin of my neck, and I can feel his growing erection press against my stomach. My knees weaken when he finds that spot behind my ear and nips gently. I begin to lose my balance and slide down the wall. And just as Sam always does, he catches me. Because he never lets me fall. He's my safety net in a world full of danger.

He pulls me up and holds me in place, between his firm chest and the wall. His hands are tangled in my long hair as he peppers my lips with soft kisses. It feels so good, I can't stop. But I need to. After a moment, I find the strength and resist, finally pulling away. Our breaths are ragged as we come to the realization of what's happening and a look of pain and apology flashes across his face. His hands fall from my hair, and he pulls away from the wall.

"I can't do this, Sam," I whisper.

He exhales loudly as he drops his forehead to mine. "Go to bed, Em," he says, his voice conflicted.

I'm stunned as he pulls away from me so easily and leaves me standing in the dim living room. I press my fingers to my lips, still numb from Sam's touch. A million thoughts flitter through my head as I slink down the hallway to Sam's bedroom. I slow as I pass the bathroom. The water is running, which means the shower is on and Sam is in there.

Conflicted with my emotions, I finally retreat to his bedroom, where I disrobe and slip into a t-shirt. Falling into his bed, I pull the sheet around me and try to sleep. Minutes pass and I hear heavy footsteps echo on the wood floor. Suddenly, the front door slams closed, and the roar of the engine of Sam's car fades into the distance.

SEVEN

Alex

I'm temporarily stunned when the unmarked car I'm riding in pulls up to a small house in the same neighborhood I grew up in until my mom died. In fact, it's just around the corner. The houses are old, small, but many have been fixed up. The neighborhood is just on the outskirts of downtown Phoenix. These houses are now considered historical. All of them are bungalow style, modest in size, with large front porches. I'm getting the chills from how this house so closely resembles the one I grew up in.

"This is it," the U.S. Marshal says as he kills the engine. "It's small but has everything you'll need. It's close to the offices downtown for when we need you to come in for recorded statements, and you'll have twenty-four-hour protection. We've been using this house for years and never had a problem. I don't intend to have one now." His eyes scan the exterior of the house before he looks up and down the street.

I unbuckle my seatbelt and open the car door, practically feeling the ghosts of my past rub up against me as I get out. My chest tightens when I think about how close I am to the home I shared with my mom. I glance to my right. Down at the end of the street, on the corner, sits the Newman Market. It used to be Newman's Bodega, but now it's been renovated into a small gourmet neighborhood market. When we drove past, I could see the buckets of fresh flowers and a fresh fruit stand on the front sidewalk.

It's almost eerie. I remember walking these streets as a boy, to and from school and church. The memories are so vivid that it feels like just yesterday I was walking down to the bodega with a dollar in my hand and coming back with a bag full of Mexican candy. I smile at the memory, but then hastily tuck it away.

Pulling my backpack from the back seat, I follow the marshal up the front steps. A porch swing hangs in front of a large picture window and small pots of plants line the concrete porch. He inserts his keys, one at a time into the three locks that secure the front door. Finally pushing the door open, we step through the threshold and into a fully refurbished house.

The interior has been painted, and the furnishings are modern and clean. The kitchen has been gutted and simple, stone countertops have been put in place in addition to white wood cabinets. A small glass kitchen table sits just inside the kitchen. Down the hallway to the right are, I presume, the bedrooms. The setup is almost exactly the same as the house I grew up in.

"Bedrooms are down there," the marshal points down the hallway, "and out back on the patio is a small workout set up. Weight bench, punching bag, et cetera. We try to make you as comfortable as possible, but this gig doesn't come with a gym membership." He chuckles to himself. Bastard.

I point to my shoulder and shake my head lightly. I won't be working out for a while. He acknowledges me with a short nod and heads into the kitchen. I step away from his tour and walk down the hallway, looking through the bedroom doors. All the rooms are set up exactly the same, but I choose the room that has an attached bathroom. Tossing my duffle bag onto the bed, I pull out the few clothes I have and begin stuffing them into the tall dresser. There's a television on top of the dresser and a small wooden desk shoved against the wall. A bookshelf holds an array of books from Dan Brown to EE Cummings. The house is small and a far cry from my luxury condo, but it's cozy.

A moment later, I hear footsteps, then the marshal stops just outside my door. "Fridge is fully loaded. Once a week, we'll restock, but if there's anything in particular you want or need, you let me know. One of the guys will pick up anything you want."

"Thanks." I offer him a short smile.

"Per our briefing earlier, you'll always have twenty-four-seven protection. Most of the time, it'll be one guy. Transports to and from court, you'll have multiple. You are able to go and do things, but my advice…lay low. You've got an advantage that many don't. No one should be looking for you. Let's not get cocky and take advantage of that." He raises his eyebrows at me.

I nod and let out a deep sigh, and he leaves to do a walkthrough of the house. He checks windows, tests security cameras, and locks doors.

Lying down carefully, I support my shoulder and place my other hand behind my head. My eyes dance across the textured ceiling, looking for a place to land. I'm supposed to be thinking about my new name, a career I could be successful at, and the city I'd like to relocate to, but all I can think about is Emilia. Beautiful Emilia. Seeing her stopped my heart today. I wanted to run to her and pull her into my arms—but then I remembered why I'm doing this, to protect her. It was best I let her walk away without seeing me.

A lump forms in my throat as I think about her—being without me, moving on, living the life she's always deserved. Anger courses through me when I think about who'll get to love her, hold her, touch her, and raise my baby with her. My anger bubbles to the surface when I think of her with Sam. I know it's selfish, and I know she has every right to move on—but not with Sam. Not with my brother.

My eyes snap open to the sound of someone banging on the front door. I sit up, reaching for the drawer on the nightstand where I'd keep my gun. My heart is racing, and I panic as I feel around the empty drawer and remember that I no longer have access to a gun. Three loud knocks again, and I wince when my shoulder falls from the support pillow. The house is dark and silent, except for the rampant knocking. Pushing myself off the bed, I stumble toward the wall and feel around for a light switch. With a quick flip, light floods the room, and I squint against the brightness.

"Open up," I hear as I jog down the hallway and near the front door. I recognize the voice as Sam's. Still, I feel cautious, my gut telling me to make sure he's alone, and he is. Twisting the deadbolt locks, I open the door carefully. My eyes scan for anyone other than Sam, and I see the marshal positioned in his car on the street in front of the house.

"You going to let me in or make me stand out here?" Sam raises his hand to show me a six-pack of beer. I open the door and step aside, allowing him in. Sam isn't one for social visits, so I'm curious as to why he's here—with beer. Dressed in athletic shorts and a t-shirt, he's definitely not here for business.

He steps over the threshold and sets the glass bottles down on the small table in the entryway. "How are you liking your new digs?" he asks, pulling a bottle from the small cardboard carrier.

"It's not bad," I say, closing the door and locking all three locks. "I take it you're not here on business?" I eye the glass bottle in his hand as he raises it and presses it to his lips.

"Nope. We need to talk." He pulls another bottle from the carrier and hands it to me, twisting off the cap first.

I take a pull of the crisp beer, the carbonation burning the back of my throat. "What do we need to talk about?" I ask inquisitively.

Sam walks around the living room, his eyes scanning everything—the windows, the doors, and the paintings on the walls. He finally stops; turning around to face me, then takes another drink of his beer, holding up the bottle as he finishes it off.

"A couple of things." He grips the empty glass bottle, his jaw ticking, nostrils flaring. I can tell he's upset, but I'm not going to ask him about it.

"What first?" I wipe the condensation from the bottom of the bottle on my t-shirt.

"Emilia." He stares at me, his tongue wetting his bottom lip.

I hate the way he says her name, like he has a right to her.

"What about her?" I eye him suspiciously.

He swallows hard and takes a deep breath before he closes his mouth and looks away from me.

"Is she okay? Is something wrong?" My voice is aggressive as I dig for more information.

He nods, opening another bottle of beer as he holds my stare. "No. I mean, yeah, she's fine. She had her follow-up appointment for her head. She's been cleared, so that's good." He seems to relax slightly as he tells me she's okay.

"Good. And the baby?" I swallow hard. Our baby.

He shakes his head. "She hasn't seen the doctor for the baby yet."

"Jesus, Sam, she needs to see the doctor."

"I know this," he says, frustrated. "I'm doing the best I can. She's stubborn, and I've got you to deal with, and Antonio." He sighs, visibly frustrated again.

I chuckle and shake my head.

Sam frowns. "What?"

"She's stubborn, you said. I had to laugh, because if there is one word to describe her, stubborn just might be the word." I laugh again, and he chuckles along with me.

"That's the first thing we may ever agree on," he says quietly and takes a long pull on his fresh beer. "So the other thing we need to talk about," he says and rolls his neck, loosening the tension. "Look, this isn't easy for me to tell you…" He pauses, taking another drink. "We need to use her to lure Antonio out of—"

"No fucking way. No!" I yell at him He watches my clenched fist nervously as I yell at him. "It's your job to protect her, not use her to get him. No. Fucking. Way. You promised me-"

"I know what I fucking said," he snarls. "And we can't find him. We need her to bring him out of hiding."

"Over my dead body," I growl. "Where is Andres? Use him."

"Don't know. Everyone magically disappeared after the shootout," he grunts in irritation. "We can't find anyone, anywhere. Every goddamn property has been seized by the feds or cleaned out by your associates. Every alias comes up clean. We've got eyes on houses of Antonio's associates in six countries, and there is not one Estrada associate anywhere to be found. Anywhere!" He slams his hand on the wall behind him. "I'm running out of time," he says. "Emilia is our best option. She's our *only* option." I can hear the desperation in his voice.

"Emilia isn't an option. She's out of the question," I tell him coldly. End of discussion. "I made the deal to protect her. I turned everything over to you in exchange for protection of me—and for her. You promised me." My breathing is ragged and I'm becoming dizzy from yelling at him and drinking half of a beer, clearly still weak from healing.

I take a seat on the couch and stare at Sam as he paces back and forth in front of me. "I don't know what else to do," he says helplessly. "You're not the only one that cares about her, Alex. I care about her too, but I need her to catch Antonio." He glances at me out of the corner of his eye.

"Care about her? You think you care about her? You want to use her as bait, you asshole. You don't care about her," I snarl at him. "You don't use someone you care about…you don't endanger a woman—a *pregnant* woman, to lure someone out of hiding. So keep your 'I care about her' bullshit to yourself."

"I do care about her," he sneers, narrowing his eyes at me.

"You want me to sign the deal? You want my testimony? You want those files? You will not use Emilia. Do you understand me?" I'm quick to stand up and stalk toward him. "If you use her, I will walk away from this deal. I will recant every statement I've given. I will say I was coerced into providing false statements. I will fucking ruin you." I boldly tell him, anger seething from every bone in my body.

He drops his head back and lets out a chuckle from the back of his throat. "Will we ever agree on anything?" He lifts his head and looks at me, his eyes pleading for an honest answer. "Do you think that just once, we'll ever agree on anything?"

"If Emilia's involved, probably not." It's the truth. Emilia is not a bargaining tool, and I will do anything to protect her.

"Emilia aside," he says. "I think we both want the best for her, even if you think I don't."

I pause for a moment to collect myself, rein in my anger. "I don't know," I admit honestly. Even as young boys, twins, brothers bound by blood, we never agreed on anything. We had different interests, different friends. We argued more than we bonded.

He blows a puff of air from his mouth and sets his beer down. "I'll let you be," he says as he saunters toward the front door. "And I won't use Emilia."

I push myself up off the couch and follow him out onto the front porch.

He looks over his shoulder at me. "Remember when that market used to be the bodega?"

"I do. We used to ride our bikes down there with a dollar bill and come home with a shit ton of candy."

He chuckles. "Mom used to get so mad at us. She always said the sugar would ruin our appetites." He smiles at the memory. Then, suddenly, his smile falls. "I miss her, Alex. Every day, I miss her. I know you and her had a different kind of bond, and I was so jealous of that for so long…" He swallows hard before continuing. "I was at her gravesite today. First time in over twenty years."

"Why today?" I ask, curious.

He hesitates, then says, "Emilia wanted to see where you'd be buried. Alex, I hate lying to her. We were right there, and I figured if I took her to see Mom's headstone, and I told her you'd be buried next to Mom, she could finally begin to heal and move on."

I still as he tells me he took Em to where I'm supposed to be buried. "How did she handle it?"

"Like I expected. She lost it. She was hysterical. Crying, then screaming at you, then laughing, then she went quiet and prayed. I was able to finally get her out of there, but seeing Mom's headstone—" His voice breaks, and he goes silent.

"I miss her too, Sam. God, every single day, I think about her."

"First thing we agree on," Sam says quietly as his eyes stay focused down the street.

"It is." I sigh and lean against the concrete pillar. "It's weird being back in the old neighborhood," I admit. "I mean, I lived what, less than four miles from here, but I haven't been back in this neighborhood since Dad sold that house to the old couple after Mom died. No good reason to come back here."

"It's just around the corner, you know." Sam leans against the opposite pillar.

"Yeah, I remembered when the marshal brought me here this morning. This house looks so much like our old house."

"It doesn't look like that anymore," Sam says meaningfully, twisting his car keys in his hand.

"You've seen it?"

He lets out a small laugh. "I own it."

"What?" I'm shocked.

"Yeah, the old couple put it on the market about five years ago. I bought it from them."

I can't believe it. He bought it? "Why? That house holds so many bad memories. That's where Mom was killed."

"It was where she was killed," he says, barely above a whisper, "but it's the only place I have good memories of her—of us. The meals she'd cook for us, the Christmases we had there. The tire swing in the backyard. Everything good that happened with her, happened in that house. I couldn't lose those memories, so I bought the house." Sam's voice breaks as he speaks.

"That house tore our family apart," I correct him.

"Wrong." His eyes are strong but not defensive. "That house did nothing. Antonio tore our family apart. He destroyed the only good thing you and I had in our lives—her."

He's right. "Another thing we agree on," I reply in a hushed tone.

"I've remodeled the house, taken away the parts where the bad memories lived, but the bones are there. She's there."

I nod, understanding Sam for once. The bones are there because Mom was the bones of our family. She was what kept us all together, the glue.

We stand on the front porch in silence as I absorb everything.

"I'd like to see it," I tell him.

He turns his head and nods, his face somber. "Anytime. I'll need to make sure Emilia isn't there, but it was cathartic for me—buying the house."

"I remember the day we moved out," I say, reliving the memory like it was yesterday. It was a horrible day that I long ago buried, but the memory is crystal clear in my mind. "I remember you sitting in the back of Tio and Tia's car..." I pause as the memory flashes through my head. "Tio was yelling at Dad, begging him to let them take me with you, but he wouldn't budge."

"I was so scared," Sam says, raking his hands over his face. "We had just lost Mom, our family was being torn apart. Everything we knew came to a screeching halt."

"It did," I admit.

"I was so angry that Dad chose you and left me behind—discarded me like a piece of shit," Sam says with a hiss. His tone is bitter, angry. "You were always the one that they loved a little more. You were Mom's favorite, it was no secret." He smiles genuinely at me. "She baked for you, always comforted you first when we fought or were upset. But when *he* chose you—and left me behind, it made me hate you. I realize now I should've never hated you." He nods to himself, as if he's coming to some realization. I can see the pain he's been carrying around for all these years and I feel terrible. "It was him I hated. I despised him for taking you from me. You were all I had left. My brother, and he took you from me and you never once looked back. I know we were nothing alike, Alex, but you were my brother." His voice is a combination of hurt and anger, and I'm shocked.

We've never talked about any of this. We were so young, but clearly what happened impacted both of us dramatically.

"I hated both you and Dad so much, that I made it my mission to do whatever it took to bring you down. To end you both," he says resentfully.

"I guess jealousy goes both ways," I admit to Sam. "I was jealous that you got to stay in the same school, and Dad pulled me out. I was jealous that you got to live with Tia and Tio, and I lived with Dad. Maybe you had the life that I always wanted." It's an honest admission. I wanted his life. He looks at me in shock and I narrow my eyes at him. "You think it was sunshine and roses for me, but it wasn't. Sure, Dad sent me to the best schools. He ensured I went to college, and had the best of everything—but the best of everything means nothing when you have no family."

"Dad and the business were your family," Sam says snidely.

"That's not family. I lost my family when I watched you drive away twenty years ago."

This is the first honest conversation Sam and I have ever had with each other. We've never had the opportunity to discuss our mother's death or the events afterward that separated us. We both are the products of the environment we were raised in, but blood is always thicker than water. Although we're separate in every way possible, there is one thing that we'll always be—brothers.

"Every birthday, I grew to envy you more," I admit. "Selfishly, I knew you were having a party and you were loved. Tio was just like Mom. He made every birthday better than the year before. I wanted that. Instead, Dad would order us a pizza and we'd watch baseball until he'd disappear to manage business. Every year. Every single year, it was pizza, beer, and baseball."

I run my hand through my hair as I think about those years. "You have no idea how much I fucking hate baseball," I say, and laugh.

"I love baseball," Sam says with a chuckle.

"For twins, we couldn't be more opposite." I kick the toe of my shoe against the side of the concrete porch and it feels good to finally reconnect with Sam. "I'm glad you came by, Sam."

"I am too," Sam agrees. "It doesn't really make up for lost time, but we only have a few weeks left anyway."

"What do you mean?" I ask, confused.

He hesitates. "When you officially sign the deal, you agree to not have contact with anyone from your past. That means me too. Even though I'm a federal agent, I won't know anything. The U.S. Marshals office handles all of that. It's a fresh start, a clean slate for you." He pats me on the shoulder and takes the steps down from the patio.

"Sam," I call after him.

"Yeah?" He stops and turns around.

"You said earlier, 'you *were* my brother.' I *am* your brother. I'll always be your brother. Even if you hate me. Even if you deny me, I'll always be your brother. Thank you for everything you've done for me."

A look of contentment settles across his face as he pulls his keys from the pocket of his shorts. "You're welcome," he says before he jogs to his car. I give him a short wave and watch as he pulls away from the curb, his Mercedes maneuvering down the narrow street. His taillights disappear as he turns and heads home, and it's not until he's gone that a combination of relief and unease settle in.

I look up at the sky, the stars dancing in the darkness, and I can't help but feel lighter. Yet at the same time, I feel heavier with the weight of the knowledge that, in a few weeks' time, I will never talk to my brother again. I'm both comforted and saddened that this will be one of our last conversations. Ever.

EIGHT

I sit in my car, in my driveway, the engine idling as I replay everything Alex said. I should be happy we finally talked, but sadness is weighing heavily on me. I'm realizing now how misdirected my anger has been for years, and for that, I am angry with myself.

I'm distracted, lost in thoughts of the past and the future I'll never have with my brother when a shadow slips past me. I've learned from experience that distraction can get you killed, and that's what I've been—distracted.

Before I even hear the gunshots, I see bursts of light, hear glass shattering, and then feel pressure.

One.

Two.

Three.

I feel all three shards of metal pierce my chest and I gasp for breath. I glance down and see blood staining my shirt. I want to run to the house where Emilia is, but I'm paralyzed in fear.

Emilia. I promised to protect Emilia.

The shadow approaches, and I see his face—Saul Trujillo. He lifts his gun one last time and pulls the trigger, hitting me in the chest again. Four. I gasp, and he sprints away. Paralyzed from shock, I panic when the light from the open front door spills into the darkness. Emilia's long hair dances in the air as she runs down the steps of my front porch.

The panic.

The screaming.

The fear in her eyes.

"Sam!" she screams at me. "Sam. God, no." She yanks on the handle, but the doors are locked. With a shaky hand, she reaches through the broken glass and presses the lock release, yanking the door open, desperately trying to get to me. Reaching across me, she pulls my cell phone from the center console and frantically presses the screen, finally screaming into the phone.

Crying.

Tears.

Begging.

She pleads with someone on the other end to send help before her pleas turn to me. "Sam, stay with me. You can't leave me," she begs me. I feel myself slipping away and my heart aches that I pulled Emilia into this mess. If I could go back and do it over, I would. I wish I could tell her this. My lips move, but I can't speak. I try to clear my throat, but I'm tired. I know I'm losing blood and slowly losing consciousness.

Emilia holds my head in her soft hands. "Look at me, Sam. Help is coming. Stay with me, okay?"

I blink once and try to nod. Forcing myself to get her information, I'm able to finally muster out, "Saul."

"Saul did this?" She glances around feverishly, and I want to tell her to run, she shouldn't be here.

I nod and try to swallow.

"Sam, don't talk. Just stay with me." She presses her hand to my chest, and I can feel her body shaking against me. "Stay with me," she whispers. "Help is coming. I can hear the sirens. Do you hear them? They're close." She tries to remain calm, but I can see the fear in her eyes, her beautiful eyes. They should be twinkling and dancing in the moonlight, full of laughter. Instead, they're full of fear and panic as she pleads with me to stay with her.

"Alex," I sputter as my eyes go fuzzy.

"Alex?" she says, confused.

And that's when I slip into the darkness.

NINE

Emilia

Tight hands grip my shoulders. I feel those hands pulling me away from Sam, and I buck against them. I don't want to be pulled away. They can't make me leave him. But I'm too weak, and I stumble to the ground, my knees hitting the hard, concrete driveway. Loose rocks scrape against my palms. On all fours, I struggle to breathe, finally losing my composure. I gasp for air as my stomach turns and bile rises into my throat.

"Ma'am, are you okay?" a gentle voice asks, and I feel hands again, this time touching my back.

No. No, I'm not okay, I want to tell him, but I can't breathe, I can't talk. All I can think about is Sam.

I watch through hazy tears as they pull Sam from his car. There is a flurry of activity, hands pumping his chest, tubes from his arm, and piles of white gauze covered in blood. I've seen this scene one too many times. Images of Alex lying on his floor with blood pooling around him. I struggle to breathe around these images of horror I seemingly can't escape.

"Can you talk to me?" the gentle voice asks, and I finally fall from all fours to my bottom and begin to cry. I sometimes feel like the only thing I'm good at is losing people I love and crying. "My name is Jeff. Can you tell me what happened?" His blue shirt and pants tell me he's with the fire department and here to help us.

I look up to a pair of the kindest eyes I've ever seen, dark brown and sympathetic. I want to answer him, but I don't have words, so I pull my knees to my chest and bury my face there.

"Let me see your hands." He tugs lightly on my arms. Looking up, I see him pouring cool water into my palms. Using small gauze pads, he wipes away dirt and gravel from the shallow scrapes.

There's a commotion behind him as they lift Sam onto a stretcher and rush him down the driveway to a waiting ambulance. Flashing lights line the street from police cars, fire trucks, ambulances, and even unmarked vehicles.

"There she is," I hear a voice say, and when I look up, I see Agent Hoffman walking toward me. "Emilia, are you okay?" He squats down next to the firefighter wrapping my palms in bandages.

"Is he alive?" I muster as I choke down tears. "I can't lose him," I sputter. "I can't lose both of them."

"Yes, he's alive, but…" He pauses, his face twisted in worry. "I need you to tell me exactly what happened."

I manage to take a deep breath and try to calm myself enough to talk. "I don't know. I was inside the house, and I heard the gunshots. They were so loud. I opened the door and saw Sam's car in the driveway and a man running away."

Agent Hoffman jots notes while Jeff pours water gently over my knees and wipes them clean. "What did the man look like?" His eyes narrow on me.

"I don't know. I saw the back of him. It was so dark, and I could just make out a figure running. But Sam said it was Saul." I rack my brain to remember the dark figure running away, searching my memory for anything I can share that might help.

"Saul?" he asks, confused. "You asked him who shot him and he said 'Saul'?"

"Yes."

"Did the man running look like Saul Trujillo?"

"I don't know. I just saw a man running."

"So you said it was a man, but it could have been a woman?" he asks, clearly agitated.

"It looked like a man. The way he carried himself."

He blows a puff of air through his nose with a slight shake of his head. Finally, he looks away from me.

Agitated, I bark at him. "Agent Hoffman, I'm telling you what I know."

His head snaps back to me. "You're not protecting your boyfriend and his family, are you?"

Really? Is he serious? "My boyfriend is dead! And I just told you Sam said it was Saul. I'm not protecting anyone!" I yell at him and I narrow my eyes when he throws Alex's name into this so casually. "And since I seem to be the last to know everything, you'd know that Sam is my boyfriend's family."

He glares at me and shoves his pen into the pocket of his dress shirt, and I can't help but grit my teeth. "I didn't see who did it, Agent Hoffman. But if I did, I'd tell you. I'd do anything to protect Sam."

After a moment, his face softens, and he gives me a short nod, turning his attention to Jeff. "Is she okay? Can she go, or does she need any further medical attention?"

Jeff answers Agent Hoffman, but addresses me. "You're all cleaned up; however, you need to watch these scrapes. You may need to see a doctor if there's any sign of infection."

"Okay," I answer quietly, my hands stinging.

"Emilia, this is an active crime scene. I'm going to bring you to the office until I can find a safe place for you to stay, and I'll need a formal statement."

"Okay," I say again. It seems to be the only thing I'm capable of speaking right now.

Jeff stands up and helps me up as well. "You good?"

"I am," I lie because I'm not good at all. I'm far from good.

My legs are weak and my stomach lurches as I pull out of Jeff's grasp just in time to vomit.

"Jesus," I hear him say behind me.

"She's pregnant," Agent Hoffman says quietly. "I forgot about that. And she's recently had a head injury."

I puke some more as I listen to Agent Hoffman give him the run down on me—from my concussion to early pregnancy. Anger roils through me as he talks about every little detail of my life like I'm not here. I should be angry with Hoffman, but I find myself suddenly angry with Sam for telling him such private details in the first place—but then, I'm business to them. A means to an end. It all makes sense to me now as I see how I'm just a pawn in their game.

A gentle hand rests on my back as I hold my hair and spit. "Emilia, I think you should come with us. Just get checked out."

"No," I say quickly, standing back up. "I'm fine. Really. I was cleared for the concussion. I think it's just nausea from the pregnancy."

"How far along are you?" He presses two fingers to my inner wrist and looks at his watch.

"I'm not sure. Early. A few weeks," I tell him, looking away in embarrassment. He's quiet and, when his hand falls from my wrist, I look back at him. There's a concerned look on his face, and I look between him and Agent Hoffman, who stands back with his hands on his hips. "I just found out a week or so ago. I'm going to find a doctor. I'm fine, really. I just need to sit down and drink some water."

"Okay. You need to see an obstetrician, though, and watch for signs of infection on those hands and knees." Then he bends down to collect the soiled gauze pads, water, and wrappers.

"I will." I wrap my arms around my waist and look at Sam's Mercedes, which is now covered in bullet holes and broken glass. It all feels so surreal. How do these things keep happening?

Yellow crime scene tape is wrapped from a tree trunk, across the driveway, and secured to a mailbox to keep everyone out. A news van pulls up, and that's when Agent Hoffman finally moves.

"Let's go." He wraps his arm around my shoulder. "I don't need anyone seeing you until we figure out what we're going to do with you."

"What's that mean?"

"That means this," he gestures to Sam's car riddled with bullet holes, the driveway covered in crime scene police tape, the police laying down evidence markers, "wasn't supposed to happen—"

"Are you blaming me for this?" I cut him off.

He exhales loudly. "I don't know, Emilia. I don't know who's to blame. But what I do know is that anyone connected to you ends up shot—or dead." His tone is accusatory, like this is my fault. But he's right, and my heart skips a beat.

In a daze, I let Hoffman guide me to his unmarked car, and I slide into the front seat. He pulls some tissues from his center console, and I wipe my mouth and blow my nose while he settles in and plugs his phone into the charger. I reach across me and buckle the seatbelt, then he pulls away from the curb, zigzagging through the dark neighborhood and out into the busy downtown streets.

After minutes of silence, his phone rings. "Hoffman," he barks into the phone. "Yes. Adams is with me, and we're en route."

I twist my fingers into knots in my lap and glance over at Agent Hoffman. I catch him looking at me out of the corner of his eye before he says softly, "Affirmative. Subject was accounted for at the time of the shooting."

I assume he's talking about me, and my heart races. Do they think I'd actually do something to harm Sam?

"Yes, sir," he says before hanging up the phone.

"I heard what you said," I tell Agent Hoffman as I turn and look out the window. "I'd never do anything to hurt Sam. Ever."

I can hear him sigh, but he doesn't respond. He just weaves through the series of one-way streets toward the downtown ATF offices. We pull up to the parking garage, and he scans us in with his badge, pulling into a reserved space.

"Do you believe me?" I ask as he opens his car door.

"Believe you?" he questions.

"About Sam. That I wouldn't hurt him."

"I don't trust anybody these days," he says quietly. "No offense."

Good to know, I guess. Although I wonder what could make a man so distrusting. Probably the job. Still, it hurts to think he doesn't trust me, and a chill runs up my spine as we walk quickly to a secure door where he badges us through. We remain silent in the elevator, but once we reach the main floor of the ATF offices, there is commotion everywhere.

I stare at everyone and frown. It wasn't even this busy when I was here with Sam during the day. People are on phones, others are gathered in small groups and talking quickly, and people filter in and out of several conference rooms that line the perimeter of the office space. The entire office is buzzing with activity, except for Sam's office, which is noticeably dark.

"Wait for me in here," Hoffman says, opening the door to a small conference room. He flips on the lights and gestures to the large wood table. "I need to make a few calls first." He rubs his hand over his face. "I want to see if I can get an update on Sam, and I'll be back in little bit. Make yourself comfortable."

The door closes behind him, and I immediately notice how cold the room is. Cool air pushes through the vent just over the table. I pull out a leather chair and take a seat, running my hands over my arms to warm them. Minutes pass and I finally rest my head on top of my hands against the shiny wood surface. As I close my eyes, I whisper prayers for Sam.

A while later, I hear a voice that jars me awake.

"Emilia." A hand gently nudges me. "Jesus, you're freezing."

My teeth clatter as I lift my head, rubbing my blurry eyes. "Did I fall asleep?"

"Yes, and you're freezing," Agent Hoffman says as I push myself up to sitting. He's frantically pushing the buttons on the thermostat on the wall. "I'll be right back. I have a sweatshirt at my desk." He jogs out of the room, and I yawn and stretch, rubbing the goose bumps on my skin.

"Here." Agent Hoffman rushes back in the room with a grey sweatshirt and a bottle of water. "It'll be big, but it'll keep you warm." He hands it to me, and I pull it over my head. It's fluffy and warm to the touch. I wonder why he's suddenly being so nice to me, but honestly, I'm too exhausted to really care.

"University of Iowa?" I ask as I take a swig of the water he brought me.

"Yeah, just undergrad."

"Good school." I remember once wanting to attend college there, back when I had dreams. Dreams that were shelved because when you have no money, your dreams simply become surviving.

"It is," he says, settling into a chair across from me. "But enough about Iowa." He pulls out a pen and sets it on top of his notepad. "I need to get your official statement, Emilia. This has really escalated, and quite frankly, I fear there is nothing Antonio Estrada won't do." He pauses and laces his hands together on the table; his tone is less condescending now and more concerned, the gravity of the situation bearing down on us. "I know you told me at the house, but I need you to really think about what you saw. Even the most minor details could be something big for us. Think about clothing, hair, height, weight."

"Okay." I nod quickly, wanting to help. Anything for Sam. "But before we start, do you have an update on Sam?" I rub my cold hands together nervously.

"He's in surgery. He took three bullets to the chest," he says quietly, his eyes full of concern for his friend. "I don't know how bad it is yet, but three to the chest is never good." He looks down at his hands, hesitates, then asks, "Do you know why he was out without his weapon? I've worked with Sam for years, and he never leaves without his weapon." He looks at me curiously.

"I don't know." My eyes tear up because I'm sad and worried and I feel so helpless. I wish there was something I could *do*. "He left after—"

"After what?" he interrupts, eager.

I blink and gulp, not wanting to admit this out loud, but it doesn't look like I have a choice. "After he kissed me. And then he suddenly stopped when I said I couldn't do this. He pulled away and told me to go to bed." His eyes widen, but I ignore it and continue. "He left shortly after that. He didn't tell me he was leaving or where he was going. I heard the door close and his car drive off. I was so confused, I just went to bed. Hours went by and I couldn't sleep, so I got up to get a glass of water, and that's when I heard the gunshots. I was standing in the kitchen, and then I ran to the door. I wasn't even thinking it was Sam that was shot; I assumed it was him shooting." My voice is so thick with emotion, I can barely get the words out. Somehow, I find the strength to finish.

"That's when I saw Sam's car. The headlights were on, and I could see him in his car, and then the man running away."

Hoffman scribbles notes in his notepad and rubs his head simultaneously. "What happened next?"

"I ran to him. His window was busted out, and I tried to open the door, but it was locked. I reached through the window and pressed the lock release and pulled the door open. That's when I saw how bad he was."

"Was he trying to speak?"

"He was, but I pulled his phone from the cup holder and called the police. I knew he was badly hurt."

"Did he say anything other than that Saul Trujillo shot him?"

"No."

Hoffman continues to scribble on his notepad, writing frantically.

"Wait," I say. "He did say something else."

He stops writing and looks up, waiting. "What?"

I glance away, trying to make sense of it. "He said Alex's name. More than once." When my eyes return to him, they're full of questions. "Why would he say Alex's name?"

"Stay here, Emilia," he says quickly, jumping up from the table. He rushes from the room and I'm left in a haze of confusion.

TEN

Alex

"I said, no, you motherfucker!" I slam my hand on the wood conference room table. "I have no idea where that piece of shit is. I've been cooperating with everything you asked of me." I ball my hands into fists on top of the table. Saul. Fucking Saul.

"First of all, keep your voice down!" Agent Hoffman yells at me. He leans forward and narrows his eyes. "So then why is Emilia Adam's telling us that Sam said your name right after he admitted Saul Trujillo shot him? Did you order that hit?"

Why the fuck won't Hoffman listen to me! "Goddammit, no, I didn't order a hit on my own brother, and I don't know why he told Emilia my name. He had just left the house. He brought over some beer and wanted to talk. So we talked. Then he left. Less than ten minutes later, there were sirens everywhere, and my house was under siege. Your detail out in front of my house can account for everything I just told you."

"What did you talk about when Agent Cortez was at the safe house?" Agent Hoffman asks, leaning back in his chair and running his hands through his hair.

I sigh and lower my head. Like I was going to tell that asshole all our personal shit. No fucking way. "A lot of things. There was a lot of air that needed to be cleared, so we cleared it."

"What else?"

"Emilia. We talked about Emilia," I say quietly.

"What about her?" he asks suspiciously.

I hesitate, but I finally decide to share what Sam and I discussed. "Agent Cortez wants to use Emilia to draw out my father and his associates. He expressed concern that you all couldn't locate him."

"And what were your thoughts on that?"

"I told him the only reason I made the deal was to keep her safe. If he used her, the deal was off. He agreed."

Hoffman huffs, then smirks at me. "Looks like we didn't need to use her. They already knew where she was. Do you want to know my theory?"

"Not really, but I bet you're going to tell me anyway."

A smug grin pulls at his lips. "Damn right, I am. Your father knew where Emilia was all this time. My guess is Saul Trujillo was there to take care of her, and Sam arriving home spooked him. Sam ended up the victim instead of Emilia. Your father is a very smart man. He doesn't want murder charges for a federal agent on his sheet. He left the dirty work and the pending charges to his go-to boy, Saul."

I seethe as he talks, and bob my knee up and down anxiously. Sadly, I believe this may be exactly what happened. "How is he?"

Hoffman stops tapping his pen on the table and just looks at me. "Sam. How is Sam?"

Yes, you prick. Who the fuck else would I be talking about? I raise my eyebrows in answer.

"Last I heard, he was still in surgery. I was told we'd get an update soon."

"I'd like to go to the hospital."

"Yeah, that's not really an option," Hoffman sneers at me.

"Then signing that deal really isn't an option." I cross my arms across my chest in defiance.

"Are you going to hold this fucking deal over my head while you throw your little temper tantrums?"

"Yes." I don't lie. "I will use this deal to my advantage in every way possible. I'd like to see my brother."

"Obviously, we'll have to see what happens in surgery, but I'll do my best to make that happen as soon as possible."

"Now let's talk about Emilia." My tone is serious, filled with worry.

His face twists in annoyance. "What about her? She's really not your problem anymore."

"Problem?" Did he really just label Emilia a fucking problem? "She was never a problem. Where is she?"

"Right now?" Hoffman asks dumbly.

"Yes. Right now." For fuck's sake, what does it take to get an answer from him? "Where is she, and where do you plan to move her now that Sam's house is a crime scene?"

Hoffman pulls his leg up and rests his foot on the opposite leg. His lip twists into a smirk, and I want to punch him.

"We're relocating her," he says smugly. "She'll be under twenty-four-hour protection until she decides to leave."

"What do you mean 'leave'?" I can feel my blood pressure begin to rise.

He gives me a pointed look. "She's not required to stay in protective custody, Alex. She's free to walk away anytime. We can't use her against your father. She isn't a witness. She can get an apartment or hop on a plane and leave tomorrow if she wants. However, while we're investigating Sam's attempted murder, and she wants protection, we'll grant it to her. Just not witness security like you."

She's free to leave. "So where are you relocating her to?"

Hoffman rolls his fingers on the table, then suddenly stops.

"We're offering for her to stay with Jeffrey Martin. He agreed, considering the circumstances. I mean, he is her father, after all."

I jump up from my chair. "Like hell she is," I growl. "That piece of shit doesn't give two fucks about her!"

"Sit down Mr. Estrada, and I recommend you lower your voice right now!" he yells back at me, then glances nervously at the door. "Martin has been removed from the case." He grins at me. "Conflict of interest and all when we brought to light that his daughter was pregnant with Antonio Estrada's grandchild." He rolls his fingers animatedly on the wood table. "He wasn't happy about removing himself, of course, especially for a daughter he doesn't even know. But as we filled him on the situation and her impeding danger, he agreed to temporarily let her stay with him. It hasn't been announced that he's removed himself, and due to the circumstances, he has full protection for the foreseeable future. It just makes sense Emilia stays with him." He shrugs.

"She would never agree to that," I hiss at him as I sit back down.

He smirks at me. "People do a lot of things we wouldn't think they would when they're desperate."

"Are we done here?" We'd better be, because once again, I want to punch Hoffman's fucking face into the ground.

I toss and turn all night, thinking about Emilia, about Sam, and about what to do. The right thing would be to sit tight and follow the path we were on, but that gnawing feeling inside of me tells me that the *right* thing will be the *wrong* thing in the end.

The alarm clock flashes three thirty-seven in the morning, and moonlight peeks through the cracks in the wood shutters. I slide out of bed and shuffle across the wood floors and into the attached bathroom. Turning the shower on, I let the hot water fill the bathroom with steam, then pull the sling over my shoulder and carefully let my arm fall. As I pull the bandages and gauze off, I find the wound in my shoulder. Bruising and stitches remain over the spot where my father shot me. In a million years, I never believed my father would shoot me, but then, never did I believe he'd kill my mother, his wife, either.

Standing in front of the mirror, I look at myself. This is where my world has led me. Drugs, guns, violence—I never really wanted this, yet here I am entrenched in the middle of it.

With a heavy sigh, I step into the shower carefully and let the hot water soothe my aching muscles, my racing mind. I lift my arm carefully and allow the stream to gently pulse against my shoulder. It's a combination of relief and pain, much like the life I'm headed toward, a life where I may not have to look over my shoulder at every turn, but a life without Emilia or our baby.

I finish my shower, manage to brush my teeth, and get dressed again with little discomfort. I decide to not bandage my arm and only use the sling if I notice any pain. In the kitchen, I make a pot of coffee and pour myself a mug. The night looks so inviting, I decide to sit outside. After unlocking the plethora of deadbolts on the front door, I slide into an oversized Adirondack chair on the front porch. It's still dark, only the streetlights illuminating the quiet street. There are two cars parked in front of the house, my security, and both men nod at me when I take note of them.

I sip my coffee and listen to the birds chirping as the morning sky begins to lighten. When a car turns the corner, making its way down my street slowly, my heart pumps wildly. As long as I'm here, I'll probably always feel like I'm being hunted, like someone is constantly after me. Sinking down in my chair, I allow the half wall of the porch to hide me, then I relax when I realize it's my security detail changing out, and I push myself back up.

The two agents talk, then shake hands. The new one jogs up the cobblestone walkway that cuts through the middle of the yard.

"Michael Hansen, Federal Marshal," he announces himself and holds out a hand for me to shake. I reach for it hesitantly and shake it. "Nice to meet you," he says, placing his hands on his hips and looking up and down the street. "We advise that during daylight hours, you stay inside, or at least restrict your outside time to the backyard."

"Seems a little restrictive," I say, sipping my piping hot coffee.

"At least until we can track Antonio Estrada and his associates, then you'll have more flexibility." His eyes stay focused on the street, his gaze darting from house to house, car to car, taking in every little detail of the neighborhood. I can tell he's good at what he does.

"So if I request to go somewhere during daylight hours, can that be arranged?"

"It can," he says, risking a quick glance at me. "We just need the details so we can arrange for proper security. We'll need to know where, how long you plan to stay, those kinds of details so we can determine in advance what we'll need to protect you while you're out. This includes any kind of doctor's appointments as well. If you could get us a list with dates, times, office locations, we'll make sure the proper arrangements are made."

"Okay."

"Is there somewhere you need to go today?" He quickly looks me up and down, assessing my condition.

"Nah, not today. But I would like to visit my mother's grave. It'll most likely be the last time I do that before I fully enter the witness security program. I shouldn't need more than an hour."

He nods slowly. "That's low risk, but I'll run the details past the senior marshal and see to it that it happens."

"Thanks," I tell him quietly, sipping my coffee again.

"If there's anyone else, or any other place you'd like to see, I'd also like a list of those people and locations. The sooner I get that, the sooner I can get them scheduled."

I think about it for a moment. "Father Mark from the church downtown. I think that would be it. My mother's gravesite and Father Mark," I say as the reality of everything settles in. I clear my throat, forcing back my emotions, and look to Marshal Hansen. "Any updates on my brother?"

He turns his attention back to the street, narrowing his eyes on the man walking his dog. I'd laugh, but the dog walker could be an assassin my father hired for all I know.

"Nothing new. It's not looking good, though," he says quietly. "Hoffman told me you'd like to see him, but his family is with him right now."

"His family? I am his family."

"Sorry." He looks somewhat regretful. "I meant your aunt and uncle, and your cousins."

"Ashley and Adam are there?"

"I'm sorry; I didn't catch their names, but yes, a male and female."

"Thank you. Let me know if there are any updates." I push myself up from the chair, suddenly feeling the drain of no sleep.

"I will, and let me know if you need anything else."

I simply nod and lock the deadbolts behind me.

ELEVEN

Emilia

I awake with a start and feel an immediate pain in my stiff neck. Through hazy eyes, I catch a glimpse of the orange sky peeking through the metal slats of the conference room blinds. I fell asleep here?

Blinking fully awake, I realize that I've been in this conference room since Agent Hoffman brought me here last night. Rubbing my eyes, I push myself up from the table and stand on wobbly legs. Opening the door, I peek outside and find Agent Hoffman on the phone at his desk. A woman walking by smiles at me as I run my fingers through my messy hair. I feel like hell. I probably look it too, in my denim shorts and Hoffman's oversized sweatshirt.

I stroll over to his desk, where he looks up at me, a phone pressed to his ear. He holds up a finger, gesturing for me to hold on a minute. One glance around his barren office and I can see there are no personal touches, except one picture tucked into the corner of his desk. It's of him when he was younger in a football uniform with what looks like his parents. Otherwise, his office is devoid of any personal artifacts, only piled with stacks of files and a laptop computer.

After ending his call, he spins in his chair and looks at me. "Good morning," he says and rubs his temples.

"Morning," I respond, my stomach growling almost simultaneously.

"Sorry about the sleeping arrangements. You fell asleep while I was making calls, and I didn't want to disturb you."

"It's fine," I lie. My neck is sore, and I'm exhausted.

"Emilia, I found somewhere for you to stay," he says, his eyes shifting between me and the hallway behind me. "It's safe. There's twenty-four-hour protection—"

"Where?" I interrupt him.

"Here in Phoenix. I assumed you'd want to stay at least until we got some news on Sam."

"Where, though?" I press. I can't imagine feeling safe anywhere at this point.

He shifts uncomfortably in his chair, and I have a feeling I'm not going to like the answer.

"With me, Emilia," a husky, faintly familiar voice says from behind me.

I jump and turn slowly. My stomach drops as I'm greeted with my own hazel eyes. "With you?"

"Yes. Agent Hoffman called me last night and I agreed. I think we have some things to catch up on."

It takes a moment for everything to sink in, but even after a moment, I still can't believe it. They want me to go stay with my father? My father who abandoned me? My father who rejected me? My father who's really never been a father at all? And they think I should trust him?

"You want to catch up *now*?" I finally say, sarcasm dripping from my voice. "Don't you think it's a little too late?"

He sighs loudly and looks at Hoffman.

"Emilia," Hoffman says, trying to reason with me. "We don't have anywhere for you to go where you'll be safe. You're free to walk out of here right now, but you'll be a sitting duck and you know it. Saul got to Sam, and we believe you're next. This is our only option for you, and I suggest you take it."

I blow a puff of air through my nose and drop my head. I should be ecstatic. I should be jumping at this opportunity. But the open wound in my heart from his initial rejection blinds me from believing I'll ever truly know him.

Still, I nod. "Okay," I say quietly.

Both my father and Hoffman visibly relax when I agree.

Fifteen minutes later, I'm sitting in the backseat of an unmarked police car and being escorted to my father's house. He's next to me, staring out his window. His knee bobs up and down nervously, and he runs his hand up and down his thigh—over and over.

It takes us less than ten minutes to pull into the gorgeous neighborhood my father calls home. I recall each perfectly manicured lawn and the exquisite ranch-style homes as we weave through the winding streets. Being here brings me back to my first few days in Phoenix. It's hard to believe how drastically my life has changed since then.

Another car with additional security pulls up in front of the house while we pull into the driveway. Two agents exit the car at the curbside and sweep the house before we're given the all clear to enter. Reluctantly, I follow my father up the familiar stone sidewalk, then pause on the front porch.

A sense of sadness overcomes me as I remember the last time I was here, the rejection and hopelessness I felt.

My father holds the front door open and watches me as I hesitate to cross the threshold. His head drops slightly as I finally enter his home. I'm greeted by modern marble floors in shades of white and grey. Everything is clean, modern, and neutral. Giant vases full of bare branches sit in corners. Mirrors and paintings fill the walls, and light grey furniture sits atop oversized throw rugs.

The place looks like he had a professional decorator. Everything is pretentious, just like my father.

After a long moment, he finally breaks the awkward silence. "So your room will be down there." He nods down a long hallway off the living room. "Second door on the right is the guest room."

"I don't really have anything to unpack," I admit, a flush crawling over my face. I find myself once again embarrassed by my lack of belongings. Bitterness simmers just beneath the surface when I see how much my father has and how my mom and I had nothing.

"We'll get you some clothes," he says quietly, just above a whisper.

"I've got some at the house, I just have to get them." We stand in awkward silence again, and I finally turn toward the hallway. "I think I'm going to go rest, if you don't mind. It's been a really long night."

"Sounds like a good plan. Maybe we can talk when you're more rested." For the first time since he waltzed into the ATF offices, my father looks me in the eye, but I don't know what to make of it. I don't know if the emotion I see there, the hope in his eyes, can be trusted. He left me. And my mom. He left us both. I don't know him. My father is a stranger.

I simply nod in response and escape down the long hallway to the second door on the right. Closing the door behind me, I turn to see a large wooden bed covered in a white and grey chevron print comforter and draped in a sheer canopy. I eagerly kick off my shoes and sink into the fluffy bedding. An air conditioning vent directly over the bed blows cold air directly at me, and I pull the covers back on the bed and slide in. The combination of cool air and comfortable bedding allows me to fall into a peaceful sleep.

The click of a light wakes me, but the first thing I notice is that the room is still dark. I must've slept all day. A glance out the window shows me the sun is down and only a sliver of light is coming from an attached bathroom. I swing my feet over the side of the bed to see a shopping bag on the desk. Turning on the desk lamp, I peek inside. There's a stack of clothes, all new, still with the tags on them. I open a shoebox next to the bag and pull out a pair of Nike tennis shoes in size nine and a half. My size.

I nervously open the bedroom door, twisting the handle slowly, wondering where my father is. It opens with a small creak, and I cringe as I step out into the hallway. I pause in front of portraits in large frames that line the walls of both sides of the hallway. They're of a girl and a boy who look to be in their early teens. Both blonde-haired and fair-skinned, and my heart starts racing. I have siblings? Their photos represent a life I never had, luxuries and designer clothes and vacations in the Caribbean. Tears sting the back of my eyes in jealousy when I hear him speak.

"Jacob and Josslyn," he says from the end of the hallway. I have to swallow hard against the lump in my throat. "Jacob is thirteen and Josslyn is twelve." He moves slowly down the hall toward me. "This was taken on vacation last year." He points to the white sand in the picture, and I chew on my lip and turn to move past him, but his large frame blocks my escape.

"Mind if I get some water?"

"Help yourself; kitchen is just around the corner." He steps aside and lets me pass.

In the kitchen, I'm greeted with an amazing aroma. A large pan sits on the stove, bubbling with red sauce, and my stomach growls as I open the fridge and pull out a bottle of water.

"Hope you're hungry," my father says as he rounds the corner. "The spaghetti sauce is almost done and the meatballs are in the oven." He pulls a handful of pasta from a container on the counter and tosses it into another pan. There's a long, rectangular dining table just off the kitchen and only two place settings.

"You've been very quiet," he says, stirring the pasta carefully in the boiling water.

I twist the cap on the bottle of water and sip it while eyeing him.

"I assumed I was going to be yelled at." He lets out a half laugh and glances at me out of the corner of his eye.

"What good would that do? You made it very clear the last time I was here that you wanted nothing to do with me." My tone is devoid of emotions and I'm proud of myself for this. I don't want him to see how vulnerable I really am.

He sighs loudly and sets the pasta spoon on a spoon rest. "Emilia, I'm very sorry for that."

"For what? What you said? Turning me away? Abandoning me and Mom before I was even born?" My entire body shakes as my anger simmers at the surface. He maintains eye contact with me and lets me speak. "For some reason, I don't feel like you're really sorry at all."

"Emilia—"

"No. Give me a minute to say my peace." I take a cleansing breath. "Why now? Why did you agree to this? You didn't want me before."

He exhales loudly and rests his hands on his hips. His head falls forward, and I notice how much grey hair he has. Lifting his head, he looks directly at me. "I've always felt guilty. Every single day. I buried my guilt in work. I worked my ass off to be the best lawyer in Phoenix. I promised myself I'd provide my family everything I never gave you—and you know what good that did? It didn't do shit for me." I can see the regret in his eyes and the hurt in his voice. "I'm alone in this house while my wife—excuse me, ex-wife—is asleep in another man's bed, living with my two kids in a house across town, because I failed everyone. I failed every single person I've ever cared about. You. Gretchen, Jacob, and Josslyn."

His hands shake as he speaks, and he turns quickly to pick up the spoon. The room is quiet while he stirs the pasta. He tosses the spoon in the sink and dumps the pan of noodles into a colander, then grabs a pair of potholders and pulls a pan of meatballs from the oven and dumps them into a glass bowl. I remain frozen, watching him move quickly around the kitchen.

"Here." He hands me the bowl of meatballs. "Set these on the table and have a seat."

Like a little girl doing what her father asks, I follow his orders. My heart beats wildly in my chest as I take a seat along the long side, leaving the seat at the head for him. He sets a bowl of pasta down along with a pan of steaming hot pasta sauce. Small bowls are filled with salads next to our plates on the table.

He slides into his chair and looks at me. There's such pain in his eyes that I want to believe that he feels guilty, that maybe he did want me. His lips are twisted as if he's holding back his words. "Please, serve yourself," he finally says. We fill our plates with pasta and eat in silence other than the sounds of silverware hitting the china. My stomach twists and turns nervously, but I devour the delicious meal.

"You were hungry?" He observes my empty plate as I finally move on to my side salad.

"I was," I admit. "It was delicious."

"Thanks. It's the one meal I can cook." He cocks a half smile at me. "You shouldn't wait so long between meals. Your baby needs the nourishment."

My hand stills when he says that. I set my fork down and look at him. "So what else did they tell you about me?"

"They, meaning the agents trying to bring down your boyfriend's family business?" He raises his eyebrows at me.

"You have no right to judge me," I sneer at him, twisting the napkin in my lap.

"I'm not judging you. I promise. I removed myself from the case as soon as Agent Hoffman delivered the news about our connection. Emilia, that family wants me dead. They were using you to get to me."

"Alex wasn't using me. He didn't even know about the connection."

"Don't be naïve, Emilia. What're the chances of all the girls in the world for him to fall in love with, it just happens to be the daughter of the judge presiding over his father's trial?"

My stomach twists again because he's right. What are the chances? But my gut tells me Alex wasn't lying.

"He didn't know," I say, my voice meek in defense.

"Maybe he didn't," he admits in defeat. "But when I removed myself from the case, Agent Hoffman informed me of everything. I was shocked, that's for sure. I thought when you left here, you went back to Illinois. Emilia, I didn't know how bad it was there, I promise." He pulls a crystal glass from the table and sips his water. "They told me everything. How Alex was shot, but not before he turned over everything he had on the business. They explained you stumbled upon Agent Cortez and fell right into their agenda, the connection between Cortez and Alex, you being pregnant. Honestly, I was shocked at all the connections. You found yourself right in the center of a very tangled web."

I nod my head slowly as everything begins to sink in once again. Silence fills the space between us. I shift in my chair when my father finally speaks again. "Are the clothes okay? I wasn't sure what to get you, so we opted for comfort. Everyone wears yoga pants and tank tops." He smiles at me, a glimmer of hope in his eye.

"Who's 'we'?" I ask curiously. "And yes, they'll be just fine. Thank you."

"Gretchen picked them out. My ex. I called in a favor. She loves the mall, so this was something she could actually help me with. And since you're pregnant, she thought comfortable was the way to go."

"You didn't need to do that, but I'm very appreciative."

"I wanted to. She was hoping to meet you, but we're not as friendly as I would like to be, and she didn't want to wait around until you woke up. She'll stop by in the morning. She assumed there were toiletries you'd want or need, but didn't want to guess on what brand you wanted. She said she was glad she could help."

I have to swallow hard before I ask. "You told her about me?"

"I did. A long time ago." He pauses, lost in thought. "We never told the kids, though. I didn't expect to ever see you again, and…"

"And what?"

"And I didn't want them asking questions."

"Why? Are you embarrassed of me?" I don't know why I asked that, but it's something I've always wondered. Is he embarrassed that I'm his bastard child?

"No. Never. I'm ashamed of myself," he says quietly. "I'm so sorry, Emilia. I can't take back the last twenty-one years, but I can apologize for my actions," he says, his voice trembling.

I take a moment and sip on my water as I think about the life I never had with him. "From the ages of about five to twelve, I used to wait by the mailbox on my birthday, thinking that maybe this would be the year you'd send me a card. I would be so excited as the day came every year, and it was when I was thirteen that I remember thinking to myself, I bet he doesn't even know when my birthday is. For thirteen years, I held out hope that you'd finally recognize me as your daughter. Thirteen years. Do you realize how long that is?" My voice is full of emotion, but I keep it under control.

His eyes are full of tears as he listens to me, and his hands are folded together on the table.

"I have a question, and I hope you'll answer me honestly. Will you?"

He nods.

"Do you? Know when my birthday is?"

His eyes are fixed tightly on mine as he chews his bottom lip. Finally, he drops his head and shakes it. I blow a puff of air through my nose loudly, my heart sinking, but I bury the pain like I'm so accustomed to doing.

"I used to make up stories about you." I chuckle. "I'd tell the kids at school that you worked for the FBI and that you were on a secret mission, and that's why you couldn't be at school for the events that the other dads were there for…the concerts, the plays, the school conferences." I look at him as he brushes away a stray tear from the corner of his eye and swallows hard. "I finally stopped lying for you when I realized you didn't love me enough to even send a letter or a card for my birthday." My voice breaks. "As messed up as Mom was, buried in her depression, she always loved me. She'd make a birthday card out of scrap paper at home, but she acknowledged me."

"I'm sorry, Emilia," he speaks just above a whisper. "I'm so sorry. I did love you. I should've been there. I should've reached out to you. I *do* love you," he corrects himself.

I should be angry. I should cry—but I have no more tears left. My heart hurts as I listen to him apologize. It hurts for him—but mostly it hurts for everything I missed out on. "I accept your apology," I say, a lump forming in my throat, "but I don't believe you love me. Love doesn't abandon." I've always been told that I forgive too easily, but if life has taught me anything, it's that it's too short. I need to forgive and move forward, let go of the past and my anger. For myself and for my baby.

We sit there for a long time, my father's eyes glistening with unshed tears. It's really remarkable how much I look like him. I have his long fingers, his dark hair, and his straight nose. Our eyes match perfectly, and I notice that his lip curls slightly at the corner, just like mine.

"Thank you for making dinner. It was really good." I offer him a stiff smile and set my napkin on the table. "I'll clean up."

"Nah, I've got it. Go relax. Gretchen said there were some pajamas in the shopping bag. Go get changed. I'll clean up." He smiles shakily at me and begins gathering the plates and silverware.

Making my way back to the guest room, I pause in the hallway to look at the pictures on the wall again. This time I smile. Not from jealousy, but from a place of acceptance.

It's amazing what a hot shower and clean clothes can do for a person. I carefully remove the tag from the oversized satin nightshirt and matching pajama shorts and slip into them. I sigh when the smooth fabric glides across my skin. Brushing the tangles from my wet hair, I let it hang loose while it air dries, then open the new toothbrush and brush my teeth. For the first time in days, I begin to relax.

Right before I'm about to crawl into bed, I'm startled by the doorbell, and I snap my head to look at the clock on the nightstand. It's after ten in the evening, and I panic when I think about who's here. I crack the bedroom door open and hear numerous voices down the hallway. Slowly tiptoeing down the hall, I'm able to see Agent Hoffman along with another man talking to my father.

Catching me out of the corner of his eye, he turns quickly and addresses me. "Emilia," he looks at me uncomfortably. I wrap my arms around my stomach and try to hide the fact that I'm in my pajamas. "We have an update on Sam. He's in extremely critical condition. The doctors still aren't sure if he'll pull through, but they're cautiously optimistic."

I catch my breath and exhale at this news. "I'd like to see him."

"I'm sorry." He shakes his head sadly. "Right now, they're not allowing any visitors other than family."

"I'm his family," I argue. Everyone looks at me like I'm crazy. "Alex is his brother, and I'm pregnant with his niece or nephew. I'm family. He's all the family I have left."

My father outwardly cringes when I say that. I didn't mean to hurt him, but it's true. He's the one that chose to leave. Maybe he regrets that, but he and I have a long path to real healing, if both of us allow for that.

Ignoring my father, I plead with Hoffman, "Please let me see him."

Hoffman sighs and looks to the agent standing next to him.

"It's not up to me. We can bring you to the hospital tomorrow and see if they'll let you in, but don't hold your breath."

"Okay." I nod, gulping back tears. "Thank you."

"We'll bring her by in the morning," my father says to Hoffman. They shake hands, then he escorts them to the door. After locking the door, he turns, startled to see me still standing there.

I want to explain. Even if he chose to abandon me, I don't like hurting him. "I didn't mean—"

"I understand, Emilia. You don't need to apologize. I was absent your entire life. I hardly expect for you to acknowledge me as family now. I have to accept what I did and how that has affected you."

"I just meant that he's all I have left of Alex." I hate saying that out loud. "They're two different people, but yet they're so much alike. When Alex died, Sam vowed to make sure I'd be okay... That my baby would be okay—"

"Emilia. You don't have to explain. I understand." He smiles sincerely at me, reaching out and rubbing my upper arm in a slightly awkward show of fatherly affection. "Unless you're headed to bed, you're welcome to join me in the living room. I was just going to watch some TV."

"Okay." I give him a small smile.

He settles into the large, velour couch and turns on the news. I sit on the matching loveseat while he scrolls through the channels, but at nearly eleven at night, there's nothing on but news and infomercials. He scrolls through the channels and sighs.

"Want some ice cream?" he asks, turning off the TV and

tossing the remote control onto the large ottoman in front of the couch. "I've got strawberry or chocolate."

"Strawberry, please," I answer him and a smile spreads across my face.

"Coming right up," he says, jumping up from the couch.

I pull a throw over myself from the back of the couch and stretch out. Oddly, I feel comfortable here. A minute later, my dad rounds the corner with two bowls. He hands me a large bowl with three generous scoops. My eyes bulge, and he laughs at me.

"Oh, eat it." He laughs. "You could use a little fat on those bones."

I shake my head and disregard his comment. I've been thin, ridiculously thin my entire life—but he wouldn't know that.

"So, Emilia," he says, licking his spoon. "How did you get involved with Alex Estrada?" He casts a sideways glance at me before dipping his spoon back in his ice cream bowl.

I push my ice cream around the large white bowl, and my stomach turns as I think back to that day. "Remember the day I came here?"

His hand stills, and he looks at me. "I do." That look of regret is back.

"After you sent me away, I went back to the motel I was staying at to get my belongings and figure out what I was going to do. I had fifty dollars, not even enough to buy a bus ticket back to Illinois—" I pause when I think about it. "I was so scared. I didn't know how or what I was going to do."

He sets his bowl on the ottoman and leans forward, his arms resting on his knees.

"Anyway, as I was walking down the frontage road, Alex stopped. He could see I was upset."

"So you just got in the car with him?" His brows furrow as he disagrees with my actions.

I nod. "I did. I had bumped into him the night before at the motel, and I felt a strange connection to him." I still remember every detail of the first time I saw him. The clothes he wore, his watch, his shoes—his cologne. A lump forms in my throat, but I'm able to swallow it down and continue. "It was so hot that day, and like I said, I had nothing. No money. I didn't know where I was going—I was hopeless. Alex saved me."

"You do realize how dangerous that man is? Right, Emilia?"

"Alex wasn't dangerous with me," I tell him softly. "He was caring, considerate, and honest. He didn't want that life—but that's all he knew. That's how he was raised."

My dad shakes his head slowly. "Emilia, the Estrada family isn't honest. They aren't nice people. They smuggle drugs, people, and they kill anyone that gets in their way."

I wince at the truth of that. *But Alex wasn't like that.* "I didn't know what Alex did when I met him. He came clean after a while and told me everything. He doesn't murder. He doesn't smuggle. He manages the business side of things—money, et cetera."

"Money made at the hands of innocent people. He may not pull the trigger, but he's just as guilty."

My breaths quicken, and tears fill my eyes. "It doesn't matter anymore, does it? He's dead," I stutter.

"It does matter because you're not safe. You don't have enough information for witness security protection, but you have enough that you're dangerous to the Estrada family. It's a real predicament, Emilia." His voice is caring and concerned.

I feel his disappointment in me, and while it shouldn't matter what he thinks—it does. "I know," I admit. "That's why I'm leaving. I decided it's safer if I disappear on my own."

"Where are you going?" he asks, surprised by my news.

"Safer if I don't say." I give him a small, sad smile and wipe the tears from my cheeks with the back of my hand.

"Emilia, someone needs to know where you are."

"Maybe in time," I reply reluctantly. "Once I know it's safe, after they're able to catch Antonio and Saul, I'll be able to tell you…But right now, I have to think about my baby, and it's just better if I disappear."

"When? When are you planning to do this?"

"Soon. I don't have an exact date. There are a couple of loose ends I want to tie up here first, and I'll need your help in arranging it."

"Anything you need," he says sincerely, and I believe him. His face is twisted with sadness, but I can also see that he understands. He knows I'm right, but doesn't like to be wrong either.

"I'm going to head to bed. Is there anything you need before I turn in?"

"Yes, two things. Tomorrow, I'd like to go to Alex's gravesite."

My dad's eyes widen in surprise, but he just nods and listens.

"I know his funeral was supposed to be today, but with Sam being shot, I don't know if it happened. Do you?"

"I don't know," he says carefully, strangely. "I can surely find out, though."

"Regardless, I need to go there before I leave."

"Okay," he says quietly.

"And lastly, do you have a computer I can borrow?"

"I do. In the office." He points down a different hallway on the opposite side of the house. "Just login as a guest; you can access the Internet from there."

"Thanks," I tell him, and he steps out, bowl in hand.

As I head to the office, I make a mental list of everything I need to do to put my plan in motion. Sitting down at the oversized mahogany desk, I feel small in the large, leather chair. Everything is neat and modern and in its place. A picture of a blonde woman is framed on the desk. I assume this is Gretchen. She looks remarkably like my mom, and I wonder momentarily if that's why he was attracted to her. Logging in, I pull up my email, my bank account, an airline, and all the pin boards I've made on the site Sam showed me. These simple boards hold my plans…my future.

When I get to my bank account, I gasp in disbelief. Eight

hundred and fifty thousand dollars was wired to my account sometime in the last couple of weeks. Alex. He must've done this before he was shot in an effort to hide money. I glance around the room in a panic, wondering who I need to tell, but for now, I use only the money that I made at Café Au Lait.

I purchase a one-way plane ticket and print the itinerary, then scroll through the pin boards, a strange excitement brewing in my belly. Shutting down the computer, I head to bed for the first time with a sense of hope…a fresh start, a new beginning lies just in front of me.

TWELVE

Alex

"Right, here. Pull over right here," I instruct the agent shuffling me around town today. The car slows to a stop and the gravel under the wheels crunches under its weight. "Am I okay to spend a few minutes alone, or do you need to be right next to me?" I ask, curious how this all works.

The agent looks over his shoulder and scans the empty cemetery. The place is empty despite a small group of men working on the landscaping across the way. "I can wait here. Take as much time as you need." He pulls out his cellphone and starts tapping at the screen.

My heart races as I step from the car and cross the plush green grass. I remember the day we buried my mom…it was late summer, eerily similar to today. The sun was bright and made the cemetery beautiful. Shocks of color shone from the floral arrangements and the trees, and even though the trees are taller and fuller now, the cemetery looks exactly the same.

I spot her resting place before I even reach it. Just beyond the towering oak tree. But I stand frozen in place when I see her name on the granite headstone. It looks smaller than I remember, although still beautiful. Treading carefully across the grass, I kneel next to her plot. "Mama," I whisper as I run my fingers through the soft blades of grass. "I'm so sorry," I muster out.

I remember her smiling face in the photo I had of all of us, the same one Sam has. Her long, dark hair, her light brown eyes…her caring smile.

And I remember Father Mark's words to me. "Visit your mother. Talk to her." And I do. I let it all go. I mumble it all through tears. How much I've missed her, how much I love her. The terrible things I've done, and the amends I'm trying to make.

I tell her about Sam, and how I'm trying to do right by him. I tell her about Emilia, our baby, and trying to do right by them as well.

Everything comes out. Emotions I believed I was incapable of feeling, buried under the surface, bubble to the top and spill over. I feel such comfort here in her spiritual presence. I can almost feel her hand on my back, her fingers running through my hair, and her arms wrapped tightly around me. I swear I can smell the lightest hint of her perfume and hear her sweet voice whispering to me that everything is going to be okay.

I confess my sins and pray. I make apologies and promises, and vow to be a better man. After hours of this, I feel emotionally and physically spent, but far more at peace than when I came.

Not yet ready to leave, though, I sit with my back pressed to the hard bark of the oak tree, taking deep breaths and drawing the warm afternoon air deep into my lungs. I can smell the fresh cut grass and the light scent of the oleander bushes that line the perimeter in the distance.

I'm in a weird state of peace when I see a figure coming closer. Suddenly, everything comes to a sudden stop as I watch her. Her long, thin legs dance across the grass. Her hair bounces around her shoulders. One arm is wrapped protectively around her still flat belly while the other one moves with each step.

Oh shit.

In one quick motion, I slide around the base of the tree,

allowing the large trunk to hide me. I make eye contact with the agent in charge of my security, and he motions for me to stay down. I nod and motion to him that Emilia is okay, safe, and he nods back, ducking behind his vehicle and watching us intently.

As she nears, my heart is fucking pounding. Blood rushes through my head, momentarily silencing the world around me. *My girl.* As she comes to a stop where I was sitting an hour ago, she lifts her shaky hands and covers her mouth. It's now that I realize she's staring at my name engraved on the granite headstone. Tears fall from her eyes as she gasps for air, then she sits and buries her face in her hands.

Guilt ravages me as I watch her fall apart. I fucking hate that I'm putting her through this.

Her words are quiet and sad, her spirit broken, and I can't stand it any longer. I don't hesitate a second longer before I step out from behind the tree. She's slumped forward now, her hands on her knees. I can't watch this anymore. I can't take it.

Jogging over to her, I wrap myself around her. "Em, Em, Em… I've got you. I've got you, Em."

"No!" she screams and fights against me. "No," she cries. She must not realize I'm real. Exactly what I was fearing.

"Em, it's me…stop." I try to console her.

Finally, she frees herself from my grasp, falling to her back. When her eyes register me, she loses it, unleashing a string of blood-curdling screams. From the corner of my eye, I watch both our security detail sprinting toward us.

Standing up, I warn them, "Stop! Stop. I'm not going to hurt her." I wait for things to click with her, but she's rolled to her side in the fetal position. "Em, please. It's me. It's Alex." I kneel next to her, brushing the hair off her face.

"Don't hurt me," she mumbles, shaking her head as if she doesn't believe what she's seeing. And she shouldn't. To her, I'm dead.

"Emilia, I'm alive," I whisper. "I have a lot to explain, but I need to you to focus. Pull yourself together," I urge her while our security detail are holding guns and watching us closely. "I'm not going to hurt her! For fuck's sake, back the hell off. Put the fucking guns away!" After a hesitant moment, my guy slowly backs off and holsters his gun, but Emilia's doesn't. I see him talking to the agent assigned to me, and he nods, but he doesn't fully retreat.

"Em." I try to pull her into my lap, but she pulls back. "God, look at you." I feel sick as I take her in. She's still insanely thin, and she looks beyond exhausted. Her normally hazel eyes are bright green in contrast to the red bloodshot whites of her eyes. As she begins to realize what's happening, she begins to hyperventilate.

"Emilia, listen to me. Please. We only have a couple of minutes. I was never dead. Sam wanted to you to believe I was because I was going into witness protection. I always intended to take you with me, but they wouldn't let me do that. Emilia, look at me!" I take her head in my hands and lift her face so she's looking at me. "I turned everything over so I could be with you, start over, and everything just went wrong. I'm so sorry."

"You let me believe you were dead," she stutters through her ragged breathing.

"I didn't have a choice." I always had a choice, but I did what I thought I had to do for her.

She still looks horrified, but her features are starting to shift toward anger. "So why are you telling me now?"

"Because…because I can't live without you, Em. I need you. I realize that now. All of this was for you, to protect you—but I need you with me. I'm not alive without you. I may as well be dead if you're not with me."

"Ms. Adams." Her security details approaches. "We need to leave."

"I said, back the fuck off!" I growl at him.

"Mr. Estrada. We're not doing this here," my security detail says sternly. "We need to leave."

"I'm not leaving her," I yell at him. "I'm not leaving you ever again," I whisper against her hair. "Ever."

The two men look at each other, and one of their cell phone rings.

"Em, I need to talk to you—tell you everything."

Her security detail approaches her. "Ms. Adams, we need to get you out of here now." Then to me, he bites out, "Mr. Estrada, this is your last warning to let her go."

"I want to talk to him," Emilia says, her voice shaking with emotion. "I'll talk to him."

"Very well. The office." Her guy reaches for her hand, and she accepts it.

Pushing myself up, I watch anxiously as he leads Emilia to their car. Her eyes search for me, and she rests her head against the window as they drive away.

"Let's go, Estrada!" my detail barks at me as he jogs to the car. "You're going to have to explain this to Hoffman, because he's fucking pissed!"

"How in the hell does this happen?" Hoffman screams at me, his fist pounding on the wood conference room table. "I mean, what're the goddamn chances you'd both pick the same fucking day, at the same fucking time? If I wasn't so fucking angry, I'd tell you to go buy a fucking lottery ticket, because shit like this doesn't happen on our detail." His nostrils are flaring, and I admit it's amusing seeing him so riled up.

"I didn't see them roll up," my security detail admits, taking some of the heat off of me. "It happened very fast. There was no way he could get out of there without being seen. He handled it the best he could."

"By outing himself? It is your job to protect him! That is a bullshit excuse!" Agent Hoffman props his hands on his hips and fumes. "What if that had been Antonio? You'd be picking up body parts right now," he scoffs at him. "Get out of here." He points to the door.

"Yes, sir," he answers quickly and sneaks out of the room.

Hoffman paces the floor and runs his hand through his hair. "She's agreed to see you, Estrada. Take your time, but say your goodbyes. I want that deal signed and on my fucking desk tomorrow, *comprende*? This is your last goddamn chance, or I'll fucking put a bullet between your eyes for your father." After that, he storms out and slams the door so hard the glass window rattles.

I could care less about his tantrum. I'm just glad they're letting me see her again.

I bob my knee as I wait for them to bring her to me. Every second I'm away from her, I feel like my lungs are slowing, caving in on themselves. Minutes feel like hours, and my anxiety kicks in as my mind runs wild. Maybe she's not coming. Then the click of the door handle tells me someone is here… and there she is.

Long, brown hair and hazel eyes stand before me. Fear and confusion dance across her face. She stares at me as if I'm not real. Judge Martin and her security detail stand just behind her.

"I could feel you," she says just above a whisper as she steps further into the room. I sit motionless as I watch her inch closer to a chair across from me. "I could sense that you were with me," she says, this time a bit louder. "Something told me you weren't gone."

"I'll always be with you, Em."

"Why did you do it?" she asks, her voice breaking.

Judge Martin remains standing in the doorway, watching us, and my eyes bounce back and forth between him and Emilia until he leaves and closes the door behind him. We might be alone in here, but I know we're being watched.

"Because I had to, Em. To protect you. I'd do anything to protect you." She has to know that by now.

The pain in her eyes says she might not. "So you thought I'd be better off thinking you were dead—you were all I had, Alex. You were…everything."

I watch the tears collect in her eyes, and she bites her bottom lip in an attempt to keep it from quivering.

I desperately want to go to her, hold her, but I wisely stay away. "You were supposed to be part of the deal. I asked for witness protection for both of us. I intended for us to start over. Remember you said we could escape somewhere? That was my plan. But they wouldn't give you witness protection. It was Sam's idea to fake the death in an attempt to keep you safe."

"How would that keep me safe?" she asks, incredulous. "Help me understand that."

I take a deep, calming breath, which does nothing. "If you knew I was alive, would you have tried to find me?"

Her eyes fall to her fingers, which are all twisted up in themselves. She nods her head, and I see the tears fall from her eyes to the table.

I close my eyes momentarily so I don't have to watch her cry. "That's why I went along with it, Em. I needed you safe. Without you safe, I have no reason to live." Unable to help myself any longer, I reach across the table and pull her hands into mine. "I was willing to let you go so you could live a life you deserved—with someone who deserves you and could give you everything I couldn't. I loved you enough to let you go."

"Love doesn't let go, Alex." Her voice is soft but full of conviction. "Love hangs on even when there's nothing left to hang on to." She starts sobbing, and I squeeze her hands tighter, sighing in frustration. She's right, of course. She's always right.

"Emilia, I—"

"I'm pregnant," she blurts out. "I'm pregnant with your baby— our baby. I'm scared and I need you. We need you, Alex. I don't want to do this alone. I don't know if I'm strong enough to do this without you." She buries her face in her hands, and I jump out of my seat and round the table.

"You are the strongest person I know," I tell her as I take the seat next to her and pull her into my arms.

"Stop it, Alex!" she yells at me. "I need you. We'll run away. My plan. It'll work. We'll have lots of babies—"

I press my finger to her lips, stopping her. "I want that for you, Em. But it's too dangerous. I can't give that to you. Antonio will always be looking for us—for me. I won't put you or my baby in danger—I won't do it."

Her hand slaps the table in anger. She's falling apart, and I can't do anything to stop it.

"Emilia, look at me." I pull her head into my hands and force her to look at me. "There is no one in this world I'll ever love as much as you. Please don't make this harder. This is for you—for our baby."

In one quick movement, her hand connects with my cheek. The sting startles me, and then the burn settles in, and a piece of me dies when I see the hurt in her eyes. I release her head and back away from her.

"Lies," she says with a hiss. "All you've done is lie to me. You lied about who you were. You lied about your past. Don't you dare lie anymore—and don't you dare tell me you love me when you don't."

"You think I don't love you?" I ask, feeling like I'm breaking apart. "This is all because I love you. This is all for you."

"Lies," she snaps. "Tell me one truth, Alex. One truth and I'll leave you alone."

"You want a truth, Em? I'll give you a truth. You are the only woman I'll ever love. Ever. That's the truth. So you believe what you want to believe, but I'm willing to give up everything for you…because I love you."

Tears roll down her cheeks, and she gasps for breath. I can see in her eyes she wants to believe me.

"And I'd do this a million times over for *you*—even if it really kills me—because I love you."

She wraps her left arm around her waist and she braces herself on the edge of the table with the other as she walks toward the conference room door. Vomit rises in the back of my throat as I watch her walking away from me. I'm not sure what I expect next, but it sure as hell isn't for her to walk away. I watch, frozen in my seat as she backs away from me, fire and pain and disappointment in her eyes, and she heads toward the door.

"Emilia, wait!"

She stops, pausing before she turns around. I walk toward her, pulling the chain from my front pocket as I approach. "This is yours."

She gasps when I pull the compass necklace from my pocket and dangle it in front of her. Placing it in her shaky hand, I tell her what I told her when I gave her the necklace. "You'll never be lost again, Em. You'll always have me even when I'm not with you."

Then, as if the sun is rising on us and our shitty situation, she throws herself into my arms and I hold her as she cries into my shoulder. I hold on to her like I've never held on to her before— because as much as she needs me, I need her more.

Our embrace is tight, firm, unrelenting; only I know I have to let go. "I love you, Emilia. I promise I did this for you. I know it doesn't make sense now, but it will someday," I whisper into her hair. She nods against my shoulder, and I run my fingers through her hair at the nape of her neck, soaking in the feel of her, the scent of her.

"Promise me you'll take care of my baby," I whisper, and her sobs become louder and she nods again against my shoulder. I peer over her shoulder, and I see Judge Martin step through the conference room door, gently pulling Emilia away from me. Agent Hoffman enters the room with a paper and pen in hand, and Emilia suddenly bucks against the judge.

"Don't sign the paper, Alex!" she screams. "Please," she begs me. "Don't sign the agreement, Alex. Don't throw *us* away," she cries. Please," I hear her yell from the hallway as the door closes. Her cries eventually fade as she's pulled down the hallway.

Tears flood my eyes, and I sit down at the table, pressing my palms to my eyes. I hear Agent Hoffman set the agreement in front of me and slide a pen across the table until it lands in front of me. Wiping my eyes, I stare at the white sheet of paper.

"Sign it," he says gruffly.

I pick up the paper and reread the agreement. The terms are simple. Everything is spelled out in black and white. It should be easy. It's exactly as I told Emilia—it's for her, to protect her.

But I can't do it. Not yet.

"I'm not ready." I push myself up from the table, the chair falling over as I shoot up. "I'd like to go back to the house."

"Sign. The fucking. Agreement," Hoffman grinds out. "Quit fucking playing games, Estrada."

"You have everything you need. Whether or not I sign the agreement shouldn't mean anything to you."

"It should to you." He smirks. "A signature on that agreement is your ticket out of prosecution. If you don't sign it, Alejandro, you're not exempt from charges."

I glare at him. "Then you shouldn't care if I sign it," I seethe. "You'd love nothing more than to see me rot in a jail cell." I clench my fists as he walks over to me.

"You're right, I would. But your brother sold his goddamn soul to get you that agreement. He made promises he won't be able to keep and called in favors he'll never be able to return—all so you'd be safe. I owe it to him to make sure you sign the agreement. Witness security was his idea, not mine. I would've let Antonio pump you full of lead. One less problem I would need to deal with." His shoulder clips mine as he stalks away. He throws the door open so aggressively it bounces off the wall, and I hear him shout, "Someone take his ass back to the house. I'm done with him."

THIRTEEN

Emilia

I'm not sure how I have any tears left, but they keep coming. I shift slightly in bed when I hear a light rapping at the door, just before it cracks open.

"Emilia." My father says my name quietly before peeking in and finding me curled up.

"Just checking on you." He comes over and sits on the edge of the mattress. "It's been an emotional day for you, I know—"

"Did you know he was alive?" I question him. It seems like everyone knows everything about me, and I know nothing about anyone.

He swallows hard, but looks me directly in the eye. "I did."

"Why?" I ask quietly through my tears. "Why didn't you tell me the truth?"

"Because I couldn't. He wanted to keep you safe, and so do I. The witness security program is difficult to get into. You have no idea how many defendants are denied entry and how many of them end up dead." His voice is agitated. "When Sam Cortez told me everything that happened, and how they were going to use the shooting as a front to distract Antonio, I couldn't disagree with his plan."

So he's known everything all along? "But when you saw how much pain I was in, why couldn't you tell me?"

He lets out a long-suffering sigh. "Because it's like Alex said to you this afternoon, Em. You would've gone looking for him, and it's too dangerous." He shifts on the bed. "And I know you won't believe this, but I care about you. You're my daughter. And yes, I've been a shitty father, but I couldn't knowingly push you toward a man running a drug cartel."

"Used to," I remind him bitterly. "He gave it up—he gave it all up." *For me.* And now I won't even be able to have him. He's gone.

"He did," he says quietly.

I push myself up and lean against the headboard, pulling my knees to my chest. "I'm leaving tomorrow."

"Where to?" he asks, a hint of sadness in his voice.

"Somewhere I've always wanted to go," I try to force a smile. "I told Alex about it once—I thought it'd be the perfect place to start over."

"You're not going to tell me?"

I shake my head a little. "No, not right now. It's probably better that nobody knows where I am anyway, plus I think I need to do this on my own. For me and the baby." It's time I started taking care of myself. It's time I started depending on myself and no one else.

"Well, you at least have to call and check in," he suggests, hopeful.

"I don't have a phone." I cringe. "I gave the one Alex gave me back to him, and it hasn't been a priority for me."

"Emilia, you can't go off the grid," he says, concerned. "Someone has to know where you are."

I'm touched by his concern, I am. Even after all this time, it's nice to know he's always cared about me. "I'll find a way to get in touch with you, I promise. But there are a few things I need to do tomorrow before I leave." Shoving my emotions aside, I begin to set my plans into motion.

"Sure, we just need to let security know so they can plan for it."

"Okay." I nod at him. "And I need to get to a store as well. I don't have a bag for the clothes you got me."

"I've got a suitcase you can have, and Gretchen must've stopped by because there were more clothes and a bunch of toiletries on the front porch."

"Okay," I say softly. "Would you please pass along my gratitude to her?"

His eyes soften, and he looks sad. "I will."

"I'm sorry things didn't work out for you two," I tell him as he pulls at a small string on the comforter.

"I am too. I'm learning that I've made a lot of mistakes, Emilia. I've neglected a lot people that I love. I put unimportant things in front of people, and it's hard to reverse that damage."

"First step is acknowledging you made a mistake," I say quietly.

"Very true. I plan to make amends, but it'll take some time for them to let me back in, I think." His sad eyes look at me and beg for forgiveness.

"In time," I whisper to him.

"In time," he repeats.

I roll the large suitcase down the marble hallway and set it near the front door.

"You all set, kiddo?" My father asks as he leans against the wall by the front door, waiting for me.

"All set," I tell him as I tuck my plane ticket into the new purse that Gretchen purchased for me. Labels mean nothing to me, but I can tell this purse must've cost a small fortune.

"I'm glad everything fit in the suitcase. I was worried after yesterday's surprise delivery of clothes."

"Me too," I remark as I look at the bulging suitcase. "She went a little overboard." I cringe and look back to my father. Gretchen bought maternity clothes, shoes, clothes that fit me now, undergarments, more pajamas, workout clothes, dresses, jackets, and even makeup. "I almost couldn't fit it all."

"I can see that." He laughs. "If there's one thing Gretchen's good at it, it's shopping and spending money. I'm just glad she was able to help you get a few things."

"I'll replace the suitcase for you."

"Nonsense. It's a suitcase. I can get a new one tomorrow." He walks over to me and plants himself in front of me, resting his hands gently on each of my shoulders. "I really wish you'd tell me where you're going. I know I don't deserve your trust, but I'm worried about you."

"In time," I whisper, and he cracks a smile.

"In time," he repeats. "I'll get this in the trunk of the car. Security is out front, waiting for us, and both locations have been approved and cleared. You ready?"

"I'm ready." *As I'll ever be*, I think as I slide into a pair of leather ballet flats.

I close the door behind me and slide into the unmarked car in the driveway next to my dad's Mercedes. As we pull out, I look over my shoulder at the house my father lives in, taking it all in. I feel at peace knowing I'm leaving with different memories than the first time I left here.

A chill runs up my spine as we enter the cool hospital. I'm surrounded by two agents and my father, but for some reason, I feel vulnerable, exposed. The elevator delivers us to the intensive care unit, and we check in at a small desk before I'm led down the hall to his room. I closely follow the nurse, who updates me on his condition.

"He's still heavily sedated. Conscious, but he's not responding to verbal commands yet. His injuries are extensive—quite honestly, we're all shocked he made it," she says. "He has serious internal injuries, and there's still a chance he won't fully recover."

I can only nod, my stomach twisting in discomfort.

"Take your time with him. Talk to him, but don't expect anything in return." She smiles at me.

The sound of the breathing machine is the first thing I hear. There's a tube taped to his mouth, and I swallow back the bile rising in my throat. He looks so helpless, lying in the bed. His chest is covered in bandages and his skin is ashen. Machines all around him are beeping and dinging quietly in the semi-dark room.

I stand next to the bed for several minutes, taking in the sight of Sam battered and bruised. Finally, I slide my hand into his and give it a gentle squeeze. "Sam, it's Emilia. They finally let me see you," I whisper to him. There's no reaction, but like the nurse said, it's to be expected. "I wanted to see you before I left. It's too dangerous here, Sam. I have to go. I know it's not what you wanted, but I'll be safer there." A lump forms in my throat, but I'm able to choke it down.

"Sam, we all love you so much. Fight. Fight so hard." With my other hand, I brush a lock of hair away from his forehead. "I'll be careful, I promise," I whisper before pressing a soft kiss to his forehead. I hate saying goodbye, especially when I don't even know if I'll ever see him again, let alone if he'll live.

I spend a few more minutes in the quiet of Sam's room, reflecting on everything that's happened and plans for the future. Fear has planted its evil roots so deep inside me that it's almost crippling, but I know leaving is what I have to do for my baby and for me.

Then, out of nowhere, his hand gently squeezes mine, and I have to swallow back the tears. He knows I'm here. "Sam," I whisper. "I have to go now, but I'll be back," I tell him as his hand relaxes. The growing lump in my throat subsides when I leave the room and find a large group of people outside Sam's door.

"Emilia," my dad calls to me. "This is Natalia and Thomas, Sam's aunt and uncle. The couple who raised him."

"Nice to meet you," they both say in unison.

"We've heard a lot about you," Natalia says. She's a beautiful older woman, I'd guess in her late forties or early fifties. Her mostly black hair is cut into a chin-length bob, with just a shock of grey hair tucked neatly behind her ear

"I've heard a lot about you as well." I smile as I remember the stories Sam told me about them. "Sam has said wonderful things about you both. Natalia, I'm wondering if I could have a brief word with you?" I ask her and step aside, hoping she'll oblige.

"Of course." She follows me a few feet away from where all the security detail are abuzz in conversation. "Is everything okay?" she asks, a concerned look spreading across her face.

"Yes." I nod my head quickly. "I just wanted to ask you…" I pause momentarily to take a deep breath and look around. "Could I get your contact information? I want to be able to reach you to find out how Sam is doing."

"You're welcome here anytime, dear. I'd never ask you to stay away. Sam considered you family, and that means we do as well."

"I'm leaving town," I tell her discreetly, and her eyes widen. "It's safer."

She nods in understanding.

"I just want to be able to check in on Sam—"

"Of course," she cuts me off and begins digging through her purse. She scribbles an email address and a phone number on the back of a receipt and hands it to me.

"Thank you." I smile at her and shove the paper in my purse, then step around her.

"Oh, and Emilia." She reaches for my arm, stopping me. "I

know Alex is still alive. Be careful with him." Her eyes harden and drop to the necklace that dangles from my neck.

She has nothing to worry about. My throat tightens around the newly forming lump. "He let me go in exchange for witness protection," I tell her, my voice shaking.

She nods, but her face doesn't change. "With Alex, nothing is what it seems. Be careful, sweet girl." Then she lets go of my arm.

I make my way over to my dad and the agents, who are now waiting for me, and we head out. Even as I'm leaving, and knowing I'm going on to make my new start, Natalia's words still hang over me like a dark cloud.

In front of Café Au Lait, I wait for the all-clear signal from the agent. When he gives it, the additional security detail in the front seat jumps out and opens my door. We walk side by side into the coffee shop, and the first thing that greets me is the delectable smell. I've missed this place. The little bell above the door chimes as we enter, and Jax looks up from the counter.

"Sunshine!" he yells and drops his pen on the counter. He jogs around the pastry cabinet and meets me with open arms and huge hug.

"Jax," I say, falling into his arms.

"What's wrong, sunshine?" he asks, sensing my mood immediately.

"That noticeable?" I ask him as I pull out of his embrace.

"What's going on?" He guides me to a small table in the back. A girl I don't recognize waves him off and begins cleaning tables and restocking the pastry case.

"I'm leaving."

He quirks an eyebrow. "Leaving where?"

"Did you hear about Sam?" I ask, changing the subject.

He gives a sad nod. "That other agent, I think his name is Hoffman, came in and told me. I'm so sorry, Em."

"It's just time for me to get away before anyone else gets hurt—"

"Wait, you're not blaming yourself for this…"

"No, but it just seems that lately, anyone associated with me ends up shot. First my mom, then Alex, now Sam…it's just safer if I sneak away and lay low."

"I agree with that," he says and rubs his short beard.

"I'm going to miss you, Jax. Thank you for taking a chance on me."

"We're going to miss you, sunshine." His somewhat sad smile is warm, and I know I'll never forget him. "Promise you'll keep in touch?"

"Promise. But before I go, any chance I can get a large cinnamon coffee?" I've been craving one for weeks.

"Anything for you." He jumps from his chair and heads over to the counter to make my coffee, handing it to me when he's done. "I'll be waiting to hear from you, sunshine."

"In time." I wink at him and give him another hug. My security detail pulls open the door when he sees me approach. He scans the sidewalk as we head to the car that's illegally parked on the street. Perks of being a federal agent.

As I get in, I hear my dad on his phone, and I direct the agent to take a left down one of the side streets. "That large church, right there. Park over there."

I point to the meters on the side of the road, and he smirks. Then I remember that he already knows where he's going, as we had to get approval. He's polite, though, and humors me. My dad gives me the side eyes when he sees we're at a church, but he continues on with this phone call and I jump out.

I jog up the steep concrete steps to the front doors of the large stucco church and pull the wood door open.

"Emilia," I hear Father Mark say as he comes toward me with a giant smile. "Come here."

He gestures to a pew, and as we sit, an unusual calm sets in. All my anxiety over leaving, my sadness over Alex and Sam, is briefly tempered.

"I'm so glad to see you."

"I've been wanting to come by for a while, but things have been—"

"Yes, I know," he says, interrupting me. "Complex is the word I'd use." He smiles at me.

"Yes. Complex," I agree with him. "I'm coming to say goodbye." I stare straight ahead at the large crucifix hanging on the altar, loving how the sun shines through the stained glass windows, casting a rainbow of colors throughout the church.

"You're leaving?"

I nod and, for the first time today, I can feel my emotions taking over. A lump forms in my throat as I turn to face Father Mark, and I inhale deeply. "I am."

"Give it to God, Emilia. Let it out," he says calmly. And I do. I break down and forgive the God I've forsaken. I forgive him for all the yelling and cursing I've done. I beg him to help me with frustration and loneliness I'm feeling, and I beg him for the strength to carry on as I leave, and for the safety of me and my baby.

Through it all, Father Mark sits and waits patiently, giving me the strength to hand it all over to God, to trust that he'll know what to do with my anger, my pain, and my prayer.

After a moment, Father Mark shifts in the pew. "Emilia. You remind me so much of Emma, Alex and Samuel's mother. She was resilient and strong, and had so much determination and fight within her. You're going to be just fine." His smile is so confident I want to believe him. I have to. I have no other choice.

"I'm so blessed that Alex gave me the opportunity to get to know you. I'll be praying for you."

And something in those words tells me that I'm going to be okay, that I'll make it through all of this. Peace replaces the anger and hurt I've been harboring and calm settles in. I take a deep breath and smile at Father Mark. "Thank you for not judging me."

"Emilia, we'll all have our judgment day," he says wisely. "I'm just here to guide you until then."

I stand up and Father Mark joins me. "I've got a car waiting." I gesture toward the street.

"Don't let me keep you." He steps back. "Take care of yourself, Emilia. You're going to do just fine."

I turn around and give him a long hug, and I smile when he hugs me back. I know now know why Alex and Sam have found comfort here, and I take one last look around the large church. I know that faith will be an important part of my life as I rebuild, and I'm so thankful that Father Mark was my steppingstone.

With a wave, I push through the door and jog down the steps to the waiting car. As we drive down the streets, I take in everything, from the brown rock to the palm trees to the stucco buildings that make Phoenix unique. Less than ten minutes later, we're pulling into the airport, and I take a deep breath. This is really happening. And I've never been on a plane before.

"Agent Wilcox will be escorting you to the gate," my father says quietly as I stare out the window. "Emilia," he says, resting his hand on top of mine, and I turn to look at him. "I am so proud of who you've become." His voice is full of regret, and it tugs at my heart. "You're the strongest person I've ever met, and you're going to be an excellent mother." He stops to clear his throat. "Please be careful and let me know you're okay."

"I will," I tell him with a nervous smile. "Thank you for letting me stay with you. It's been really nice getting to know you. That's all I ever wanted when I came to Phoenix. I just wanted to know you."

He nods and hesitates. "I'm sorry for the way I treated you. You deserved better than that—"

"I forgive you," I tell him immediately. "I just wanted to meet my dad," I say and smile. "And I'm so lucky I got that chance. You're all I have now, so me leaving here doesn't mean you won't see me again. You know I have to do this."

He visibly relaxes and squeezes my hand. "You better go or you're going to miss your flight."

Agent Wilcox has already left the car and is waiting on the curb with my luggage.

"Thank you for everything," I say as I open the door and step out. Through the window, I see him lean back against the seat, and I wave. He raises a hand to wave back at me as the car pulls away, leaving me with Agent Wilcox.

"Ready?" he asks, pulling the large suitcase behind him.

"Ready," I tell him and my heart races. Nerves take over and my knees tremble as we enter the airport.

We make it through security in record time after I check my bag. I guess it helps when a federal agent escorts you to your gate. They let you skip to the front of the line, and no one questions anything. As we sit in the leather seats at the gate, agent Wilcox taps his finger on his leg.

"Ms. Adams," he says, looking around the gate area.

"Yeah."

"Couple of things I want to go over with you." He leans forward, inching closer. "I think you're crazy for leaving, but since you are, I wanted to give you some advice." He takes a drink of water from his water bottle and twists the lid back on. "Be aware, this'll keep you alive. Take note of everything, and I mean everything." He waits for me to nod, then continues. "Double and triple check the locks on your windows and doors. Make a spare key and hide it somewhere, but do not hand one out to anyone. Remember exactly how you leave things. If anything at any time looks or appears to be out of place, get the hell out of your house. Leave. Don't wait. Just go."

I nod again quickly.

"Be aware of your surroundings. Stay in public places and away from secluded areas. Always look to see if you're being followed. But most importantly, be careful of what you say to whom. Keep all mention of the Estrada family and this case under wraps. You have no idea who is connected to them, understand?"

"Understand," I say as my heart pounds with the weight of what I'm doing.

His eyes remain serious. "It's going to be easy to get lazy in time. You'll get comfortable and confident, but that will get you killed. Don't let it consume you, Emilia, but make a routine. You check things when you leave, when you come home, you look for signs, but at the same time—live." And with that, his seriousness lessens.

I take it all in, stressed at the amount of what I'll have to do, but I can do it. I can. And I will.

At the boarding announcement, he stands. "This is you. I'll be here in the gate area until the plane starts taxiing. Take a deep breath." He smiles at me.

I pull my purse up onto my shoulder and grip the ticket in my hand a little tighter. "Thank you."

"You're welcome." He nods at me.

"And take care of my father, please."

He gives a curt nod. "Happy to."

I board the plane and find my seat against the window. Buckling myself in, I press my forehead against the cool plastic window of the airplane and close my eyes. As I feel the plane pushing away from the gate, I try to calm my nerves. I have to remind myself over and over that a new beginning is only a few hours away.

FOURTEEN

Alex

Lies.

That's all I'm really good at.

I learned from the best.

I know exactly when and how to lie so that something works to my advantage, but I hated that my lies hurt Em. What she doesn't know is that this lie will lead me back to her.

The pain in her eyes when I told her I had to let her go just about killed me, but I needed to buy myself some time. I need to see Sam. I need to right my wrongs and absolve my sins before I can give myself to her. It wouldn't have been safe if she knew my plan, because I know my girl…she wouldn't have left.

There's a knock on the front door, and I freeze, contemplating if I should answer it. Peeking through the blinds, I see that the security detail is out front, but they're not on alert. I walk quietly over to the door and look through the peephole to see Agent Hoffman. Quickly, I unlock the door and pull it open.

"Agent Hoffman," I greet him and step aside so he can enter.

He steps through the door and stands in the middle of the living room. "You're not going to sign the witness protection agreement, are you?" His brows are furrowed, and the vein that runs between his eyebrows is raised. He's angry but not as livid as he was the other day.

My face goes hard. "I'm not."

"Motherfucker." He swings a punch into the air. "One goddamn thing. Just one. That's all your brother wanted for you—protection. Do you have any idea what we did to get you that deal?" His hatred of me is clear in his eyes. "No, you wouldn't, because you're too fucking selfish to think about anyone other than yourself." He begins pacing in circles around my living room. I close the still wide-open front door and lean back against it as I watch him come unglued.

"I don't know if he's going to make it," he says, his voice strained. "But he made me promise to make sure you didn't fuck up this deal. I'm in this with him, and even though I wish you were dead, I owe it to him to make sure you're safe."

"I will be safe," I tell him as walk to the center of the room. "Look, I was going to take the deal. I was prepared to sign the papers and go…until I found out Emilia was pregnant. I can't abandon her and the baby."

He shakes his head. "You're a real asshole, do you know that? You'd leave her when it was just her, but now that there's a baby involved, you won't do it?" He snorts.

"I can't," I admit. "I can't leave them. For the rest of my life, I'd regret this decision. I'm trying to right my wrongs, can't you see that? I've given you everything you need to bring down my father, the Estrada organization, and most of their associates. But I cannot sign that deal. I can't go into hiding."

We stare at each other, each of us holding our ground.

"So what do you want?" he finally asks, breaking the silence.

"Immunity. That's all." Not that that's such a small thing. "I'll still give you everything you need. I just need immunity. For Emilia. For our baby."

He drops his head in frustration. "You know this is a risk, don't you? For all of you. You might get them killed."

"They're more vulnerable without me. You know that." My stomach turns at the thought of Emilia on her own without protection—without me.

After a long moment, he finally nods in agreement. "All right then. Immunity was part of the witness protection agreement. I'll tell them you'd like to forgo just the protection portion."

"Thank you," I tell him. "I appreciate everything you've done for me."

"It's not for you, Estrada," he bites out. "It's for your brother. He's been my best friend and partner for years. This is for him. Don't mistake my helping him as kindness toward you."

"Understood. Speaking of my brother, I'd like to visit him…tomorrow."

"I'll see what I can do." And with that, the door slams behind him as he leaves.

"It's your lucky day, Estrada." The voice pulls me from counting to three hundred and thirty-seven as I rise from my last sit-up. The morning sun is beginning to warm the air, and sweat rolls down my temples from my hairline.

"What makes it my lucky day?" I ask Hoffman as I push myself up from the ground and grab a hand towel to wipe my head. I've seen more of him in the last two days than I'd like to, but right now, he's my ticket to my brother.

"You've been granted permission to see Sam." Relief settles in my stomach.

"I'm family. I shouldn't need permission," I growl.

"You're a criminal and your brother is a federal agent," he reminds me smugly. "Everyone needs permission."

"Well, then, thank you," I say, mostly meaning it. I'm not going to get into a pissing match with him this morning over what relationship I have with my own brother.

His eyes narrow in disgust. "Don't thank me; thank your aunt. She's the one that approved it."

"My aunt?" I raise an eyebrow.

He shakes his head. "Yep, now go shower. We need to be there in a half hour. Apparently, they're going to start pulling back on the pain meds, and they'd like you to see him before they start."

"Okay. Give me fifteen." I rush to shower and get ready. One glance in the mirror shows how rough I still look. I haven't shaved in three days, and my face is covered in a short, sparse beard, but there's no time. I dress quickly and brush my teeth, then find Agent Hoffman on my couch, sipping a cup of coffee while scrolling through his phone.

"Ready?" I ask him.

"Everyone's waiting on you, Estrada. It's like we're moving the fucking pope with how much security you need," he says, his voice dripping with disdain.

I ignore that and head outside. Everyone is in position as I walk to the waiting car, and we move through the Phoenix streets quickly. In the hospital parking garage, I stay put until I'm told to move, then we move quickly. A back storage elevator is used to bring me to the intensive care unit where Sam is still kept, the same elevator I left this hospital in just weeks ago.

The floor is quiet yet busy. Nurses and doctors move from room to room, and all kinds of medical equipment lines the halls. My stomach drops as we near a room where I see Cortez written on a white board hanging just to the right of the door.

"Can I go in?"

"Yes," a female voice says from behind me. I turn to find a nurse in blue scrubs and a white sweater. "He's still heavily medicated. We've begun to decrease his medication already. He may not respond, but he can most likely hear you. And he may be in pain, so don't be alarmed if he responds with abrupt noises."

"He can hear me, though?"

"He can if he's awake. He's been more alert in the last

twelve hours, responding to some of our questions by squeezing our hands or blinking. He's still intubated, so he can't talk. His tube will be coming out later today as well. He's made great progress, though. I really didn't expect this outcome, to be honest."

"The Estradas are almost invincible," I say and smile.

"He's a Cortez." The sharp voice startles me. "Everything about that boy is a Cortez," my Uncle Tommy says. "He was never an Estrada." My Uncle Tommy was my mother's brother and denounced the Estradas after she was murdered.

My Aunt Natalia walks up behind him and wraps her arm in his. "*Mijo*," she says quietly, hesitating. My uncle wipes a tear from his eye, and she takes a step forward. "Please go see your brother. We'll wait for you down the hall. And I'd like to speak with you for just a minute before you leave."

My uncle laces his hand through my aunt's, and I watch them walk slowly down the hall, hand in hand, toward the waiting room. My stomach clenches, and I realize I miss them. I miss everything that we were when we were all a family. I miss my uncle building us a tire swing. I miss the parties and the holidays. I miss my family.

Shoving the thoughts away, I turn to open the hospital door. The swishing sound of his breathing machine is the first thing I notice. Next are the bandages taped all over his chest. A sheet lies over his bottom half, stopping at his abdomen.

"Hey," I whisper. "I'm sorry I haven't come sooner. They wouldn't let me."

His eyes are closed, both arms at his sides. His hands are curled just slightly, and his fingers twitch occasionally. It hurts to see him like this, all because of me.

"I hope you can hear me," I lean in, resting my forearms on my knees. "I'm so sorry you got hurt. If it's the last thing I do, I'll make sure Saul pays for what he did. I will make sure he doesn't get away with this."

At that, Sam's fingers twitch wildly, and his pulse quickens as displayed on the monitor next to his bed. He can hear me.

"Sam, listen," I say quickly. "I know you can hear me. I need to tell you that I'm not taking the deal. I can't do it. I can't walk away from Em and the baby. I know how hard you worked to get me that deal, but I can't do it." Tears fill my eyes as I look around and see the destruction I've caused—Sam lying injured in this hospital bed, my Uncle Tommy, who can barely look at me, down the hall, Emilia and the baby, gone. All because of me.

"I'm so sorry for all the pain I've caused you. For the anguish I've brought to you. I only did what I knew to do. I know you don't understand, but I need you to know how sorry I am."

I inhale sharply as the heart rate monitor settles, and his pulse stabilizes. "For the rest of my life, I'll work on making it up to you and to the family. Emilia left, Sam. I'll stay and do whatever it takes to help Hoffman with the case, but as soon as I'm able to, I need to find her. I've abandoned a lot of people in my life, but I won't do that to them. Please understand that this is the only reason I'm walking away from the deal. Everyone will have my full cooperation. I promise. I know my word doesn't mean much, but from here forward, it will."

I pause, wondering how to say goodbye. "You have no idea how much I appreciate everything you've done. Love ya, man." Before I stand up to leave, I whisper a quiet prayer for Sam.

As I leave the room, a nurse walks over to me. "Your aunt would like to speak with you. She's waiting in the lounge at the end of the hall."

I look to my security detail, and they nod in approval. My stomach twists in anxiety as I walk the length of the hall. White, vacant walls guide me to my family, a family who has disowned and hates me. I push through the door and find my aunt and uncle sitting side by side.

"Tia. Tio," I address them humbly.

"*Mijo*," my aunt says, standing up, her voice raw with emotion.

"Come here." She holds her arms open and waits for me. I hesitate, but finally, my feet carry me to the family I've missed—my mother's family.

Pulling me into her arms, she presses her face to my chest and mumbles in broken Spanish how much she's missed me. A lump forms in my throat as she holds me. My uncle stands and waits, finally interrupting our reunion by also wrapping his arm around both of us. Finally pulling away, my aunt invites me to sit down.

I sit in the lounge chair across from them.

"Alejandro," my aunt says quietly. "We've missed you so much."

"I've missed you too," I tell them and take a deep breath. It feels so good to see them.

"I'm proud of you for finally cooperating with the government," my uncle says, grudgingly proud. "Sam had been keeping us informed. We knew you'd wake up one day and realize this is not the life you were meant to lead. All we could do was pray for you," he says, his voice crackling with emotion. "Your mother would finally be so proud of you."

Finally he says, and he's right. My mother would be just as disgusted with my behaviors and choices, until now.

I nod solemnly. "I'm still cooperating. I'll give them everything they want or need, but I'm not taking the witness security protection."

"Why not, *mijo*?" my aunt interrupts.

"Emilia. She's pregnant."

My aunt gasps and closes her eyes. "She left."

"I know. She had to, for her protection. She doesn't know I'm coming for her."

"*Por que, mijo*? Why didn't you tell her? We saw her yesterday. She was so scared." My aunt hasn't changed a bit, still speaking in half Spanish, half English.

"For her safety. If she knew I wasn't taking the deal, she would've wanted to hang around and wait for me to be finished here. Until Antonio and his henchmen are caught, it's not safe here. I have a pretty good idea where she's going. It should be easy to find her."

"If it's easy for you, that means it's easy for Antonio," my uncle snaps. "She's not safe—no one is safe until that murderer is off the streets." My uncle shakes his fist in the air. "I'd murder him with my own two hands—" He cuts off suddenly, his head dropping forward. I know he never got over my mother's death. For being her older brother by six years, they were unusually close.

His words shock me, though. I didn't know they knew what my father did. I thought it was my secret—mine and my brother's— this whole time. "Sam told you?"

"He did," my aunt says and rubs my uncle's arm. "We had our suspicions, but it's just sickening to finally have the truth."

"I was just as shocked. I mean, I knew he was a horrible man, but I never suspected he killed her."

"He was too big of a coward to pull the trigger," my uncle mumbles bitterly. "He had someone else do it. I know him. He loved her—but she got in his way, and that coward didn't have the balls to do it himself." He uses the back of his hand to wipe tears from his eyes. "I have prayed for years to have answers, but now I don't know if living in ignorance or knowing the truth was easier."

I listen to my uncle break down, and I feel sick. The pain he's carried all these years and the hatred he has for my father has trickled down to me.

"I'm so sorry," I say somberly. "I loved her just as much as you did, and I miss her every single day, and I'm sorry for any pain that I personally caused you."

My aunt shakes her head. "No, *mijo*. We know that you became a product of that environment. We don't blame you."

"I blame myself. I could've left. I *should* have left."

"He would never have let that happen," my uncle says honestly, his voice sad. "We tried so hard to convince him to let you come with us. I'm not sure why he let Samuel go so easily, but he…he had his eyes set on you. There was no escaping this for you. For a long time, Samuel was so hurt that your father turned his back on him. But as he grew, he understood that he was blessed. Everyone felt so much sorrow for you. Living that life."

"Everything we used to do when I was young, I miss. The birthday parties, the holidays, the barbecues—"

"Antonio hated that stuff," my uncle blurts out. "Anything that he didn't plan, anything that made your mother or you boys happy that he didn't provide, he didn't want to be a part of."

The air is thick with emotions. My Uncle Tommy sniffles as he finally gains his composure, and my aunt just rubs his arm gently, trying to calm him.

"Uncle Tommy," I say, getting his attention. "Remember when you built Sam and me that tire swing in the backyard of our old house? You tied it up and it was so high that Sam fell off and broke his arm?"

He smiles and a low chuckle rumbles from deep within. "I do, *mijo*."

"The tree is still there," my aunt says with a smile. "Sam made sure when he bought the house and fixed up the backyard that the tree remained untouched."

"I still can't believe he bought the house," I remark.

My aunt smiles. "I can. Everything he loved was once in that house. All his good memories were there. It's very sentimental to him. Your uncle here helped him remodel most of it." She rubs his arm. "You should come see it, Alex. It might be cathartic for you. I have the keys. We can go anytime."

"I don't know," I say honestly. That house was once everything good, but also the beginning of everything bad.

"Sam said he's the most at peace there."

"That's how I feel at her grave," I admit. "I feel her there."

"And Sam feels her at the house. When was the last time you were there?" my aunt asks.

"The day we moved. I haven't been back since. Ironic that my witness security house is just around the block from it."

"Sam mentioned that. He was concerned you wouldn't be happy about that."

I shrug. "Nah, I can't complain about anything Sam has done for me." It's the truth, even though I hated him when he was after me.

As we sit there, my mind starts to wander, and I think about what it would be like to see the house again.

I run my hands up and down my thighs, wiping my sweaty palms on my jeans. "Let's do it," I say nervously. "Let's go see the house. I'll have to ask first. They usually do a security sweep first."

"Ah, yes," my aunt says knowingly. "Well, why don't you go request that."

I nod and head over to my detail where they're clustered together, laughing and talking. As I approach, the mood turns more serious. They're not happy about my request, but after one phone call, we're all set. Sam's house has had round-the-clock surveillance since his shooting. The house is clear and can be accessed immediately.

I close my eyes for the short drive back to the neighborhood as I fight to bring back the memories I've tried so hard to bury. I remember the one of my mom smiling as she works in the kitchen, stirring a pot on the stove or baking cookies. I unbury the memory of the barren backyard, except for that large tree with the tire swing. I find the memory of the front porch where Sam and I would sit for hours and play checkers, or draw hopscotch in chalk on the ground. I let those memories free, and I feel them. Feel the love within them.

As the car slows and parks at the curb of Sam's house—my childhood home—I have to take a deep breath. The brick bungalow-style house looks almost identical from the outside. New landscaping has changed the curb appeal, and shutters have been added, but it otherwise looks almost the same as it did twenty years ago when we left.

I step out of the car and follow the flagstone pavers to the front porch. Potted plants adorn the sides of the steps. My aunt fidgets with the keys in her hand, finally turning the lock and pushing the front door open.

My brain works overtime as I take in the newly remodeled space. It's perfectly combined with touches of the old peppered with new. The kitchen was opened up and made modern, but not so much that I don't recognize it. I can still see my mom standing at the counter with her small mixer in hand. The wood floors are original but have been sanded and treated. They look just as I remember but darker. New windows and doors have been put in, but the style is identical to the original.

Modern furniture is mixed with rustic Mexican décor that I'm sure Sam got from my Uncle Tommy, who still has family in Mexico. A few walls have been knocked out to give the area between the kitchen and living room a more open concept, but I still see the corner of the living room where our Christmas tree sat, and the back porch where I stored my baseball bat and glove.

My aunt stands back, letting me wander and remember. I run my finger across the brick mantel of the fireplace, and I find myself standing at the patio door that leads to the backyard.

"Go ahead, *mijo*. You should see what he's done out there."

With a breath, I twist the lock on the French doors and pull one side open. The back patio is just as I remember it as well. Covered, but he's stained the concrete to look like stone, and added another world to the backyard. A large pergola sits just off the patio, covered in flowering vines. Large outdoor furniture rests beneath it with a small fire pit in the middle. A custom-made built in barbecue and wet bar are just off the pergola.

But what takes my breath away is the tree. The long over-reaching limb where that thick rope used to hang with a large tire attached is still there and prominent.

Sam and I spent hours every day playing on that swing. My mom would sit on the back porch and drink lemonade as she watched us. I can't help but smile, and it amazes me how something so simple can hold the fondest memories.

"I told you, *mijo*," my aunt says as she wraps her arm in mine. "He left it."

"It's just like I remember, only bigger."

"Everything he loved about this house he left untouched."

I nod as I see, clear as day, Sam swinging from the tire. He's leaning back, his brown hair blowing in the breeze. A giant smile on his face and laughter rolling off his tongue.

"So many memories," I say, squeezing my aunt's hand.

"So many," she repeats. "I'm going to go inside. Take your time out here."

She lets go of my arm, and I sit down in the patio chair to ponder. The memories are so fresh, so front of mind as they take me back to the happiest days of my life. But when I open my eyes, I'm reminded of my reality, and the good memories suddenly vanish.

Heaving a sigh, I push myself up from the chair and head back inside. My aunt is on the couch waiting for me, but it's Emilia's leather bound notebook on the coffee table that catches my attention.

"That's Emilia's," I mumble, lifting it from the table. It's sitting on top of a thin Apple laptop computer. I flip the cover open and find pictures with notes and lists tucked under the front cover. I'm curious but immediately feel guilty for looking through her personal belongings.

"She never came back here," my aunt says quietly. "Her father told us she left with only what she had at his house."

"Which had to be nothing," I mumble. "She came here with nothing and left with nothing. At least nothing of importance. This was all she cared about." I hold up the leather notebook.

"Take it with you," my aunt says. "If it's important to her, Sam would want her to have it. And that computer." She points to the laptop. "That isn't Sam's. I bet it's hers. Take it."

"I'm going to look and see if there is anything else she left." I head down the hallway, peering into the bedroom that Sam and I shared as kids. Our room, which used to hold bunk beds and a large chest, now looks to be storage for Sam's odds and ends. Even the closet has been reconfigured and built into a bookshelf.

The small hallway bathroom has also been completely updated. New fixtures, tiles, and paint have transformed the small space.

The closed door at the end of the hall holds my biggest nightmare—the master bedroom and the attached bathroom where I found my mother riddled with bullets. My stomach turns with each step as I draw nearer. At the door, my hand stills on the knob, and I close my eyes. Sweat beads along my hairline, bile rising into my throat. I close my eyes and will myself to turn the doorknob.

With a deep breath, I turn the handle and push the door open, then I exhale loudly as I see how different the room is. Sam has changed everything.

Everything.

I thought I'd be upset if this room changed drastically, but I'm relieved. The bathroom off the bedroom has been extended and remodeled and a new tub was installed along a different wall. This is the only room in the house that has truly changed, so much that it feels like a different space altogether.

Across the room, on top of the chest of drawers, sits the same picture I had in my room at the condo. The one Emilia confronted me with. I cross the room and pick it up. Happiness. Everything in this photo was my happiness. *Was*.

With a sense of loss, I refocus and place the picture back and scan the room, looking for any of Emilia's belongings. A stack of clothes is sitting on a chair, and her bag is on the floor next to it. I shove the clothes into the bag and carry it to the living room.

"You okay?" my aunt asks as she shuffles from foot to foot nervously.

"Yeah. I am now."

"He did good," she says with a smile and a gleam of pride.

"He did. I was so nervous to come back here," I admit.

"You needed to. I think we're all still searching for closure. Emma's death ripped this family apart, and we've never been the same. Your uncle helped Sam with the remodel, but he still has a hard time coming over here."

"Where is he?"

"On the front porch." Her eyes are tender. "It's where he usually ends up if we're here too long."

"I'm going to go talk to him."

"I think that's a good idea. I'm going to make a quick phone call and then lock up. I'll meet you out front in just a bit."

I find my uncle on the porch swing, deep in thought, his legs dangling. "Tio," I say quietly, not wanting to startle him.

He turns his head, his face somber and eyes misty. "*Mijo.*"

"You did good. The house is…" I don't know what word I want to say. Perfect is wrong, because it's not perfect—my mom isn't there. Nice seems insincere.

"Just a house," he supplies quietly. "It used to be a home, but that died when Emma died. Alejandro, I owe you an apology. I was so angry at Antonio, and that anger boiled over and became directed at you as well. You were just a little boy when all of this happened. I know none of this was your fault. I should've fought harder for you. I should've done anything to get you away from that monster."

I feel his sincerity, his pain, and his regret. But I don't blame him. "I think we all have regrets," I say as I take a seat next to him on the porch swing. "I don't want any more regrets."

"I don't either." He puts his arm around my shoulder. "I've missed you, *mijo*. And I know you need to get to Emilia, but I'd like to spend some time with you too."

Butterflies fill my stomach and a smile pulls at my lips. This is what hope feels like—and goddamn, I've missed it.

FIFTEEN

Emilia

As the car crawls along the old pebbled street, my fingers grip the steering wheel so tightly my knuckles are white. "Forty-seven-fifteen," I mumble as my eyes scan the house for the address. After a few seconds, I spot the numbers under the carriage light of the attached garage.

This is it.

Feeling nervous, I pull into the short driveway.

A minute later, a small pickup truck pulls up behind me, and my heart races as an older gentleman hops down and hobbles over to my car. "Ms. Adams?" he asks with a smile. My nerves begin to settle when I see his friendly smile.

"Yes," I nod at him.

"I'm William Anders. Ready to see the house?"

"I am." I step out into the foggy air. It's overcast here, and the air hangs heavy with the moisture of impending rain.

William slides a key into the deadbolt, pushing the door open. The ad I found online said the cottage had been recently built. Everything looks new and untouched.

"I haven't had a chance to furnish it yet," he says as he walks toward the kitchen. "My wife wanted to pick out all the furnishings, but she's recently become ill."

"I'm sorry to hear that," I tell him as we walk into the kitchen. I listen to him as I walk around the empty, open space. This place would be perfect for the baby and me. "I love it," I say softly as I run my finger along the wooden window frame.

He gives me a lopsided smile. "Sweetheart, you haven't even seen the best part. Come here."

I follow him through the living room and into the dining area just off the kitchen. Suddenly, my eyes go wide. In front of me is a pair of sliding glass doors that open to a wood patio. Beyond that is the Pacific Ocean.

This can't be real, I think as the waves crash against the sandy shore and tall grass that is whipping in the wind. "It's beautiful," I whisper because I'm in total awe. This place is everything I've ever dreamed of—peaceful and quiet, and the ocean. I've never seen the ocean.

"Wait until it's sunny." His eyes look wistful. "It's heaven here, Ms. Adams. You'll never want to leave."

"I don't plan to," I say under my breath.

He waves me over. "Come on; let me show you the bedrooms and you've about seen it all."

Reluctantly, I leave the breathtaking view and follow him back into the house.

"You said you wanted two bedrooms, so here is the guest room."

I'm pleasantly surprised to see the walls in this room are a pale yellow, almost cream color. This would be perfect for the nursery. It's a decent size with a closet and window that looks out onto the beach. *My baby will get to see the ocean every day.* That thought brings me so much contentment, I feel a smile taking over my face.

"And here is the master. This room is the largest in the house. My wife wants to move here someday, and she went crazy when we designed it."

The room is huge. One wall is almost entirely a giant bay window with a sitting area built into it. Bookshelves line both sides of the window and over the top. It's like I'm in a magazine. There's so much space in here, I don't even know what I'd fill it with.

"The master bath is over here." He points to the door connected to the bedroom. "And the walk-in closet is on the other side of the bath. There's an oversize Jacuzzi tub," he adds with a grin.

Without needing to see more, I blurt out, "I'd like to rent the place. For at least a year, maybe longer. Are you willing to do that?"

His eyes bulge, and he starts stammering.

"I'm pregnant and moving right after the baby is born is of no interest to me."

He looks me up and down like he doesn't believe I'm pregnant. I understand. I don't look like it, not yet.

"This is exactly what I need," I tell him, hoping I'll convince him.

He blinks a few times. "I guess I could write a long-term lease. Usually people just want to vacation here, spend a couple weeks..."

"I'd like to stay for a year," I reiterate, "maybe longer."

He still seems hesitant. "Ms. Adams—"

"Mr. Anders, please. I won't even ask you to furnish it. In fact, I'd really like to pick out my own belongings."

As if he finally believes me, he grins wide. "I feel like this is too good to be true."

"It's not," I assure him.

He claps his hands together excitedly. "Well, let me get a contract put together. You can't stay here tonight." He glances around at the bare floors. "There's a little hotel in town, though, or you can drive to Portland or Salem. That's probably where you'll want to shop anyway," he says, rubbing his head.

"I'll probably stay in town tonight. I want to check it out," I tell him. "And then head into Portland tomorrow to order some furniture. Can we meet back here tomorrow evening around five to sign the lease?"

"That works for me." He nods, looking pleased, and we walk back to the living room. The hallway reminds me of the hall at my father's house, and I can't wait to fill my walls with pictures.

"If you don't mind, I'm going to go sit on the patio for a little bit before I head into town," I tell him.

"You bet. You can get back to the front from the side of the house. Just walk around."

I step out onto the back patio, and he closes the door, locking it behind me. There are three steps that lead down to the sandy beach, and I sit on the top one, enjoying the breeze and the view. The wind has picked up, and I can smell the sea salt in the air. I rub my arms to keep the chill at bay as I watch the waves come in one after the other, folding onto the shore.

Starting to feel giddy, I unlace my tennis shoes and kick them off. I still can't believe I'm here. It feels like a dream. But when my toes hit the soft sand, it starts to all sink in. The sand is coarse and reminds me of the sand at the beach back home in Illinois.

I look up and down the beach in both directions. Not a soul to be seen. Small, older houses are scattered every few hundred yards up and down the coastline, close enough to be called neighbors, but far enough apart for privacy. This is my heaven.

I tiptoe closer to the water and, when a wave thunders up the shore and hits my toes, I gasp, catching my breath. It's cold—but it's the ocean. I take a few steps further until another wave encases both of my feet, and I can't help but smile. I bend down and run my fingers through the cold water before standing up again. Tipping my face to the sky, I close my eyes and take in the smells and sounds. This is what I always dreamed of. And even though Alex set me free—it is because of him that I'm here.

I'm thankful for all the clothes Gretchen purchased for me, especially for this jacket and pair of fleece lounge pants keeping me warm in this rain. After settling into the cutest little boutique hotel, I walk down to the local drug store for an umbrella and some snacks.

I'm the only one around it seems in this cute downtown area. The adorable street boasts a drug store, a small grocery market, a bakery, and a small flower shop all nestled between offices and other small businesses. I pause outside a vacant brick building, right between the flower shop and a small bookstore. A 'For Rent' sign is hanging in the large glass window, calling to me like a beacon.

Peering through the glass, my mind immediately goes to work. I scribble down the phone number on the sign, then shove the paper in my purse and rush back to the hotel, just as the rain begins coming down harder.

Later, I sit in the bathtub, soaking in bubbles as I make plans. Finally, I feel like my life might be slowly coming together.

A knock at the door pulls me away from the spiral bound notebook in my lap. For the last hour, I've been frantically jotting down notes, questions, and plans.

"Room service," the voice calls. I check carefully, paranoia still front of mind. When I see the waiter all in uniform, I let him in. He sets my breakfast tray on the desk, and I lock up behind him. While I sip on my cappuccino and eat my bowl of oatmeal, I look at the grey skies outside and make my to-do list.

Ninety minutes later, I'm pulling into a shopping center in Portland. The next four hours are spent picking out furniture for the bedroom, living room, and kitchen. I also fill my car with kitchen essentials and linens. My last stop is the cellphone store, where I pick up a new phone—not that I have anyone to call, but more for emergency purposes.

The drive back to the beach is quiet and, while I'm still not comfortable driving, I manage just fine. I'm ten minutes early to meet Mr. Anders at the house, and I sit on the front steps, waiting for him. I love the air here. It feels cleaner here. My head feels lighter. Every bone in my body is telling me this is where I belong.

Mr. Anders gladly accepts my check for eighteen months' rent up front and, with a signature, the house is mine. He even helps me unload my car full of small appliances and household supplies that I bought.

I make a quick call to schedule delivery of the furniture, then I go over my notes in my notebook, crossing off items that I managed to get done today. Tomorrow, I'll tackle the remainder. It feels good to piece my life together, and a sense of confidence takes over, knowing that I'm doing this on my own.

My fingers wrap around the keys in my palm. I can't believe it —my first house. Well, it's not officially mine, but having a safe, clean, beautiful home on the beach is nothing short of a dream come true for me, and I can't help the swell of pride that fills me.

With no furniture, though, I can't stay here tonight, so I head back to the hotel for the night. After my exhausting day, I'm asleep before my head even touches the pillow.

The next morning, I wake up and sit in bed for a while. I have to make a call, and I'm nervous. I dial the numbers and my heart races, wondering if he'll answer.

"Hello." His voice is hoarse when he answers.

"Hi, Dad."

"Emilia, hi!" He clears his throat. "Thank you for calling." I can hear the relief in his voice and I can't help but smile, my nerves suddenly calm.

"How are you?" I ask him as I pull myself from the comfort of the bed and saunter over to the desk. I flip through the room service menu as my dad fills me in on what he's been doing.

"Sam's awake," he says.

I freeze. "What?"

"They slowly withdrew the heavy pain meds the day after you left. I heard yesterday he was almost sitting up. Of course he's in a lot of pain and not ready to leave the hospital, but it's progress."

I'm in awe. And so happy. "I didn't think it would happen that fast."

"I didn't either," he says happily. "But from what I understand, it appears he'll make a full recovery. I'm sure he'll never be one hundred percent, but he's alive. That's what's important."

"It is," I say with a smile on my face.

"Thank you for calling," he says tenderly. "I'm so relieved to know you're safe."

"I am." For now. Hopefully forever.

"Are you happy?"

"I will be. I'm not there yet, but close."

"Good." He sounds pleased, and it's nice to know he cares. "The number you called from shows up on my phone. You need to get that blocked. Get a private number. And do not leave a personalized voicemail, or let anyone know this is your number, okay? If the phone company gives you any trouble, let me know. I know a few guys who can make a call for you." He laughs into the phone. It's so good to hear him laugh.

"All right, Dad. I gotta go. I just wanted to call and check in."

"Call me again soon?"

"I will."

We end the call, and I have to sit down, Sam heavy on my mind. I'm so happy he's awake, but I'm sad that I didn't get to talk to him before I left. I order room service and take a long, hot shower in the meantime. As I eat breakfast, I page through my to-do list and begin making some calls. I have an appointment with a real estate agent to see the space on Main Street at noon. I take my time getting ready, actually styling my hair into long, loose waves, and putting on make-up.

When I arrive, I take my time perusing the street, weaving through the clusters of people gathered in small groups. There are bistro tables outside a small deli, families eating and laughing together. It makes me smile.

I stop at the flower store where a large flower stand is stationed on the sidewalk in front of the store. Large bouquets sit in buckets of water. Roses, carnations, and mixed bouquets so fragrant pull me over to take a closer look. I pull a huge bouquet of lavender roses mixed with lilacs. The smell makes me smile, reminding me of home. One of the only nice things about our trailer was the enormous lilac bush behind it. I'd cut the flowers and place them in an empty mason jar in the center of the small table in our trailer. Mom would sit and smell them for hours—always commenting on how perfect their smell was. Pleasant and light, not overwhelming. They remind me of her.

I run my fingers across the soft petals and inhale the sweet scent of the flowers, making a note to stop by after this meeting to pick them up. When I see a man in a suit unlocking the doors of the building just a couple of doors down, I tuck the flowers back in the bucket of water and head over to meet him.

I take a deep breath as I approach the glass doors, butterflies fluttering around in my stomach. *You can do this*, I prep myself as I reach for the door handle.

"Mr. Jacobson?" I ask. The man twirls around to meet me. "I'm Emilia. We spoke on the phone."

"Yes, hello." He smiles kindly. "Pleasure to meet you. Thank you for wanting to look at this space. It used to be a small clothing store," he tells me as he walks over to a wall and presses some buttons. Lights come on, and I notice the beautiful silver track lighting. "Back there are two dressing rooms that could easily be converted to offices," he continues. "This counter can be removed or relocated," he says, running his hand across the top of a Formica counter. "You said coffee shop?" He quirks an eyebrow at me.

"Yes. Coffee shop." I smile at him. The space is perfect. I

envision a new long counter with light stone countertops. Tables of all sizes, small and high, and long and low to fill the space. Goose bumps crawl across my skin as I see my dream come to life in my head.

"Well, the space is for lease or sale. Obviously, certain build out requirements would be written into the lease. With a sale, you're pretty much free to do whatever you want."

I nod as he talks numbers and figures, the pros and cons of leasing versus purchasing and vice versa. He asks about my business plan, my knowledge of the coffee business, then offers me resources that can help with all of that. We agree to meet at the deli tomorrow so that I have the opportunity to speak to some of the local business owners to get a feel for how their businesses are faring.

I spend the rest of the afternoon speaking with the owner of the bookstore next door, the deli owner, and even the small gift store clerk. Everyone is extremely friendly, helpful, and more than willing to share information on their sales, tips, advice on working through the peak vacation times during the summer. Everyone's excited to hear about my plan, as apparently no one has ever opened a standalone coffee shop here before.

The next morning, over terrible coffee at the deli, I sign a two-year lease with Mr. Jacobson. The building owner has agreed to the build out request, and I've received approval to proceed. Life feels like it's finally falling into place for me. Although I worry that, like every other time in my life, the other shoe is about to fall.

The next morning is cool and crisp, and my nose tingles at the slightest hints of fall. I grab a coffee from the coffee cart in the lobby of the hotel and check out. I'm moving into my beach house today, and I could not be happier.

Shoving my suitcase into the back of my rental car, I drive the few miles out to the cottage to wait for the arrival of all my furniture. I was able to schedule everything to be delivered this morning.

While I wait, I wash linens and dishes and silverware, finally finding everything a place in the cabinets. I make a grocery list and add it to my to-do list for the day. When the men arrive, they begin unloading couches, and chairs, and tables, and mattresses, a desk, a table, and things I don't even remember purchasing. It's overwhelming and exciting all at the same time as I'm directing where everything goes.

Home.

Happiness.

My home is almost complete. I tuck sheets around the new mattresses and put the finishing touches on the bed with the comforter and throw pillows. The grey walls complement the black and white paisley bedding with bright yellow accent pillows. The bedroom furniture is a deep brown, almost black, espresso color. I fold bath towels and tuck them into cabinets and finally begin hanging the clothes that Gretchen purchased for me.

Another trip to Portland is in order to get the last of the remaining things for the house—and to return my rental car. That means car shopping. A pit forms in my stomach because this is something I've never done before. I only wish I didn't have to do it alone.

With my to-do list in hand, I head out to Portland for the second time in three days. The hour commute doesn't bother me. I love the time that driving gives me to just think, to plan, to prepare.

First stop, the car dealership.

Fortunately, I have an idea of what I want. I test drive a small SUV, and then sit down with someone to pick out a vehicle that matches everything I want—color, options, and price. I don't even have to call in a hostage interrogator. The entire ordeal was fairly painless, and four hours later, I'm walking out with a new car. They even follow me to the rental car return at the airport.

I stop at a shopping mall in the suburbs just outside Portland to get a warmer jacket and spend an hour purchasing additional clothes. I've never had money to buy whatever I wanted; it was always just the necessities and always at the local thrift shop.

It's dusk as I'm pulling onto the freeway and still have about a forty-five-minute drive home. My pulse quickens when I realize it'll be completely dark when I get to the house. The entire drive home, I talk to myself, tell myself how ridiculous I am for being so paranoid. No one knows where I am. No one here knows who I am, or what I know. When I'm almost there, I finally feel the calm settle in. My headlights shine on the dark house, and I pause before turning off the car, then take a deep breath. Fear rips through me as I think about entering my dark house—alone.

Killing the engine, I grab my shopping bag with new clothes and jog to the front door. I fiddle with the keys in my shaking hand and look over my shoulder as I feel around for the lock. Slamming the door behind me, I toss the bag of clothes aside as I lean back against it and close my eyes.

"Calm down," I tell myself. "Calm down." I fear that I'll never truly get over the anxiety I feel—always feeling like I'm being hunted. I bend over, grab the shopping bag, and head back to the bedroom. I run a hot bath as I hang up the clothes I bought today. I splurged and bought a new notebook to journal in, plan, and take notes. It's beautiful and bound in yellow leather. I set it on my nightstand and head to the bathroom.

As I soak in the oversized bathtub, bubbles up to my neck, I move my hand to my stomach. It amazes me that it's starting to feel harder, yet there's still no noticeable bump—at least when I'm clothed. I can see the difference in my body, but from the outside, no one else would know I'm pregnant. I begin to relax as I see my plan coming together. A home for my baby. A business plan. I feel like my life is finally coming together and I'll be able to provide a stable life for us.

I brush out the wet tangles from my hair and slip into my

pajamas, ready to call it a night. I can't help but double check the locks on every window and every door…and that's when my heart stands still.

In the center of my new kitchen table sits the very bouquet I was looking at this morning, only twice as big. Fear shoots through me like a knife in my back, and I run to the last room I have yet to check, but every door and window is locked.

Who was here?

And when?

My mind races with questions as my knees give out, and I sink to the plush carpet.

Was it Antonio? Saul?

Pushing myself up from the floor, I race to the living room to grab my phone from my purse. But when I dump the contents onto the couch, I discover there is no phone. I left it in the car—which is parked in the driveway.

Shit!

I double check every window and door again, second-guessing myself. Frantically, I run from room to room in a panic until I go mad and finally fall into bed, crying myself into a restless sleep.

When daybreak hits, I manage to get myself to the kitchen to make a cup of coffee, and I sit at the kitchen table, staring at the flowers. I pluck a lavender rose from the vase and twirl it around under my nose, inhaling the sweet scent of the flower as I sip on my coffee.

At least it's light out now, and I finally feel comfortable enough to venture outside. I change quickly and grab my car keys so that I can retrieve my phone from the car, but I startle and scream when I open the front door.

Someone's there.

"Jesus Christ, you're going to give an old man a heart attack, screamin' like that!" Mr. Anders jumps back. My hands are clenching my jacket, and I'm too shocked to even respond. "You okay, Ms. Adams?"

I try to catch my breath, barely managing a nod. "Sorry, just a little on edge this morning."

"I came by to tell you I dropped some flowers off on your table. I normally don't let myself in, but I came by to see if you were all settled in, or if you needed anything, since I don't have a phone number for you and that giant vase was sitting on the front porch. It was getting cold, so after I knocked and you didn't answer, I just set them inside. I didn't want them to die."

I take a deep, calming breath. So they were on the porch, not inside my house. That's somewhat comforting. "So you didn't see who left them?"

"No, ma'am. They were just sitting here."

"Well, thank you for bringing them inside." Even though I know only he was in my house, I'm still on edge. "And let me get you a phone number. I just got a new phone yesterday. It's in the car." I step down the sidewalk as I press the unlock button on the car. Pulling my phone from the center console, I look up the number to give to Mr. Anders.

He enters it into his old flip phone at an agonizingly slow rate, and I wait patiently as he finishes.

"I'm glad you stopped by, actually," I tell him, shoving my phone into the pocket of my jacket. "I met with Mr. Jacobson, the real estate agent for the vacant building on Main Street yesterday. I'm leasing the building to put in a little gourmet coffee shop. I was surprised when Mr. Jacobson recommended you as someone who could help me with the build out."

Mr. Anders' eyes widen with excitement. "Would be glad to. We'll need to walk the space and draft up some plans, but I'd be happy to manage the project for you." He looks at my new car and then back to me. I know exactly what he's thinking—I'm too young to be opening a business, buying a new car, paying rent for eighteen month's upfront. So I'll save him the trouble of asking, or making assumptions.

"I recently inherited a little bit of money," I say sheepishly, still feeling uncomfortable about having all that money in my account. "Nothing crazy, but enough to get me settled. I want to raise my baby in a stable and safe environment. I like it here. I've always wanted to live by the ocean, and one of my favorite jobs was working at a coffee shop. I feel like when I moved here, the stars aligned. I found your house and the vacant building. Everything just kind of fell into place for me in the last four days." Which is still so hard to believe.

He smiles at me and shoves his hands in his pockets. "I'm not here to tell you what to do, sweetheart, but you're young. After this coffee shop build out, invest your money. I've owned businesses all my life. If you're careful, you'll be able to turn a profit on that shop within a few months. We've never had a coffee shop here."

"I know." I smile at him. "And I'd like to make it more than just a coffee shop. I want it to be an Internet café as well. I want it to be the heart of the town, where people come and spend time, stay a while and visit. I'm making sure it's wired with the best Wi-Fi so the summer tourists have a place to come."

He nods warmly. "You seem like you have a great concept. I have no idea what an Internet café is, but anything paired with coffee is good." He chuckles. "You got plans today?"

"Other than getting groceries, I'm wide open."

He smiles at me. "There's a little diner just off of Main Street. They have the best breakfast you've ever had for under five dollars. Shitty coffee, but the breakfast is delicious."

I laugh at him.

He joins in with a chuckle. "I'd love to take you to breakfast and hear more about your plans. Then we can swing by the space, and you can give me a general idea of what you're planning to do. I can get my drafter in here tomorrow, and we'll get some plans drawn up right away. Once we get those finalized, I'll apply for any necessary permits, then we'll get started. If all goes smoothly, I could probably have you in business in six to eight weeks."

"Are you serious?"

"I never joke with a pretty lady." He gives a deep belly laugh. His eyes pinch closed when he laughs and I can't help but smile at him.

"Then yes, let's go have breakfast and talk." I lock up the house and follow Mr. Anders in town.

SIXTEEN

Alex

"He's awake and wants to speak with you," my aunt says over the phone. "I know you're leaving, but please come by before you go."

"Okay," I mumble and rub my eyes. The clock reads five thirty in the morning. Why is she calling so fucking early? "I'll stop by later this morning. I wanted to stop by my mom's grave first."

"That's a good idea," she agrees. "Agent Hoffman told us last night that you've been given immunity, and that they don't need anything further from you. He figured you'd be leaving to find Emilia as soon as possible. I begged him to give us your phone number. We all want to say goodbye, *mijo*."

I sigh into the phone, not because I'm upset but because I'm not good at goodbyes. I'm not used to feeling my emotions, and lately, that's all I've been feeling. I wanted to stop by my mother's grave one last time because, until my father and Saul are caught, it won't be safe for me in Arizona. Even after they're caught, I'm not sure it'll ever be safe here for me. The Estrada family has many ties, many connections, and I just gave all of the information I have to the feds.

"I'll be by later this morning," I tell her and roll over, hoping to catch a few more minutes of sleep.

We hang up, but now I'm awake, and all I can think about is getting to Emilia. She made it very easy to find her. Too easy almost. With her laptop that I got from Sam's house, I found her Pinterest board marked Oregon, and everything she pinned led me directly to her, right down to the town she's living in. I'm only certain because I've had security on her for the last twenty-four hours, and he found her within two hours of landing in Oregon.

My sweet, naïve girl.

I'm only somewhat calm because he'll be watching her until I get there. He's been giving me updates every few hours, and I've finally been able to breathe better knowing she's safe.

I get up and make some coffee as I finish packing up the few items I have left—which isn't much. Amazing how you can go from owning an empire to being a pauper pretty damn quickly.

I pack Em's laptop and her journal in my backpack, then shower and get dressed. Before I go, I spend some time on the front porch, enjoying my coffee and the last Arizona morning I may ever see. Although I have many bad memories here, some of my best were created in this place. And while I'm not thrilled to leave—even with the lack of safety—love is about sacrifice, and I'm sacrificing everything. But Emilia is worth it. She means more to me than my own life. Worth every risk I'm about to take.

The federal marshal who's been parked out front all evening opens his car door and stretches. He offers me a nod before he walks up the paved path leading to my front porch. He takes the steps two at the time and stands in front me.

"Looks like this is the end of the line," he says with a shake of his head. I know all the marshals think I'm crazy for turning down the protection, but it's the only way I'll be able to be with Em and our baby. I have to do this.

"It is." I stand up and offer him my hand, looking him in the eye. It's interesting how these are the guys I've been escaping for so long, and now I'm on their side. Funny how life changes. "You guys have the toughest job," I say. "Protecting those that don't deserve protecting. Thank you for everything you've done for me."

He nods. "Take care of yourself," he says with a firm handshake.

"I will. I'll leave the keys on the table just as Agent Hoffman requested." I gesture over my shoulder.

"Sounds good," he says, offering me a wave as he jogs down to his vehicle. I watch him get into his car and leave, and I realize how vulnerable I am. My Range Rover sits in the driveway, a little going-away gift from Hoffman. Although all of my belongings were seized, they were generous enough to give me my car. I've made arrangements for it to be delivered to Oregon. There's no way I have the patience to drive it there myself, knowing Em is just a few hours away by plane.

With a sense of peace and loss, I grab my suitcase by the front door, lock up, and toss the keys in the planter. Wheeling my luggage down the sidewalk, I take one last look up and down the street in the neighborhood I grew up in. Then, leaving it all behind, I shove the suitcase in the back and slide into the driver's seat. The leather seats are pleasantly warm from the morning sun.

At the cemetery, the green grass is covered in a late summer dew. It's so peaceful here, now I wish I'd come here more often. When I reach her headstone, I kneel down, the knees of my jeans damp from the dew, and I press my fingers to the grooves of her name. Bowing my head, I pray.

I pray to God, I pray to my mother, I ask for forgiveness, and I make promises to be the man and father that Emilia and our baby need.

As the birds chirp, I fight with my emotions. Remorse, anger, hope, and love all vying to break free. Remorse for the past, anger at my father, hope for the future, and love for Emilia and our child. It's up to me now to choose which I will let guide me, and I choose hope and love.

In my last moments, I beg my mother for forgiveness and ask

her to help guide me in this new life, then I promise to visit when it's safe to come back. Swallowing down the lump in my throat, I run my fingers over the smooth granite headstone one last time. I'm about to turn and leave when I hear my name.

"Alejandro," his voice calls from behind. A voice I'm all too familiar with. Snapping my head around, I find my father and Saul standing about ten feet away.

Fuck. No…

My stomach falls, and my knees lock. "Father." I try to appear calm.

He looks different as he steps forward. Tired. Worn. "I knew you'd come here," he says, glancing down at the headstone. "You two had such a strong bond," he says, his voice laced with jealousy.

"As did you and Sam," I tell him, anger leaking into my voice. "Speaking of Sam, why didn't you choose him for the business? Why did you let him go and take me?" My voice begins to shake with anger.

"Ah, son…It was because Sam was so much like me. We wouldn't have worked well together. Now you…you were always the pleaser. You wanted to make everyone happy. You do as you're told." His lip curls as he speaks.

"Not anymore," I growl at him. "I'm doing what makes me happy."

His dark eyes hold mine and he swallows hard. I see him wrestle with emotions. Trying to remain in control, but his facade is cracking.

"I never wanted this life," I tell him. "I wanted a normal life. A job, a family, friends—"

"You had family, friends," he interrupts me.

"No, I had you," I seethe. "You are my father by blood and that's all. Family doesn't murder each other," I throw a finger at my mother's headstone. "You murdered the one person that actually made us a family."

His eye twitches as I yell at him.

"You took my family away from me when she was buried and you gave Sam away. They are my family. Not you. Not your 'business family,'" I shout at him. "That's not family. That's business."

He nods and purses his lips.

"Emilia and our baby are my family now," I tell him when I see Saul slowly moving toward us. I look back to my father, who's watching me and, for the first time, fear hits me.

This is where they're going to kill me. On my mother's grave.

I look back and forth between my father and Saul, who has his hand shoved into the pocket of his suit jacket.

"He killed her, and now you've brought him to kill me too." It's not even a question. I just know. I blow a puff of air through my nose. I narrow my eyes on him, feeling betrayed and also hurt. "You're such a fucking coward. Can't even kill me yourself, can you?"

My uncle's words play through my head. He was a fucking coward then, and he's going to be one now. Willing to do what he thinks is necessary, but not willing to get his own fucking hands dirty.

"I want you to do it." My voice is cold and hard as I stand up taller. "Go on. Be the man everyone thinks you are." I give an upward nod, challenging him. "Pull the trigger." With a slight smirk, he calmly pulls his gun from the holster in his jacket, then points it at my chest. I can feel it in his eyes, the hesitation, that maybe a part of him remembers I'm his fucking flesh and blood and doesn't want to kill me. But the rest of him has blackened over time. There's really no heart left in him. I'm not sure there ever was.

"Do it," I tell him, my heart beating so fast I can hardly breathe. I look at the green grass beneath my feet, waiting to feel the sting of the piercing bullet through my chest.

"Pull the fucking trigger," Saul barks from behind him. "That's what we're here for."

I watch as my father's normally steady hand begins to shake, then everything happens so fast. Saul lifts his gun, his face full of hate, and points it directly at me. He's about to discharge, but my father is faster. A shot rings out, and I'm spattered with blood and brain matter. It takes a moment for me to register what's happened when I see Saul fall to the ground, a hole in his forehead.

Fuck.

"It ends here, *mijo*. All of it." My father kicks Saul's foot. "I should've done that a long time ago." He shakes his head. He turns back to look at me, and the hate I've always seen in his dark eyes has turned to regret. His face is tired, haggard. "I should never have dragged you into this world." He chokes back his emotions and rubs his forehead.

"I know you won't believe me, but I never intended for Emma to get hurt. She overheard Saul on the phone, and he panicked. He thought she was going to rat us out."

"All she was going to do was take us and run," I interrupt him.

"I know that," he says, "But Saul wasn't going to let that happen. I told him to give me some time to figure things out and he killed her. He handled it."

"He killed your wife, and you continued to keep him as your best friend for twenty years. Do you know how fucked up that is?"

"I do. But he's the only one that had the connections I needed to build the business. I needed to keep him close. You know that saying, 'keep your friends close and your enemies closer.' And because I trusted him. He's one of the few I believed I could actually trust."

"Pathetic," I growl at him. "You didn't even trust me," I sneer.

"I did," he argues. "You did good by our business."

I shake my head in disgust. "Because I had to."

"And now you don't," he says quietly. "You're free to go,

Alejandro. I love you, son, and if there's one thing I can give you to show you how sorry I am, it's this. Everyone believes you're dead. I've confirmed with the associates that I've identified your body. You're free, Alejandro. Go." He looks at me as I ponder what he's telling me.

"Go!" He shoos me away. Stunned, I watch him fall to his knees, much like I do every time I've come to my mother's grave. He rests his hand on the top of her headstone, pressing his forehead to her name. Then, in the biggest surprise of the day, I watch his tears fall. I have never seen him cry.

I have to steady myself with the tall oak tree as he talks to her. Begging her for forgiveness. He breaks down quietly, talking to my mother. He repents his sins to a God he doesn't believe in—a God he gave up on a long time ago. I hear him pray the Hail Mary, the Our Father. Prayers he hasn't spoken in decades. I hear him mumble the beginnings of the Act of Contrition when I finally turn and walk to my car. I've seen enough death and destruction today. Enough for a lifetime.

"Forgive me father for I have sinned," plays on a loop in my head.

I'm stumbling toward my car when I hear the shot, the one I know has ended my father's life. I have to squeeze my eyes shut and collect myself before I turn to look at him. I look over my shoulder to see him slumped over on top of my mother's grave, Saul at his side. He told me it was over, but I wonder if it really ever will ever be.

I bend over and vomit, bracing myself on the front of my car. Holy shit. He killed himself.

When I finally collect myself, I reach in to pull my phone from the center console, then call Agent Hoffman and deliver the news he's been waiting for. Somberly, I walk back to that large oak tree and sit down, resting my back against it as I wait.

I'm surrounded by death here, old and new. And yet I've never felt more at peace. A weight has been lifted from me, and the hope that I might be able to live the life I've only dreamed of begins to fill me with hope.

It takes less than three minutes before the cemetery is full of police cars and investigators from every major federal agency. I'm asked the same questions over and over as I sit with my back against the oak tree, staring at my father's body, which they've covered with a large sheet.

Agent Hoffman sits down next to me, his knees drawn up. "I thought it would feel amazing to see him dead," he says, reflecting. "But it doesn't."

"It doesn't," I repeat in a monotone voice.

"I just wanted justice for everyone he's hurt…including you."

I turn to look at him. "He can't hurt anyone any longer." Not Emilia, not our baby…Not me. It's over.

"True," he says. "You know I'm going to need you to stick around for a few more days. Just until we get the investigation over with."

I nod, figuring as much. I won't be getting to Emilia as soon as I had hoped, but it's okay because once we're together, nothing will ever split us apart again.

Hoffman continues, but I only half hear him. "…but everything you told us matches up with what the investigators are finding."

"For once, I'm actually telling you the truth," I tell him, somewhat teasing.

"Good." He pats my shoulder "Sit tight. They'll want to swab your hands for gunpowder residue to clear you in the shooting, and they may want to take pictures of your face and hands to show the blood spatter—for evidence. Once that's done, you're free to leave. Stay local. We may need you for additional questioning."

"Got it," I say with a deep sigh. I just want to be the one to tell Sam—he's family, I feel like I should do it. "Has anyone told Sam about this?"

"Haven't had a chance yet."

"Good. Mind if I tell him? I mean, I know it's probably not your procedure…but family and all," I say with a shrug.

"Makes sense," he agrees. "I'll stop by the hospital later this afternoon to talk to him if he has any additional questions."

Pushing himself up, he wanders over to the group of other agents. A minute later, a crime scene investigator approaches me, swabs me, and takes some pictures, then I'm free to go. I drive in a trance-like state to the hospital and manage to make it up to the ICU. My aunt is already there, standing in the hallway, talking to a nurse. She begins to panic when she sees me, and I remember what I must look like.

"What happened, *mijo*!" Her voice is frantic and I can see the terror in her eyes.

"Where's Tio?"

"In the room with your brother."

"Good. Come on; I have something to tell you."

She excuses herself from the nurse and follows me into the room.

When Sam sees me, I pause. The look in his eyes says he knows, and his jaw hardens, bracing for the news. "Did you do it?"

I shake my head, finally feeling a lump forming in the back of my throat. I had no idea that I'd feel anything when and if my father ever died. He was such a large figure, it was like he was bigger than death, immortal. But he was my father, after all. He raised me.

"No," I manage to tell him.

"What happened?" he asks stoically.

My uncle stands and gives my aunt his chair, then moves to stand at the head of Sam's bed next to him.

"Dad found me at the cemetery," I begin. "Saul was with him. I'm sure they were there to shoot me, but Dad shot Saul instead."

"Jesus Christ," my uncle mumbles and rubs his chin.

My aunt covers her mouth with her hands and tears fill her eyes.

"What about Dad?" Sam asks, his hands balled into fists at his side.

I have to clear my throat. "He told me it was over and to go… and then he shot himself."

The room is so quiet you can hear a pin drop. No one moves, no one breathes. Then my aunt finally jumps up from her chair and rushes to me, pulling me into her arms. She cries into my chest as she holds me, and I finally let it all out—the anger, the hurt, the tears, the bitterness, and hatred I've been holding back. Everything breaks free, including the grief I now feel for my father now that he's gone.

My uncle wipes his eyes as I see a tear break free from Sam's eye. As evil as my father was, we are all affected. We will all suffer. But I feel with certainty that we will all heal. Eventually.

"It's over," I tell him, and Sam nods.

So much death and all because of greed.

We spend the afternoon as a family in Sam's room. Sometimes, we're all lost in quiet thought; other times, we're talking and sharing memories, but the weight of my father's death has also lifted a burden that's been hanging over us since my mother's murder. As ready as I am to get to Emilia, it's going to be hard to let go of the family I just got back.

One week

Two weeks

Three Weeks

Recovery is a bitch, I think as I sit down carefully on my sofa, trying not to move too fast. Sudden movements still cause my upper body to cry out in pain. I inhale sharply as I settle in, finally releasing the breath I was holding.

"I'm telling you this is crazy," my aunt clucks away, propping pillows behind me. "You should be in a rehab facility like the doctor suggested."

"I'm fine," I groan. "I just want to be at home, sleep in my own bed—I need to heal here." *Heal.* My wounds go deeper than the physical, but I smile through the emotional pain…because I have to, because I always have.

She shakes her head at me as she scurries around rearranging things so they're within my reach, then she sets the TV remote on the arm of the couch.

"Alex is coming over," she says quietly. "He got the all-clear to leave."

"So I heard," I respond. Trey mentioned it to me this morning while I was checking out of the hospital. My emotions are mixed. Alex and I are finally at a place where we can begin building a relationship and I'm sad to lose that.

"*Mijo*—"

"Stop, Tia. I'll be fine."

But will I?

Am I truly ready to accept that Alex and Em will be together? Choking down my jealously, I take a deep breath. Alex and I are working to rebuild our relationship, and that is what I need to focus on. Emilia was never mine—as much as I wanted her to be. She's always been in love with Alex, and for Christ sakes, she's pregnant with his child.

When the doorbell rings, my aunt dashes over and opens the front door. It's Alex.

"*Mijo*," she exclaims, pulling him into a hug. "When do you leave?"

"My flight leaves at one. As long as there are no delays, I should be there early tonight." Alex steps inside, his eyes wandering, taking it all in as he sits himself in a chair next to the couch. "Hey, man, how ya feeling?" He props his foot on the coffee table like he's been coming here for years. In a way, I guess he has. This house has always been both of ours.

"Been better, but I'm trying to stay off the meds," I admit.

"Been there." He raises his eyebrows. "Take it easy. You shouldn't even be here right now."

I roll my eyes. "You're starting to sound like Tia." I glance fondly at the woman who's now standing in the kitchen next to a counter full of food, which she is undoubtedly going to make for me.

Alex sits up straighter, lacing his fingers together as he leans forward and looks at me.

"Look, I'm not good with goodbyes," he says with a smirk. "Not really my style."

I laugh at him and shake my head. He's still witty Alex.

His eyes turn serious. "But I need to thank you again for everything you did for Em and me."

I nod silently. Selfishly, I want Em. Realistically, she loves

Alex. I have to accept that…and I will—in time. "I'd do it again if I had to," I tell him with sincerity.

We sit quietly, absorbing that. Years and circumstances kept us apart, and I made a promise to myself to not let anything come in between us again. He's my blood…my family. I will bury the feelings I have for Em to forge a new relationship with my brother.

"*Mijo*, you need to get going or you're going to miss your flight," my aunt chides.

Alex sighs and stands up, extending his hand for me to shake. Sometimes, there are no words that need to be said. What should be awkward silence isn't. After a hearty shake, he gives an understanding nod, then heads over to say goodbye to our aunt.

"Take care of her," I tell him, and he turns back to look at me.

He holds my stare and offers me a tight smile. He sees my conflict, but he does what he needs to do. He's going to find the woman he loves. "I will. I promise," he says, and I know he's telling the truth. He'd do anything for her, and for that I find some comfort in knowing it won't be me protecting her.

As the door closes behind him, I swallow back my emotions and vow to leave them behind that closed door. I have to accept that this is what's best for all of us, and everything is exactly how it's supposed to be.

TWENTY-ONE

Emilia

It's been a month since I left Arizona, and Alex still consumes my thoughts. It's hard for me to forget him while I have a piece of him growing inside me. He's the first thing I think of when I wake up and the last thing I think of before I fall asleep. I wonder where he is, what he's doing—what his name is. I wonder if he even thinks about me, about us.

I pluck the ultrasound picture off the front of the fridge while I sip my morning coffee—decaf now, of course. I had an appointment with my OB, and I finally got to see my baby. He or she is growing and healthy, and so am I. Most importantly, I feel good and every day, my heart begins to heal a little more.

Mr. Anders has worked tirelessly to get the permits to begin work on the coffee shop. I have a copy of the plans here on the kitchen table, and every day, I look at them to remind myself that I have a lot to be thankful for. Today is the day that they're actually beginning the demolition of the old dressing rooms and starting the build out of a small kitchen area and office, along with two new restrooms and a huge new counter.

The fall mornings here are chilly, but nothing wakes me up

more than spending a few minutes on the back patio, watching small waves roll in while I enjoy my coffee. Eager for that very thing, I throw on my heavy coat and slip my bare feet into a pair of slippers. Sliding the glass door open, I step out onto the large patio. Cold air nips at my nose, but the warm mug of coffee warms my hands and takes the immediate chill away.

I take ten deep breaths—it's this thing I do every morning. I draw them deep into my lungs so that I can feel them burn, exhaling slowly. There's nothing better than the smell of ocean air and the burn of it in your lungs. It energizes me. As my nose turns cold and my fingers begin to tingle, I wonder if I'll be able to handle this all winter.

I'm sure I'll make do, I think with a smile. This place is too peaceful. No season will stop me from coming out here.

Since I want to be at the coffee shop to take some pictures as they begin demolition, I head inside to get dressed. I'm documenting the entire process and creating picture books to put in the shop so customers can see where it all started. We all start somewhere, people and places. Sometimes, the prettiest of things were once the most depressed. I've made two trips into Portland to shop for equipment for the shop and also purchase mugs, plates, silverware, and other supplies. Today, I plan to post a help wanted sign in the hopes that I'll be able to start interviewing employees soon. It's still hard to believe sometimes that this is all happening.

After showering, dressing, and inhaling a bowl of cereal, I head into town. It's a short drive, less than two miles. A straight shot from my house, but I enjoy the scenic drive. Everything about this town is quaint, perfect. I love it all—the small houses, the friendly people, and the beach. Parking in one of the three designated spots behind the building, next to a work truck and a large dumpster, I head inside and find men already beginning to tear down the existing walls. Quickly, I snap some pictures of them working, then stand back and take in the progress while also taking notes on other items I'll need.

"Mornin' sweetheart," Mr. Anders says from behind me as he comes in the front door.

"Morning, Mr. Anders." I give the older man a bright smile. He has been such a blessing to me. First by allowing me to rent his house long-term, and now with his help in building out the coffee shop. I don't know what I would've done without him. He knows everyone in this town, and he's been wonderful in helping me adjust to life here.

"I can't wait until I can walk through that front door and get myself some coffee," he says as he stretches his arms over his head. "Looks like the guys are off to a good start."

"They are. They beat me here and almost had all the walls down," I tell him.

"Good. I told them no fiddling around. We're watching their time and your money." He raises his eyebrows at me.

"I appreciate you looking out for me."

"Glad to help ya," he says with a smile.

We spend the morning going over the timeline, projected costs versus actual costs to date, and I show him some of the paintings I plan to purchase. We're leaving the exposed brick on the walls and bringing in artwork rich in reds and browns to fill the walls. The main space will have dark wood floors and tables, and a few plush couches with large pillows.

We met with the cable company to discuss the wireless internet needs and got that all agreed upon and set up for installation. Every day, I leave feeling like progress is being made, and it's such a great feeling.

When I look outside, it's pouring rain and dark clouds have moved in, far from the sunny morning. The guys have left for the day, and Mr. Anders decides to call it a night as well. I have a few more measurements I need to take for painting and possible window coverings, so I lock up the back door as he leaves, then take out my tape measure and jot notes in my notebook. When I stand back up, I freeze. A face I thought I'd never see again is staring at me through the large glass window.

Even though it's dark and the rain is coming down hard, I can still see him. I'd never forget that face…those eyes. My heart races as I process whether this is real or my mind playing a terrible joke on me.

And then he presses his fingers to the glass and watches me—waiting for a reaction.

I can't believe it. He's here. How did he find me? How did he get away? My mind races with questions as tears flood my eyes. But it can't be real. There's no way. As I'm trying to convince myself of that, he starts to walk away.

No!

I race to the door and fight with the lock, yanking the door open. "Alex!" I scream to him, but his dark figure is fading in the distance. "Stop!" Forgetting the rain completely, I run down the sidewalk after him.

He turns slowly as I approach, and we stand just feet from each other. The rain beats down against us, and a cold wind blows, causing the rain to feel like sleet. But I don't feel it. I don't feel the rain or the cold. I only know that he's here. He's really here.

"Why are you here?" I ask him, my teeth chattering.

He hesitates but finally answers. "For you, Em. I came for you."

"You said—"

"I know what I said. It was lies."

My heart breaks again at this admission. Everything with Alex and me has been lies. I almost begin to wonder if there will ever be truth with us.

He looks down, disappointed. "I shouldn't have come, Em."

"Then why did you?" My tone is hurt, angry.

He watches me, and it looks like he's tearing up, only I can't tell for sure because the rain is coming down so hard.

"Why did you come here, Alex?" I ask again.

"Because I love you, Em." His tone is pained. "I need you."

And that's all I need to hear. My resolve breaks, and I throw myself into his arms as the rain beats down us, but all I feel is the warmth of his embrace.

"You're shaking, Em," he whispers into my wet hair.

"Come on; let's go inside." I wrap my hand around his and pull him toward the door of the coffee shop. Inside, I rub my hands together as I try to warm them, but Alex pulls my hands into his and holds them. The warmth of his hands radiates into mine and I shiver. For a different reason now.

"We need to get you home, Em," he insists, looking concerned. "You need to get out of these wet clothes."

"I'm fine," I tell him, even though my body is saying otherwise. My arms and legs are shaking inside my wet clothes.

"Em."

"Fine," I sigh and grab my purse. I pull out my car keys, and Alex takes them from me.

"I'll drive."

"You don't even know where we're going." I narrow my eyes at him.

He quirks a smile. "I've known where you were this entire time, Emilia. The flowers." He gives me a pointed look, and my insides flood with relief. So it wasn't one of his father's people after me, trying to scare me. It was Alex.

"That was you?" I close my eyes in relief.

He nods, pleased with himself. "With a little help from a friend." He smirks, then adds tenderly, "Come on. Let's get you home."

I lock the front door and shut down the lights as we head out the back door. My close parking spot makes it easy to get out of the rain quickly. Alex adjusts the driver's seat and begins driving… right to my house. He really did know where I was the entire time. I should be surprised, but I'm not.

We pull into the driveway, and he cuts the engine before he turns to look at me. "Do you want me to come inside?"

"If I said no, where would you go?"

"Back to town. To the hotel down the street from the coffee shop. It's not far, Em. I could walk, or I could take your car and bring it back in the morning."

I almost chuckle at him, but I don't. I have questions, and we need to talk. "Come inside," I tell him. I jog up the sidewalk in the rain, and Alex meets me at the front porch.

He juggles the keys and manages to get the door open quickly. "I hate that you didn't have an alarm system," he says as he closes the door and locks the deadbolt.

"I don't even think there's a police force in this town," I say, only somewhat teasing. "Who would come if the alarm goes off?"

"There's a police force," he says, then adds in a joking tone, "I think there are four officers. Maybe five. It's not clear, but there are police." Of course he'd know that. He probably already knows everything about this town, about where I've been and what I'm doing.

"So I'm assuming you know everything that I've been doing," I say aloud, echoing my thoughts as I kick off my tennis shoes and pull my socks off. My bare toes are numb from the cold, and I wiggle them on the wood floor, trying to bring back some feeling.

"Everything." He nods and kicks off his shoes, then peels his jacket off and hangs it on a coat hook just inside the front door. His jeans are soaked, and even his shirt that was underneath his jacket is soaked completely through.

"Come here." I lead him toward the laundry room. "Let's just wash everything and dry it."

"I don't have anything to change into; my suitcase is at the hotel," he says, a grin creeping up his face.

I can feel my cheeks flush. "Right." I stop outside the laundry room. "Forgot about that."

He runs his hand through his hair, pushing it back off his

forehead before he reaches out and runs his thumb across my lower lip. "Purple," he says as he swipes at my lip. "Your lips are purple."

"I'm cold," I finally admit, running my hands over my arms.

Alex pulls the wet sweater I'm wearing over my head and tosses it to the laundry room floor. He unbuttons the jeans I have on and bends down, taking the jeans with him. When he pauses, I realize he's looking at my stomach. The tips of his fingers brush against my lower stomach. While there isn't much of a bump, my stomach is hard and firm. His touch is soft and tender. I close my eyes and welcome his touch.

With both of his hands on my hips, his thumbs rub small circles across my belly. He whispers something that I can't make out before leaning in and pressing his forehead to my stomach. He takes a moment before finally speaking. "You're freezing, Em. We need to get you warmed up." He stands up and runs his hand up and down my arms. My pale skin is full of goose bumps. "Bathtub?" he asks. His touch is welcome, and I lean into him.

"In the master bathroom." I nod down the hall, feeling breathless. With a tender smile, he slides his hand into mine and leads us down the hall. In the bathroom, he turns on the water for the tub and grabs a towel from the towel rack above the toilet.

"In," he demands as the tub slowly fills with water. I reach behind me and unhook my bra, pulling it off my arms. It falls to the floor, and Alex inhales sharply. He fights to keep his eyes on mine, but true to Alex style, they fall to my chest and lower as I undress. He remains a gentleman, though, and quickly regains his composure.

I tug at the waistband of my panties and pull them down, stepping out of them and leaving them in a pile on top of my bra. Alex holds my arm as I step down into the large bathtub. The warm water feels amazing and begins to instantly warm my cold skin.

"I'll be right back," he says and leaves me to soak. About five minutes later, he comes back with mugs of hot tea, one for him and one for me. "Sip on this," he says and sits down on the floor next to the tub. I blow on the steam and sip carefully. Feeling the warm tea travel to my belly instantly warms me from the inside.

We sit quietly sipping our tea, a million unasked questions on the tip of my tongue when Alex finally starts.

"I'm sorry for lying to you." He looks me dead in the eye. "But I did it to protect you, Em."

"How?"

"If I told you I wasn't going to accept the deal, you wouldn't have left Phoenix. Every minute you stayed, you were in danger. I needed you to leave." I can see hurt and honesty behind his words.

I blink in surprise. "Wait, so you just walked away from the deal? You can't do that, can you?"

"I asked for immunity. They accepted that. Honestly, they could care less what happens to me. If I die, I'm one less person they have to worry about."

"Don't say that, Alex," I snap at him.

"It's the truth, Em. I saved them a whole lot of time, money, and energy. I gave them everything they wanted, though."

"So if you're so worried about protecting me, why are you here? Aren't you worried about your dad finding you here with me?"

"Not anymore," he says, his eyes strangely somber.

I have a bad feeling in my gut. "Why?"

"He's dead."

It takes me a moment to process that. "Saul?"

"Dead," he says quietly. "It's over." But there's peace in his voice as he says that.

I lean my head back in the tub and close my eyes. I did not see this coming. Death is never something I'd wish on anyone, but a sense of utter relief fills me to know neither of them are alive and hunting Alex or me.

"So what now?" I ask him.

"I'm begging you to forgive me, to take me back…to love me." His voice is quiet, but there is desperation in its tone.

"I never stopped loving you," I tell him, my heart in my eyes. "But the lies, Alex…."

"We were all bound by my lies, Em. But not anymore. There are no more lies. There never will be," he promises. "I swear on my mother's grave." He reaches over and laces his fingers through mine.

After I'm dressed, I find Alex in the kitchen, staring at the ultrasound pictures on the fridge.

"Is that…?" He points to the picture.

"It is." I can't help but feel a sweep of maternal love as I walk over and pull the paper from under the magnet. "Here." I hand it to him so he can take a closer look.

"It looks like a real baby," he mumbles, completely in awe.

"It *is* a real baby," I laugh.

He rolls his eyes good-naturedly. "I know, but it's not like a peanut…it has arms and legs…"

"It's the size of a lime," I tell him. "I've been reading this book, and each week, it tells me what's happening, how big the baby is, what's developing this week. It's pretty amazing."

He hangs the ultrasound pictures back on the fridge and turns to me. "Marry me, Em." It's not a question, it's a desperate demand as if he's worried I'll leave him.

"What?" I stutter, shocked. Well, more than shocked. Never in a million years did I picture Alex proposing. "Are you serious?"

"I've never been more serious about anything in my life. All I want is for you and me and the baby to be a family." He holds my chin so that I can't look away. "All I want is you—forever."

"We can be a family without getting married, Alex." I go from freezing one minute to having the sweats the next. Where did this proposal come from? One thing I want to ensure before I accept any proposal is that we're getting married for the right reasons. Not just because I'm pregnant.

"Do you not want to marry me?" I can hear the disappointment in his voice.

"It's not that, it's just that everything has been so insane the last couple months. I think I just need to adjust to life here, get the coffee shop up and running, just get settled. You know?"

He nods, understanding but noticeably disappointed. "I'll keep asking until you say yes, Em." He cups my cheek, his eyes full of tenderness. While I'm so touched, I'm glad he's dropping the subject for now.

"Are you hungry?" I ask, desperate for a subject change. "I was thinking about making some spaghetti."

He grins. "I'm starving; spaghetti sounds amazing."

I begin pulling out the pots and pans and, while I expect Alex to disappear while I make dinner, he surprises me and begins helping. We work alongside each other and boil noodles, stir sauce, and he even makes garlic bread. I cut up some veggies to make a small tossed salad, and our meal is complete.

We fall into a comfortable silence as we set the food on the table. "I'm glad you're here," I tell him as we sit down to eat.

"I can't imagine being anywhere else, Em. What we just did, making dinner together—I want that every night for the rest of my life. Just being with you, living a normal life. Ordering pizza, snuggling on the couch, going to the movies. All of it."

I bite my lip to contain my smile. "I want that too." From the moment I fell in love with Alex, this is all I've ever wanted.

While we eat, he fills me in on everything that has happened back in Phoenix. He updates me on Sam and answers a million questions that I have about his business and what he plans to do now that he's no longer managing a multi-million dollar illegal drug and gun smuggling operation. I drill him with questions, all of which he answers perfectly. No lies, he said. I'm holding him to that.

After we clean up the dinner dishes, he starts a fire in the fireplace. I loved that feature in the house, but I've been too afraid to start one by myself. Enjoying the heat and coziness, we sit on the oversized couch in the living room, with me curled up next to him as we talk. I don't even realize I've dozed off until I feel Alex carrying me to bed.

"Don't go," I mumble as he sets me on the bed.

"I'll stay on the couch," he says, pulling the comforter back and tossing the decorative pillows onto a chair in the corner.

"Stay with me," I beg him, and he stills.

"Are you sure?"

"Never been more sure about anything," I tell him.

I crawl into bed, and I hear him take off his jeans and his t-shirt. He crawls in next to me and pulls me to him. We fall asleep wrapped in each other's arms and, for the first time in years, I fall asleep without a care in the world.

I wake to feel Alex running his finger down my arm, from my shoulder to my wrist. My eyes flutter open as they try to adjust to the bright room.

"Wake up, sleepyhead," he whispers, pressing a kiss to the tip of my nose.

"What time is it?" I ask and groan as I snuggle up next to him. My fingers trace the hard lines of his chest, and I play with the small patch of hair in the center of his chest.

"Seven thirty," he says and wraps his arms around me, pulling me tighter to him. "I want to wake up like this every morning."

"Hmmm…me too." I kiss the corner of his mouth.

"I want to kiss you a million times a day," he says sweetly and kisses my face all over, from my temples to my forehead and all the way down to my chin.

"I'd like that," I say as he finally captures my lips.

"I need you, Em," he says, his voice needy.

I know exactly what he means. "I need you too," I reply.

In one careful turn, he has me on my back and he's resting between my legs. "Are you sure?" he asks, and I nod quickly. I've longed for his touch and my body reacts hastily.

My breathing quickens as he laces his fingers through mine, then he places them next to my head as he presses himself against my center and gently pushes into me. I gasp at the intrusion, but quickly adjust to him.

"You okay?"

"Mmmhmm," I moan as he begins to move slowly inside me.

"God, Emilia," he groans. "I've never met a more beautiful woman," he says as he makes love to me. "I want to make love to you every night and every morning for the rest of my life."

"Ahh!" I gasp when he hits that spot deep within me.

"You feel so good, baby," he mumbles against my lips as he kisses me.

I hitch my legs around his waist, pulling him deeper inside me.

"You're going to make me come," he says, slowing his pace.

I smile and loosen my grip on him. He lifts my tank top and pulls a nipple into his mouth, rolling his tongue around the hard bud. As he nips at it, I can feel my climax building. My hips match his pace, and he fucks me harder. "Alex," I gasp, saying his name.

"Just feel it, Em. Just let me love you."

"I'm so close," I tell him.

"Come for me, Em. Come all over me." With a few more thrusts, I gasp as my body begins to let go. "That's my girl," he says as he slams into me.

"Alex," I say his name between breaths.

"Yeah, baby."

"I love you," I tell him just as his release comes.

He explodes into me and falls on top of me, then he kisses that spot on my neck that he's always loved. We're one. One body, one soul, one being.

"There's nowhere in the world I'd rather be than with you," I tell him as he looks in my eyes. "It's you and me forever," I whisper to him.

"Forever," he repeats, pressing his forehead to mine. "Marry me," he asks, our lips so close they're almost touching.

"In time," I whisper to him.

TWENTY-TWO

Alex

We're settling into life in Oregon, and I couldn't be happier. Life with Emilia is everything I ever dreamed it would be. I moved in with her, and I've even gotten a job. My accounting degree has actually paid off, and I'm working with a small accounting firm here in town. I'm basically just managing books, basic accounting, but it gives me something to do while also focusing on helping Emilia get the coffee shop ready. We don't need the money, but it provides me a sense of worth. I'm showing Emilia I can take care of her and our family with money earned legally.

Before I left Phoenix, Sam recommended I change my last name, something they request that everyone in witness protection do. It adds an element of safety but without completely changing your entire name. I thought about it, and felt that Cortez was appropriate. Cortez was what my mother's maiden name was, my brother's name, and every family member of mine that has forgiven me and welcomed me with open arms.

So I am Alejandro Cortez—or just Alex to Em.

Every day, I ask Emilia to marry me. She just laughs and brushes me off. I don't know if it's that she doesn't want to get married, or if she's afraid to commit to a person that has done what

I did. We've talked about the past and agreed to move forward, but deep down, I fear she'll always see the monster that I was, not the man I really am.

"Alex, hurry," she says. "We're going to be late for the first day." She hops on one foot, trying to get her shoe on.

"Don't do that!" I scold her. "You're going to trip and fall, and hurt yourself or the baby."

"Stop worrying about us," she grumbles, grabbing her purse off the coffee table. I reach out and grab her arm, stopping her. "What?" she asks, and I pull her into a hug.

"For the rest of my life, I'll worry about you and our baby." I press a kiss to her forehead.

"I know," she says quietly. "I didn't mean it like that. I meant stop being so protective."

"Never. It's my job to protect you, Emilia. So get used to this."

Pulling away, she smiles at me and presses a soft kiss to my lips. "Can we please go now?"

"Yes." I chuckle. She's been so antsy these past couple weeks, waiting to see her dreams realized, and I couldn't be happier for her. "But tonight, I get you. All of you. Dinner, dessert…." I wag my eyebrows.

She just laughs and swats my arm. "Fine. Let's go."

The grand opening was a huge success. Local businesses were extremely supportive, as well as the residents. Winter appears to be a good time to open a coffee shop in a town that has never had one. Emilia hired an assistant manager and six part-time employees to manage all the days and hours. She's planning to hire more, but these next few months will be a good gauge to see how the business will operate and what its future needs will be. I'm so fucking proud of her, I can hardly contain myself.

She works the room, meeting everyone and introducing herself.

I stand back in the corner, letting her enjoy her moment while I enjoy how beautiful she looks. Her long hair is pulled into a messy bun, and her curvy body weaves from each side of the shop and back.

Her belly has started to show, and she protectively rubs it without even knowing. She and the baby are my family, my life, and I take in my reality as I sip on a cinnamon coffee. Never did I believe I'd have this, or that I deserved it. But I'm thankful. Every fucking day.

As Emilia approaches, soft arms wrap around my waist, and I rest my chin on top of her head. "So proud of you, Em."

"I wouldn't have been able to do it without you," she says sweetly.

"Emilia." I pull her over to one of the couches tucked under the large main window. "Sit down. I want to tell you something."

Snuggling into me, she turns and waits, a somewhat concerned look on her face. "Is everything okay?"

"Yeah, yeah." I shake my head a little bit. "It's about the money I gave you."

"Okaaay." Concerns flashes through her eyes.

"I want you to know it was all legitimate money. Not money from my father's business or anything I used to do." I can tell she's surprised, and I explain. "Sam and I each got money that went into a trust when my mother was murdered. I never touched mine, mostly because I didn't need to, but it never felt right. I want you to know that everything I gave you was her money." I sigh as I take a look around. "She would've loved this place, and I know this is exactly what she would've wanted me to do with her money. You're reinvesting in a community, bringing people together."

She leans into me further and presses a kiss to my jaw. "I love you, Alex."

And because I can't help myself, I ask again. "Marry me, Em. I'm serious. I want nothing more than the rest of my life with you."

She just giggles and kisses me. "I'll think about it."

"Seriously, how many times am I going to have to ask you? You're busting my balls here, you know that, right?" I joke with her, but I'm serious. I'd do damn near anything to hear her say "yes."

"I like your balls," she says against my lips.

"Em," I warn her.

She sighs. "I know you're serious. And I will accept…when the time is right."

I frown. "What's wrong with now?" I never have been known for my patience, but I still don't understand why we should wait.

She shrugs and kisses me again. "I'm just really happy right now," she says contentedly. "I've got you, the coffee shop, a healthy baby I'm excited to meet…I just don't want to upset the dynamics."

I sigh loudly, but I can't fault her logic. I respect her thought process. "Let's go home. I need you…now," I tell her and kiss her back. Lust flashes through her eyes and she nods.

"Give me a few more minutes." She pushes herself up from the couch, grabs a napkin and empty cup from a table, and disappears into the back room. Ten minutes later, Lisa, the assistant manager, is all but shoving Emilia out the door.

I barely get through the front door of our house before I'm tearing off her clothes. I've never met a sexier woman in my life. "God, Em…what do you do to me," I say as I push her up against the wall and unbutton her blouse. She giggles and bites her lip as the silk top slides off her shoulders, revealing a lacy bra. I saw her put it on this morning, but it's somehow a hundred times sexier right now. She presses her lips to mine, swiping my lip with her tongue. "Jesus, Em," I growl at her.

"Need you," she breathes through ragged breaths.

She works the buttons on her pants and pushes them down as I impatiently unbutton my dress shirt and kick off my pants. Everything about her turns me on. From the swell of her breasts, to her puffy lips—I want all of her. I slide the edge of her panties to the side and feel her wet center. I slide a finger inside, and she moans as she rubs against my hand. My lips find her neck, my favorite part on her body, and I nip at the delicate skin.

"You're wet, baby," I whisper.

"Yeah," she says breathlessly, barely registering.

I chuckle darkly and pull my finger out, hooking the waistband of her panties in my fingers and dragging them down her long, lean legs. My fingers find her wet center again, and I move to roll her clit between my fingers, causing her to whimper. I hook one of her legs over my hip and guide myself into her—deep.

"God," she hisses as I slide in.

She feels so fucking good.

I hold her ass and her other leg wraps around me as I fuck her slowly against the wall. There will never be anything that feels as good as loving Emilia. Nothing.

Our lovemaking is hungry and needy, but still sweet and loving. It's the perfect combination of need and want. Still in the middle of it, I pull her away from the wall and walk to the couch, pulling her down on top of me. This has been her favorite position lately.

With a gasp, she guides herself up and down, pulling me deeper into her. "Love," she gasps again. "This." She rides me for less than a minute when I feel her walls begin to tighten. "So close," she breathes heavily as she presses a kiss to my lips.

"Do it, baby," I encourage her. "Let go."

And she does. Her cries are a combination of pleasure and pain. I pull one of her tight nipples in my mouth and suck hard as she climaxes, her entire body convulsing as she orgasms. I'm close as well, so I stand up and walk us to the bedroom, still inside her. She rests her forehead on my shoulder as she tries to control her breathing.

Pulling out of her, I set her in the center of the bed and pull her clit into my mouth. She gasps and her legs instinctively try to close, but I hold them down while I lick her pussy and bring her to another climax.

"Alex," she cries as she grabs my hair.

"One more, baby," I tell her, and she rocks her hips against my mouth. With that as my permission, I slide back inside of her and use my finger to rub her clit as her orgasm builds again. I thrust myself in and out of her wet pussy and, just as she explodes, I join her.

I pulse inside of her—claiming her. Then I fall forward, resting on her chest and she locks her ankles behind me, holding me inside of her.

"I love you, Alex."

"I love you too," I tell her.

We lie wrapped around each other the rest of the evening, a tangle of arms and legs. Then we make love again. I could do this all night long with her. I'll never have enough of her. As she lies on her side with her back pressed to my chest, her breathing becomes steadier, and I lean forward, pressing a kiss to her cheek.

"Marry me, Emilia," I whisper to her.

I expect one of her usual brushoffs or excuses, but I'm stunned, left speechless when she replies, "Okay," a soft smile pulling at her lips.

"Wait, you will?" I ask, shocked.

"Yes." She giggles.

Everything I ever wanted is right here, and I'm the happiest man in the world.

Alex

EPILOGUE

"Drive carefully. Don't speed. Hurry up!" she yells at me from the passenger seat. We're still about twenty miles from the hospital.

"Baby, just breathe," I try to soothe her, squeezing her hand again. For the last five minutes, she's been practically cutting off the circulation to my hand, but I'm happy to let her. "Remember what they taught you. Deep breath in, deep breath out."

"What do you think I'm doing!" she screams at me as her right hand grips the car door.

"You're yelling at me," I try to point out gently, but her panic is drawing me in. "When you're yelling at me, you're not breathing!"

Her face is the angriest I've ever seen it. "Do you really think *now* is the time to be a smartass, Alex? Just drive. *Faster*!"

Yes, ma'am. I grip the steering wheel and stomp my foot on the accelerator. Seventeen miles. I can get us there in ten minutes if I really push it. The roads are nearly empty since it's two thirty in the morning. Emilia woke up having contractions about midnight, thought they were nothing because she's not due for another two weeks, but by two, they were coming faster.

"Slow down, you're going to kill us," she barks at me.

Fuck. My nerves are rattled. Slow down. Hurry up. Nothing I do is right, and I just want to take her pain away.

"Ugh," she moans as she leans back.

"Did that contraction pass?" I ask her, and she nods, refocusing on breathing. "Good. Deep breaths, baby. We're almost there."

I keep track of how close the contractions are coming while I break about ten different traffic laws. Twelve minutes later, I'm pulling into the carport of the hospital in Salem. A man with a wheelchair greets us, and Emilia visibly relaxes.

"We made it," she says with tears in her eyes.

Relief settles in and I take a deep breath. "I was not about to let you have my baby on the side of a road," I tease her, but she shoots me a "don't fuck with me look" and I just go silent.

I give the man wheeling her in a brief run down on the timing of her contractions, and he immediately steers her away after telling me where to park and meet them.

By the time I make it up to the floor where maternity is located, they've already got Em in a room, changed, and hooked up to all kinds of machines. A nurse is jotting down her vitals while another nurse straps a large elastic belt to her stomach.

"You dad?" she asks.

"I am." I nod, feeling stressed but also beaming with pride. I can't believe we're here. It's surreal.

"Congratulations. It'll be soon." She smiles at me.

Em flashes her a dirty look, and I choke back my laugh.

The same nurse props up Em's legs and begins to explain that they're going to check her cervix. I stand next to Emilia and hold her hand.

"You're about four and half, maybe five centimeters dilated," she says. "And you said the contractions are about five to six minutes apart?"

"Yes," Em says and finds my hand again. I let her have it, even though I'm just getting the feeling back.

"Looks like you're progressing. My guess is that, by later this morning, your baby will be here. Did you and your doctor discuss pain management?"

"Yes," Em interrupts her. "I want an epidural."

The nurse smiles and laughs. "Most do. I'll call down and request the anesthesiologist. It might be a while, so practice your breathing through the contractions."

Emilia turns her head to look at me; her face is full of conflict.

"You okay?" I ask, pressing a kiss to her sweaty forehead.

She nods. "This is the last time it's just the two of us," she says quietly as her voice breaks.

"Yes," I tell her soothingly. "But this is what we wanted, Em, a family. A real family."

"I know. I'm just scared. What if I screw this up? What if I'm like my mother?" she asks, panic in her eyes.

"You're not," I stop her. "And you have me to lean on." I give her my sternest face without risking being kicked in the balls. "Is this going to be easy? No. It'll probably be the hardest thing we'll ever do. But as long as we have each other, we'll be just fine." I lean down and press another kiss to her forehead. "I love you, Emilia, and I can't wait to meet our baby."

"Love you too," she says quietly.

As we wait for the anesthesiologist to arrive, Em begins to doze off between contractions. I shut the large overhead lights off, leaving just the small lights above the bed on. Reaching out, I rub Em's belly, when I feel a little kick. I can't help but smile and think that, in a few hours, I'll be holding our baby.

I lean on the edge of the bed and get as close as I can. "Hey there, little one," I whisper as not to wake Em. "It's your daddy." My fingers trail small circles over the spot where he or she last kicked. "I can't wait to meet you. I promise to always take care of you and love you and your mommy. There's nothing in the world that means more to me than you two."

A lump forms in my throat as I talk to our baby. "I will always protect you. Always." I kiss Em's belly and realize that our lives are about to change in ways we never expected…in ways I never thought possible. But I'm more ready than I've ever been.

"Give me one more big push," the doctor tells Emilia. She's been pushing for almost two hours, and I fear she's on the brink of exhaustion.

"You've got this, Em. You're the strongest person I know," I whisper to her, brushing her hair off her cheeks.

She's flushed and sweating, and squeezing my hand harder than I ever imagined she could. Taking a deep breath, she gives everything she has.

"That's it," I hear the doctor encouraging her. "Keep pushing!"

Tears fall from Em's eyes, and her head falls back against her pillow. "I can't do this," she cries and gasps for breath.

"You can, Em. One more. Let's do this," I try to push her on. She sits up a little taller and looks at me. "Big push," I tell her.

She squeezes my hand again and begins pushing and that's all it takes. Seconds later, our baby's head is out and the doctor is clearing its nose and mouth.

"Oh my gosh," Em cries.

"One more little push, and the shoulders will be free. The rest will just follow. Good job, Emilia." The doctor smiles at her. "Ready when you are," she says, and Emilia gives one final push. The doctor pulls the baby up and immediately sets it on Emilia's chest. He or she is purple, and covered in I don't know what, but I don't care because all I care about is hearing our baby cry. Emotions overtake me and tears fill my eyes and pride fills my heart. *Our baby.*

Emilia holds the baby on her chest as she sobs and kisses our baby's forehead, while I wipe my own tears from my eyes.

Never did I think I'd have a family, and here it is.

"It's a girl," one of the nurses says to Emilia.

"Girl?" I ask, not sure I heard her correctly.

"Little girl," she says again.

Holy fuck. It's so real. I have a little girl. I can picture it all—the pink and dresses and baby dolls, and pigtails and everything inside of me melts.

"Dad, you want to cut the umbilical cord?" the doctor asks, pulling me away from staring at my daughter. She hands me a pair of medical scissors, and I cut through the rubbery cord.

Emilia just cries and holds our baby as a nurse wipes her clean. "We have to take her for just a minute." The nurse pulls our baby girl from Emilia's arms.

I lean down and wipe the tears from Emilia's cheeks, pressing a kiss to her lips. "A baby girl," I whisper to her, and she cries harder. I honestly feel like I'm living in a bubble. Nurses and doctors buzz around us, helping Emilia, and I finally sink into the chair that's in the corner of the room.

Closing my eyes, I thank God for blessing me with a second chance. A chance to do good. He's given me the best gift I could ever imagine, and I promise to not screw this up. I wipe tears from eyes as a gentle hand touches my shoulder.

"I think she'd like her daddy," a smiling nurse says. She hands me a swaddled bundle with a little pink hat on. Dark blue eyes try to focus on me as I lean in and kiss her chubby cheeks. Her nose is small and pink, and her little lips purse as her tongue presses through them. I've never seen anything so beautiful in all my life.

I kiss her again, pressing my lips to her forehead, then I whisper promises to her that I will never break. Glancing over, I see Emilia watching us, and she gives me a watery smile. At this moment, my world is complete. Love that I never imagined possible fills every fiber of who I am.

I stand up and walk over to Emilia, cradling our baby girl in my arms. "What should we name her?"

"What about Emma Grace?" Emilia swats at tears.

"After my mom?" I ask, not even considering Emilia would want to do that.

She nods.

"We could call her Grace," I offer. "Yeah, Grace. It's perfect." Fits her. My daughter. I have to say that a few times to get used to it.

"Perfect," Emilia whispers, reaching a finger out to caress the baby's cheek.

"Emma Grace Cortez, welcome to our family," I whisper with another kiss to her forehead.

three years later

Emilia

"Gracie, don't let Sam get too close to the water!" I holler at her as our two kids run toward the beach.

Grace reaches down and holds Sam's hand as their little feet sink into the soft sand. At a year and half, one would think our little boy was a teenager. He runs along the beach with no fear and loves picking up rocks and throwing them into the water.

Grace is like Alex. Protective and concerned, always looking out for everybody. Her long, curly hair whips in the wind as she holds her brother's hand tightly. She's got perfect olive skin and light brown eyes. Sam is more like me. Cautious but adventurous. His complexion is lighter, and he reminds me so much of his namesake, his Uncle Sam.

"Here you go, babe," Alex says from behind as he hands me a mug of coffee. We sit down in the sand, next to one of the small dunes, and watch the kids play on the beach in front of us. This is our favorite Saturday morning family pastime.

I sip on the hot coffee and watch my children laugh and play. Nothing makes me happier than their little laughs. "What time do you have to get Sam and Kate from the airport?" I ask Alex.

"Around two this afternoon."

"The guest room is all set up for them," I tell Alex. We built a house just down from Mr. Anders'. We're the last house at the very end of our narrow street, tucked away from everyone else, but still on the beach.

"I'm glad they're coming," he says. "We haven't seen them since our wedding."

"I know, it doesn't seem that long ago, but it's been over two years."

"Little Sam is so excited," I tell him with a smile. "The name is so fitting. You have to see the resemblance."

"I do," he says as he watches the kids closely. "Even their personalities are similar."

"That Estrada blood runs deep," I joke.

"Cortez," he corrects me. Alex changed his name, wanting to rid himself of the ties the Estrada name brings.

"Right. Cortez," I say quietly. I hesitate for a moment, then ask, "Will we ever tell them, Alex?"

"About?"

"Your family. The business."

He shakes his head. "Em, we've worked too hard to give them a good life. A life they deserve."

I nod and sip my coffee. "Did I tell you my dad is coming for a couple weeks this spring? He's renting that little house down the street. I told him he could stay with us, but he didn't want to intrude."

"He should just stay with us," he insists. "We have plenty of room. We have the guest room, and the room upstairs next to Gracie's—"

"No, I'm going to renovate that room." I have to hide my smile.

He turns and looks at me like I've lost my mind. "What do you mean 'renovate'? We just built the damn house."

"I mean, I'm pulling the bed out of there, and the nightstand, everything. It won't be an extra guest room." I've been waiting for the right time to surprise him.

"What're you going to put in there? You have a library downstairs, an office, we have a sitting room—"

"A crib," I tell him tenderly, unable to contain it anymore.

"A crib?" he asks, confused. "There's a crib in Sam's room."

"I know. But we're transitioning him to a toddler bed, so I need a place to put a crib." I smile and chew on my bottom lip.

"Wait, what?" he asks me as I giggle. "No!" he says, shaking his head.

I nod. "Yes."

"We're having a baby?" A grin stretches wide on his face.

"Number three," I tell him and wrap my arm around his. I lean into him, and he kisses the top of my head.

"Who knew that here we'd be living in Oregon, owning our own business, and having a third kid," he remarks in awe.

I press a motherly hand to my still flat stomach. "I think I'll want to be done after number three, though."

"What about one more?" he asks and raises his eyebrows. "I always wanted a big family."

"We'll see." I smack his arm. I have a hard time telling Alex no, but it's a small annoyance in my otherwise wonderful life.

My life is complete now. It's a life I never imagined I'd have. Our coffee shop is hugely successful, so much that we've expanded into the bookstore next door. I don't really even work anymore. With three managers and a full staff, I pop in with the kids and help out here and there, but most of my time is spent wiping noses, chasing kids, and making dinner.

Alex manages most of the day-to-day business needs of the coffee shop, but he still lets me make all the decisions.

Life is good. Even when it's bad, it's still a blessing. And as I look out at the sparkling ocean, my beautiful children running around in the sand and husband at my side, I can't imagine any greater gift in the world.

.   .   .

Betrayed by Lies (Sam's Story)
Available NOW!

ALSO BY REBECCA SHEA

Unbreakable Series:

Unbreakable

Undone

Unforgiven

Bound & Broken Series:

Broken by Lies

Bound by Lies

Betrayed by Lies

Standalone Titles

Dare Me

Fault Lines

Unexpectedly Yours

Always Been You

Co-written with A.L. Jackson

One Wild Night

One Wild Ride

CONNECT WITH REBECCA SHEA

Website
www.rebeccasheaauthor.com

Sign up for Rebecca Shea's newsletter
http://tinyurl.com/h8mfya2

Sign up for Rebecca Shea's new release and sale alerts
http://www.subscribepage.com/j1m3c5

Follow Rebecca Shea on Facebook:
www.facebook.com/rebeccasheaauthor

Follow Rebecca Shea on Instagram:
https://www.instagram.com/rebeccasheaauthor/

Email: rebeccasheaauthor@gmail.com